# THE WILD DEAD

## ALSO BY CARRIE VAUGHN

*Bannerless*

# THE
# WILD DEAD

*A Bannerless Saga Novel*

## Carrie Vaughn

A John Joseph Adams Book
*Mariner Books*
*Houghton Mifflin Harcourt*
BOSTON   NEW YORK
2018

For information about permission to reproduce selections from this book,
write to trade.permissions@hmhco.com or to Permissions,
Houghton Mifflin Harcourt Publishing Company, 3 Park Avenue,
19th Floor, New York, New York 10016.

hmhco.com

Library of Congress Cataloging-in-Publication Data
Names: Vaughn, Carrie, author.
Title: The wild dead / Carrie Vaughn.
Description: Boston ; New York : Mariner Books, 2018. | Series: The
bannerless saga ; 2 | A John Joseph Adams Book.
Identifiers: LCCN 2018004748 (print) | LCCN 2018001246 (ebook) |
ISBN 9780544947641 (ebook) | ISBN 9780544947313 (paperback)
Subjects: | BISAC: FICTION / Science Fiction / General. |
FICTION / Mystery & Detective / Women Sleuths. |
GSAFD: Mystery fiction. | Dystopias.
Classification: LCC PS3622.A9475 (print) |
LCC PS3622.A9475 W55 2018 (ebook)|
DDC 813/.6—dc23
LC record available at https://lccn.loc.gov/2018004748

Book design by Jackie Shepherd

Map by Mapping Specialists, Ltd.

Printed in the United States of America
DOC 10 9 8 7 6 5 4 3 2 1

*For my family*

# THE COAST ROAD

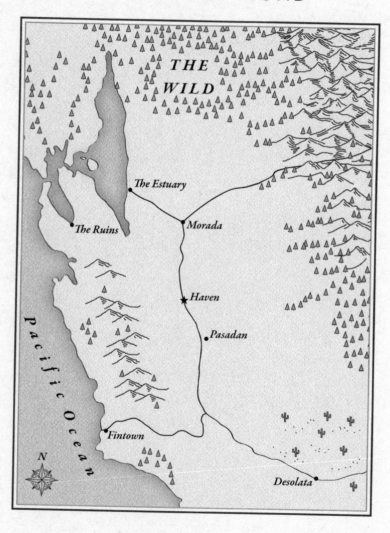

## The Precarious House

Most regions Enid visited, she could find something to love about them, some enticing and beautiful detail about the landscape, the people, the mood of the place. A reason folk would want to stay and scrape out a living in less-than-ideal situations when a dozen other settlements had more resources and less disease, and would gladly welcome extra hands. Even the rainless, baking salt flats at the southernmost end of the Coast Road had isolation to recommend them, for those who wanted to be left alone. And just to show that every place had a reason for existing, the people of Desolata household there exported the salt they collected from the flats on their own trade route.

But here in the Estuary, Enid had to consider for a while what exactly the appeal was. Over the damp marsh where the San Joe River drained, clouds of bugs rose up through a sticky haze, shimmering with heat. Squealing gulls gathered, circling on slender wings, drawn by some rotting treasure. There were no orchards here, no pastures, no rippling fields of grain. Instead, a dozen scraggly goats, stuttering their calls to one another, picked at brush along the last trailing edge of the Coast Road. Presumably, there were fish in the river to eat, along with shellfish and the like this close to the ocean. In checking the settlement's records, Enid had learned that it rarely exceeded quotas—because there wasn't enough to start with. The folk rarely earned banners, either, and had few children. Why would anyone stay in such a place? Perhaps because in the end it was home . . . and sometimes that was enough.

The sunlight here had a bronze cast that she had never seen anywhere else, and the light made the water seem molten, flashing with ripples to the horizon, broken up with stands of marsh grass and the sticks of old dead trees. If you'd lived here forever, the light might seem warm, the air like a favorite blanket on the skin.

That was what she told herself, to try to understand the people here a little better. Because at the moment, her patience was waning.

"Would you *look* at that," her new partner, Teeg, murmured, clearly amazed. A short, sturdy kid, he shaded his eyes with one hand and gripped a staff with the other. Had a manic way of moving, like he'd rather be running ahead than slowing down enough to be methodical. His shining black hair was tied in a short, sloppy braid at the back of his neck, and his lips always seemed to be pursed, like he was thinking hard. When he wasn't talking. This was his first official case as an investigator. "They said it needed repairs. I thought they meant a new roof, maybe it had holes in the walls. Does it even count as a house anymore when it looks like *this?*"

Erik, head of the Semperfi household, looked at the young investigator with dismay.

Erik's request for a mediation had brought Enid and Teeg

to the Estuary. Semperfi household had a building that needed repairs, Erik's request had stated. The community refused to help with those repairs, despite all the support Semperfi had provided to other households over the years. Records supported this assertion—Semperfi had been the first household in the region, and was an anchor. Normally, a town's committee would mediate this kind of disagreement, but the Estuary didn't have a committee. Didn't need one, the people claimed. They didn't consider themselves a town, but a loose collection of households whose members preferred to rely on themselves and one another. The regional committee at Morada set quotas and awarded banners, and medics came through a couple of times a year to check birth-control implants and general well-being. Place like this didn't need a committee until it did, and so Erik's household had to send for investigators to settle the dispute. Now that Enid and Teeg were here, it became clear to them that the building in question was far past anything resembling salvageable.

The structure, a sprawling, single-story block of a house, was old, a pre-Fall construction. Wood and brick walls sat on a crumbling concrete slab, covered with some kind of plastic siding that was cracked and disintegrating. What strips of it remained were held up with nails, twine, and hope. It might have been blue once, but it had long ago faded to a sickly gray. The siding survived only on the lee side of the house; the windward was built up with wood slats and leather hides—layers and layers of them—evidently replaced as the next bout of wind tore them off. Likewise, the slanted roof might once have had purpose-made shingles, slate tile or plywood, but the decades hadn't been kind and the surface was now patched with reeds and hides. What was left of the structure still dripped from last week's bad storm.

All that was bad enough, but the land under the house was falling away. Years of storms had eaten at the ground, mudslide after mudslide eroding it until half the house now stood over nothing but air. This last storm had made the problem critical. Huge slabs of concrete lay at the bottom of the slippery hill, the house's foundation lying in crooked, broken pieces, sliding inevitably toward the river. Tree trunks, two-by-fours, scavenged steel rebar, and rusted scaffolding precariously held up what was left. A house partway on stilts—not like the sturdy pylons of the other structures in the area, but thin and haphazard. A breeze would knock it down. Somehow it was all still standing. Clearly, the structure was at a literal tipping point. If it lost any more ground, the whole thing would fall. No amount of stopgap framework supports could possibly keep it stable. And yet, the folk of Semperfi were clearly trying.

Even the overly emotional testimonies of folk from Bonavista and Pine Grove, the first two households on the path up here, couldn't possibly have prepared Enid for how bad the wreck really was. The folk had complained about how awful the house was, that it was a waste of resources—about the worst insult possible. It never should have required investigators to decide this.

"It's a lovely view, anyway," Enid murmured, looking out over the sluggish river and golden, shimmering marshes of the Estuary. A century ago, there'd probably been an entire neighborhood, an entire city, of nice houses just like this one—or just like this one must have been, once upon a time—a grid of streets, sturdy street lamps lighting it all up bright as day at all hours of the night. Signs of that old world littered the marsh, all the way to the horizon. Canted blocks of concrete, broken frames of steel, whole berms of debris washed up on the tide.

Some of the households here made their living by scavenging. Lots of that to be had, constantly turned over by waves and storms.

Before the Fall, this neighborhood would have been miles from the ocean. Back then, flooding may not have even come close. But then it had, and the other houses fell away. Semperfi had saved this tiny little scrap of that ancient neighborhood, and there was something poignant about that. They might have had folk living in it, parent to child, ever since the Fall. But there came a point when no amount of effort could save a thing, and surely this structure wouldn't last another storm.

Erik pleaded the house's case desperately, speaking quickly, as if speed would give his argument more weight. He knew what Enid and Teeg must be thinking. "Yes, it's in poor shape, but . . . there's nothing else like it. It's lasted this long, it'd be a shame to let it go to ruin now. Wouldn't it?" He kept his voice steady, but his eyes shone with anxiety.

He was younger than Enid had expected. The head of a household wasn't necessarily the oldest member, but had typically been around some time, maybe even earned a banner and raised a kid. He didn't seem much older than Enid's own thirty years. Lanky, angular, he had skin the shade of teak and close-shaved brown hair. His face was gaunt, like he never quite got enough to eat, but he kept his hands on his hips in a confident stance.

He'd been watching for them and came to meet them as they followed the path up the hill. Ready to intercept them before they saw the house. Not giving them a chance to make any judgment on their own. Moving up the path with them, he gestured toward the house, guiding them over uneven, scrubby ground. A rangy, tawny dog named Bear had accompanied him. Now, after sniffing at the investigators' hands, it sat politely at Erik's feet. Looking up at them, it gave the uncanny impression of following the conversation.

"I know it's not easy, I never thought it would be easy. But it's still worth doing. This is important," he said.

Enid tried to see the place through his eyes. An artifact from the world before the Fall, evidence of what used to be. Like the collection in the archives at Haven, carefully stored bits and pieces, the plastic bricks of computers and radios and things that weren't any use now, but that people saved because, well, they'd always been saved.

But this was a whole *house*.

"How long have your people been keeping the place up?" Teeg asked. He made the question sound curious, rather than accusing. Just a casual conversation.

"Since the start. My great-granddad grew up in it. They stayed, all the way through the Fall, even when everyone else was gone. Scavenged the neighborhood, made repairs when everything else washed away. We've got pictures, real photos of what it all used to look like. I can show you, I can show that it's worth saving. My dad"—here he paused, swallowed back grief —"I was seventeen when my dad died, and I promised him I'd look after the place. Seventeen and keeping up the whole household, plus the house . . . I can't let him down, don't you see? I promised." Erik said this with the determination of a man going into battle.

He continued the tour with a parent's pride. "There used to be a concrete walk right there." He pointed to the path leading down the hill, back to the other households. A dip in the earth, a stretch where the scrub grew in a little paler, was in fact visible. Scanning over the hillside with fresh eyes, Enid could see all kinds of evidence of a previous vast settlement: divots in the earth where sewer and drain pipes had collapsed, mounds where ruins had fallen decades ago and been buried or scavenged, leaving only shadows behind. An unnatural straight line where shrubs had grown over a fallen lamppost. She had just been thinking of how hostile this place seemed, but this had been a city before the sea crawled inland and storms washed it away.

"That's impressive," Enid admitted.

"So you see why we want to keep it standing. We've got to!"

Enid wasn't an engineer and didn't have much mechanical inclination, but she had a thought: they could get a team of horses—a big team, six? eight?—and put the whole structure on rollers to move what was left of the concrete slab and everything on top of it to more solid ground. Even fifty yards would put it on bedrock rather than the disintegrating muddy cliff it was on now. If Sam were here, he'd have a better idea of what was possible and what was ridiculous. The undertaking would be massive, a huge and excessive use of resources, so Enid couldn't help but think it would be so much easier and more efficient to build something new and let the old rot away. Better for everyone.

Except Erik had an attachment to the old house. Enid just about understood the impulse—she loved the archives in the cellar under Haven's clinic, with its stacks of dead things from an irrelevant world. Including photographs, much like the ones Erik bragged about. Memories had their uses, and this house clearly meant something to its people.

But what could possibly justify using the immense resources that would be necessary to save such a wreck?

The look on Enid's face must have been pained, because Erik kept going.

"The household name, Semperfi—it was a motto my

great-granddad had. He was something like an enforcer—like you," he said, gesturing at Teeg's staff. "He had this phrase written on badges and things. It means never give up. That's how he got through the Fall, that's how he started all this. We can't give up now."

Enid wasn't sure that explanation of the name was exactly right—based on her reading, it had been a pretty common saying before the Fall. And she suspected that Erik's ancestor would prefer that his great-grandson put his energy to better use, into making something new that would help his household. But there was that promise. Four generations of promise.

Erik led them on eagerly. "Come inside, here—"

Teeg looked at Enid in wide-eyed horror. No assumptions, she wanted to remind him. No preconceived notions. But it was hard to stay neutral, looking at that house. *House* wasn't even the right word. That *artifact*. And like an artifact it likely held its own bit of history—precious, full of information. The photos Erik spoke of ought to be kept in an archive, where they could be protected.

Teeg held back. "You don't actually go inside there, do you?"

Erik said, "It'll be fine. Unless there's an earthquake or a storm coming up, it's fine." He started for the front door, urging them forward as if he could pull them by force of will. Fortunately, the wood-grain door was in a part of the house that was still on solid ground. The metal knob and deadbolt might have been original, judging from their scuffs and scratches, the patina of hard wear. Still intact, still functional.

Enid took off her hat, rubbed a hand through her short brown hair, which had become matted with sweat. She was

THE WILD DEAD · 9

game to enter the rickety building and grinned back at Teeg. "Maybe you should wait here and get help in case the whole thing tips over."

"That's not actually funny," he replied, following her.

Erik swung the door in; the hinges creaked only a little. The floorboards inside groaned more. The dog waited, settled on its haunches, tail wagging weakly. Sensible enough to stay outside.

The interior was dark—the window frames were visible, but they'd been covered up, probably ages ago, to keep out the weather. The only light came in through the open door. Enid's steps were audible as she stepped on some kind of warped and stained plastic-tile flooring. It had been light-colored originally, with a kind of marbling pattern still barely visible. The walls, paneled with simple wood slats, were not original. When it was new, the walls would have been smoothed and painted. There was a front room, a doorway to what looked like a kitchen, though Enid would have been shocked if any of the plumbing worked; she hadn't seen any cisterns outside. Sockets, switches, and some loose wiring were visible, but again she guessed that electricity hadn't run through here in ages; the place didn't have any solar panels or compact wind turbines—those were reserved for the household's newer cottages, farther up the path.

The air reeked of mold, the inevitable product of damp leather and ancient wood forced together and aging badly.

The kitchen had a sink, counters, cupboards—all of them cleaned over and over until the surface finishes had worn off, so they now seemed thin and brittle. From the kitchen a short hall led off to more rooms. Interior walls that must have once been present had been taken out; the space was open now. Some furniture had come to roost here and there: a table pushed into a corner, an assortment of chairs next to it. That was it.

Erik waited for their reactions, like a kid showing off his lumpy, misshapen first attempt at pottery or woodworking. Of course you'd tell him how nice it was.

Enid took her notebook from her satchel and made notes, a list of everything she saw wrong with the place, from her first impression outside to the smell inside. Even just writing a couple of words per item, this took a while. But she wanted this documented. No one could come back later and say she hadn't been thorough.

"You don't use this place much, do you?" Enid asked.

"Well. We do. Storage, when we're prepping food. We do a lot of drying and canning, and there's space to spread out and keep things dry. Usually. I mean, when the roof isn't leaking. We dry laundry in here sometimes. But that's kind of the point: if we really get this place fixed up, get some really good pylons under it, get it stable—then we can sleep people here again."

Enid kept her reaction off her face, tamping down hard on her feelings of dismay. No, no one should ever sleep here. Erik's father, the household's previous head, had died of a lingering illness—flu, the reporting medic thought. Enid didn't say so, but she wondered if spending too much time in this house might have caused his health to deteriorate. Did everyone in Semperfi have lingering coughs they couldn't explain? She wouldn't be surprised.

The place should be dismantled for salvage, and something fresh, new, with wide windows and a very solid foundation, should be built far away from the mudslides. The other households were right, however much Enid might want to sympathize with Erik. The house had survived the last storm, but the next would likely finish it off. It wasn't safe. Now it was her job to convince him of that, as kindly as possible. But all she could think of at that moment was this question: they'd hiked a week up the Coast Road for *this?*

Teeg kept his face entirely turned away from Erik to hide his look of disgust. Expectantly, he waited for Enid's reaction as a cue to how he should behave. He seemed to be trying to silently ask, *What do we do with this?*

Out of a sense of duty and professional thoroughness, Enid went through the whole house. She didn't quite know what more she was looking for. Maybe she was hoping to find a pre-Fall book that didn't exist anywhere else — a painting or a photo album that would drive some future historian to ecstasy. An artifact that Erik and his household might have overlooked, that would make the whole case — the whole trip here — worthwhile.

In the corner farthest from the front door, she found a pile of rags. Debris, it looked like — shoved out of the way. Cringing every time the wood creaked under her steps, Enid went to poke at it with her foot. Not rags after all, but a whole blanket, threadbare, big enough to wrap around a person. Shifting the cloth uncovered more: a simple leather pouch, and, inside it, flint and steel made from what looked like salvaged scraps. No charred streaks were visible, so likely no one had tried to start a fire inside the house, for which Enid sighed in relief.

"Erik, you said no one sleeps here?"

"Of course not," he answered, clearly shocked at the idea. He and Teeg came up beside her, looking where she looked.

"Then you've got a squatter." She set the pouch on the blanket, stepped back.

Erik snarled, biting off a word. Far from surprised, he was angry. Furious.

"You know who?" Enid prompted.

"It's got to be outsider folk. Wild folk from upriver. They spy on us, been stealing from us for years."

Enid's brow furrowed. "What have they stolen?" In her experience, outsider folk stayed far away from the Coast Road settlements. According to their stories, the Coast Road folk were villains, demanding tribute and stealing babies.

Erik shrugged. "Well, nothing specific that I know of. But that blanket—they must have taken that from somewhere; they sure don't have weaving like that."

"This looks like just one person, maybe trying to get out of the rain." Someone who knew they wouldn't be bothered in this sad old house. But why would such a person have left anything behind? The wild folk she'd met never had much to spare. Maybe when Erik brought Enid and Teeg here today for the tour, they'd surprised someone. Chased the person off when they came in. Enid listened for noises, anyone moving outside the house, labored breathing. Inside, there wasn't any-place to hide. She didn't sense anything. Erik was glaring at the abandoned mess. "This is another reason to get this place fixed up. Get the doors and windows fixed, so we can close it off, keep it safe—"

"And make sure no one gets killed if the roof and walls fall in?" Enid asked, brow raised. "Let's get outside, into the light, yeah?"

Outside, the sky was huge and even the briny, humid air smelled clean. A weight came off her—relief that the house hadn't killed her. She hadn't realized that she'd been worried until she breathed fresh air and the space over the wetlands opened up before her.

A dozen people waited outside.

She recognized Jess, Juni, Avery, several others from Bonavista and Pine Grove. She and Teeg had met the first of the area's households on the walk up here. Bonavista was the first household on the road into the Estuary, something of a gateway to the rest of the settlement, and Jess and Juni had spotted them as they arrived, welcoming them with more enthusiasm than Enid was used to. Jess was a lean man, his skin reddened with pockmarks from old acne or illness. He had a welcoming smile. His partner, the co-head of Bonavista, was Juni, a small woman with a round face and eager manner. Avery, the head of Pine Grove, had bragged that they were under their quota for the month—no overfishing happened here. But he knew very well that Enid and Teeg hadn't come to investigate fishing quotas. They'd all been happy to tell the investigators that Erik was mad, that the house was a wreck, that he had no business wanting to save it. She'd thought they'd been exaggerating.

Curious, the group must have followed the investigators up here, at a distance. The ones Enid didn't recognize probably came from the households farther on. She and Teeg wanted to talk to everyone; they hadn't gotten that far yet. The Estuary might not have had a committee, but the small-town grapevine was working just fine. They all knew that Erik had asked for an investigation, they'd gotten word that investigators had arrived, and now they wanted to come see for themselves.

So this was going to be more complicated than Enid liked. Teeg had moved up beside her and planted his staff. In their brown uniforms, a matched set, they clearly had authority here.

"Hola," Enid said brightly. "Can I help you?"

"Now do you see it? It's just like we told you," Jess of Bonavista said, gesturing to the ruined house with his hand flattened, angry.

"Yeah," she said calmly. "We've had a chance to look things over."

"Erik's crazy to think he can save this!"

Anna of Semperfi, Erik's partner, put her hands on her hips and jerked her head toward the investigators. "Let them decide, it's what they're here for!"

Another man, big, with a brimmed hat pulled low over a pale, flushed face, stepped forward. Avery from Pine Grove. "They need to hear all of it. It's not just the house that's the problem, it's the assumption that we should be helping," he countered.

Enid tried again. "Once we've had a chance to talk to everyone, we'll—"

Erik marched forward before Enid or Teeg could stop him and jabbed a finger at Avery. "You're just too lazy to put in the work! Can't face a little challenge, can you?" *Lazy.* Almost as bad an insult as *unproductive* or *wasteful.*

"That's not it and you know it!"

Everyone started talking at once, then. Yelling, really. They even managed to drown out the racket from the circling flock of gulls. Erik somehow made himself heard over it all.

"You're not listening! If you just listen, I can convince you, I can make you see, we can save the house! We can, I just need a little help—"

"A *little?* All the help on the Coast Road won't save it!" Jess countered.

The two men yelled at each other with just an arm's-length distance between them, flinging angry gestures that could easily turn into punches. They seemed to forget the investigators entirely.

Erik might have given this speech a dozen times, it seemed so well practiced. "After everything we've done for all the rest of you, for you to . . . to turn on us like this!" Erik pointed at each of the households in turn. Pine Grove, Bonavista, all of them. "You know we're the best builders, so you ask us to help with all your work. We help keep the bridge up. Every time it rains we help pull your dumb goats out of the river. And we've been doing it for years. Decades! From the very start, we were here before any of you. And you"—he pointed at Juni and Jess—"back when Bridge House folded, we took in half your people, even though it blew all our quotas and we didn't have the resources—"

"You were a child then—you don't know what you're talking about!" Juni bared her teeth, her face flushed. A strange-looking fury rose up in her. She'd been good tempered so far, in Enid's interactions with her. Jess touched Juni's arm to hold her back, but she wasn't deterred. "Your father didn't have a problem with it!"

"Not that he ever told you! He was too nice to say what he was thinking, but we sure heard about it at home! About what Neeve did and you all trying to cover it up!"

"We didn't! We reported it right off!"

Enid should have known someone would bring up the old case, from twenty years ago. The Estuary took care of itself, mostly. But twenty years ago, one of them had cut out her implant, presumably to try to have a baby without a banner. She'd been caught. Eventually, her household had disbanded over the incident. Juni had started the new household, Bonavista, in its place. It should have all been left behind. But something like that was never really forgotten.

A banner. What it all came down to, in the end. A household came together, worked hard, proved that the members could take care of one another, manage themselves, not waste resources, and then the regional committee would award them a banner. The right to have a child. Households, quotas, trade, investigations, all of it went toward proving you could successfully bring a new human being into the world.

Dig down far enough, it wasn't about houses at all.

Enid turned to Teeg and smirked. "See? This is why we don't start with group meetings. The shouting. All of them at once."

"Yeah, I guess so. We had enough?"

"I think so."

Teeg put fingers to his mouth and whistled piercingly. The whole group fell quiet; a couple of them even jumped back, as if the sound had been a clap of thunder. Enough quiet now so that the soft whining from the scrappy dog was audible. The animal clung to Erik, close to his feet, and seemed worried. Enid sympathized with his sense of confusion.

She looked over the gathering, a dozen people from households up and down this part of the road, come to gawk. Most folk looked away rather than let her catch their gaze. This wasn't comfortable. Ideally, they'd be having this conversation alone with Semperfi's folk in their kitchen. Someplace where Erik and his folk would feel comfortable. Or at least, where he wasn't being attacked. Then again, this way, no one could invent gossip about what the investigators told him. So they stood in the open, with the rotting structure lending undeniable evidence to back up the decision. The sun beat down on them, insects buzzed, and everyone felt annoyed.

In that quiet, another sound carried up the hill from the marshland at the mouth of the river. A desperate, panicked voice, shouting over and over, coming closer until the repeated word became clear: "Help! Help me! Help!"

Across the marsh a figure ran toward the main road at the base of the hill, slipping, recovering, momentum carrying him on. A man in work clothes, holding on to his wide-brimmed hat to keep it from flying off. His other hand was waving. The dog barked and charged out; Erik called Bear back.

"Is that Kellan?" Jess asked.

"Who's Kellan?" Teeg said.

"One of Last House's. He's usually down on the beach, scavenging."

Details clarified: brown skin darkened and weathered, dark eyes narrowed in a constant squint and radiating crows' feet, and a rough beard softening the jaw. Rangy limbs, homespun clothes hanging off him loose and comfortable. A machete and a crowbar knocked at his belt. The man seemed to be running for his life, but nothing chased him.

"Teeg, come on," Enid said, and they took off at a jog, downhill to the mud, to meet him.

"What's wrong?" she said when they got close.

The man pulled up, panting for breath, glancing back and forth between the investigators and something behind him.

"You, investigators? You're investigators."

"Yes, that's right."

"You've got to help. Please come!"

He reached out and clung to Enid's sleeve. Hardly anyone ever got that close when she was wearing the uniform. Teeg stepped forward, his free hand at his pouch where he kept tranquilizer patches. But Kellan wasn't belligerent. He was scared, upset, blinking with shock.

She held his hand, hoping to anchor him, comfort him. Get him to a point where he could explain. "What is it?"

He gaped a couple of times and then stammered, "There's a body, *a body*. Someone's washed up, she's dead!"

Enid's nerves fired, sharpened. A sense of alarm crashed over her, made her stomach clench. Teeg turned to her with a look of shock to match Kellan's.

"Show us," she said.

## Death on the Tide

Kellan led them past the bridge and down into the marsh. The tide had washed out, and brackish mud sucked at their feet as they plodded through it, water seeping into the footprints they left behind. Farther on, they had to navigate around debris—broken sections of chainlink and seaweed-covered rebar with chunks of fractured concrete clinging to them. The path became something of an obstacle course, and Enid couldn't quite see where they were headed.

The wheeling gulls circled over one spot. Usually the birds appeared alone or in pairs, no more than a few at a time, individual cries distinct. This was a flock, a cacophony, rattling. Something had drawn them here.

Kellan led them to where a pale canvas bag, probably his own, slumped on the ground, dropped when he ran for help. Ten feet beyond that, another shape hunched on the mud. The slope of a back, a length of legs stretched out. Enid, with Teeg following, strode forward for a better look. Cackling gulls scattered.

It was a woman, arms tucked in as if she'd been holding something. She wore a long skirt and a tunic. A loosely knitted kerchief covered her brown hair, tied in a muddy braid, tangled and full of grime. Simple leather shoes on her feet. She was no more than twenty years old, if Enid guessed right.

The body was soaking wet, so she might have washed down the river to the side of the bank and gotten snagged in the mud and debris there. She didn't seem beaten up enough to have washed in from the sea. It was possible she'd been lying here for days. Maybe drowned in the storm. No one in the settlement had said anything about someone missing, and that was the sort of thing people usually told investigators. So the dead woman was probably from somewhere else. But where? The next settlement, Everlast, was ten miles down the road and quite a ways inland. North of here was nothing. Far up the shore lurked the shadows of buildings, walls fallen in, roofs collapsed, steel bones rusting in place. Even a few hulls of steel ships had washed ashore. No one lived in that region. At least, not that Enid knew about.

Already Enid was making a list of what she would need to do: find out who this young woman was, where she had come from, how she'd ended up this way. At a moment like this, the number of things that needed doing was too long, almost overwhelming.

It was a whole new investigation.

Teeg caught his breath. "Oh no. What do you think happened to her?"

He stepped forward, but Enid held him back. "Take a look around. See if there's anything else that might have washed in with her. Bag, clothing. Anything out of place, anything that might identify her or tell us how she got here."

Kellan stood frozen, some dozen yards or so behind. Enid called to him. "Did you touch the body at all?"

He nodded quickly. "Just . . . just for a minute. Just to see . . . I thought she might have been alive. But she's not. She's not." He was gasping, close to hyperventilating.

"Kellan, take a breath. A deep one." She spoke calmly, slowly, to get him to match her rhythm. "Breathe slow. There you go. And another one." His shoulders were bunched up to his ears and he shut his eyes tight. He wasn't calming down. "Did you see anyone else? Anything strange?" She almost had to shout to be heard over the gulls, flocking close again.

"No, no . . . I don't think . . . I didn't look . . ."

"That's all right. Think about it a minute, tell me what you remember."

"Enid, look at this." Teeg had walked a circuit around the body. She hoped he studied the ground as he did so, surveying every inch for anything that might have fallen from her when she washed in. Enid joined him, slogging in the mud.

"There," he said, hushed, pointing.

Enid stepped closer to the body, crouched down beside it. The dead woman's brown skin had turned sallow from wet and decay. Eyes half-closed, clouded. Full lips and high cheekbones in a round face. Fingers slender and curling.

But Teeg was pointing at her neck and chest, and the streak of blood down the front of her tunic, the wide brown stain still visible even after what seemed like a good deal of time in the water. Carefully, gently—wondering, as she always did, at this need to be gentle with people who were dead, who were long past needing such kindness—Enid pressed against the shoulder, turning the body over so it lay flat on its back. This revealed a gash, across the woman's throat and arcing down her chest.

This woman hadn't drowned. She'd bled to death.

The collar of her tunic was ripped from the cut, which started at the right side of her neck and ended halfway down her rib cage. The cut itself was deep, exposing muscle, even part of her collarbone and a glimpse of rib. It tore into her windpipe as well as the veins and arteries around it. She might have suffocated or even choked to death before she bled out. A real autopsy would determine that for sure—did she have blood in her lungs, for example. But they didn't have time to get a medic up here to say for sure, and Enid didn't have the skill to do it herself. Really, the finer points were moot. The awful wound had stopped bleeding long ago and had been washed clean, making its severity all the more clear. Anyone could tell what had happened.

"She was murdered," Enid said. Stating the obvious, needing to say it, out of some sense of procedure. Saying it out loud made it real, and she didn't want anyone to argue otherwise.

She glanced over her shoulder at Teeg, who stood with a hand over his mouth and horror in his gaze. "Murdered?" he said. "Like, someone did this to her?"

"I expect so," she said. "I suppose there might be some scenario where some accident did this." She considered. What possible accident could have caused this? Could someone possibly fall on a blade in such a way as to make a cut like that? "But then she likely wouldn't be washed up in a marsh, would she?"

"No, I guess not," Teeg said. "So . . . what do we do now?"

"We start another investigation."

It pained Enid to say it—she had so wanted to foot it for home this afternoon. She thought briefly that she could maybe pass this case on to another pair of investigators . . . but no, getting more investigators here would take too long. Besides, Enid had to find out who did this thing, even if it meant delaying her return home. She supposed she ought to send a message on to Sam and the others, saying what had happened. Get word to the regional committee.

She straightened and looked over the wetlands, streams of sparkling water cutting through thick dark mud, all flat as a table, bounded by stands of grasses. They ought to be able to find some evidence. But artifacts, like whatever had made that awful cut, would sink and disappear in this kind of marsh, among a century's worth of ruins. And of course there wasn't anything so obvious as a suspicious figure running away; the woman had been dead enough time that the assailant was long gone, likely.

"Find anything?" she asked Teeg.

He was still staring at the body, and shook his head as if waking up. "No . . . I don't think so. I . . . I should look again. Just in case."

They stepped around the body, searching for anything that might look out of place. Only the body itself, Kellan's bag, and Kellan, still standing rooted some distance away.

Enid was going to have to talk to everyone in the settlement. Make a decision about what to do with the body. She didn't know where to start. But she knew what her mentor, Tomas, would have said: you pick one thing on the list and do that. Then the next, then the next, and eventually the task reaches an end. That was how they'd solved a murder once before. Or rather, she had solved it. He'd died on the investigation before they finished. A year gone and her thoughts still shied away from the memory. Now, though, she needed to remind herself of his steadying presence. *You can do this,* he'd have told her.

She had a job to do.

"All right," she said finally. "Let's see if we can get a

stretcher down here to carry her out of the mud. Find out if there's a cool space to keep her, at least for the next little while." With the water table so high in this area, there weren't any cellars. They probably ought to plan on burning the body in the next day or so, unless Enid could find out for sure where the woman had come from, then deliver her to her people. Maybe this wouldn't take too long.

Or maybe they would never find out what had happened.

She picked up Kellan's bag and carried it to him. Couldn't resist peeking inside—it gaped open when she pulled the strap over her shoulder: junk, mostly. A couple of lengths of rusted metal. Didn't look good for anything, as far as Enid could tell, but she might be wrong about that. An intact glass jar the size of her hand. A few seashells. Exactly what one might scavenge off a beach like this.

Kellan took the bag from her and hugged it to his chest. "What do we do?" he asked. His voice was tight, like he might cry.

"We're going to try to figure that out. Do you recognize her? Is she from around here?"

He quickly shook his head. "No, no, she's not from here. No."

"Any idea where she might have come from?"

He kept shaking his head, over and over. The man was going into shock, and Enid tried to anchor him, speaking calmly.

"You scavenge the coast here regularly," she said. "Have bodies ever washed up like this before?"

"Never." Fearful, he looked past her, at the lump in the mud.

"She was just like that when you found her?"

"I—I ran, soon as I saw she wasn't alive. To get help."

"And that was the right thing to do," Enid said, to reassure him. "Okay. I'll probably have some more questions for you later on. In the meantime, you know where we can get a stretcher?"

"No . . . no, I don't think so."

"Can you do something for me, Kellan?"

The tears had broken; he was crying now, and might not even be listening, much less able to do what she asked. Enid pressed on, speaking gently. "Go up to Bonavista or Pine Grove and see if they have a sturdy sheet or a big length of canvas we can use. Can you do that for me? Everyone's still waiting up on the road; someone should be able to help."

A glance told her that yes, the whole gathering who'd spent the previous fifteen minutes arguing about a broken house was still standing in a clump. They'd moved closer to the marsh, to watch the commotion, but no one else had ventured onto the mud. Help would have to be fetched.

"Kellan?"

"Yeah. Yeah, I'll go." He trotted up the way, back to the road, each step squishing as he went.

Enid returned to Teeg and the body. "You want me to go for the stretcher instead?" he asked.

"I think Kellan can handle it. He needs a job to get his mind off this. Meanwhile, you and I can keep those birds away." The gulls had backed off at their approach, but dozens of them now circled, waiting for their chance at the body.

Enid studied the mud again. The depressions from their footprints formed a series of tiny puddles. All were recent, belonging to her, Teeg, and Kellan—arriving, circling, and leaving again. This meant the woman hadn't walked here recently, hadn't been killed here in the past day or so—and in the meantime the flowing water of the tide had erased any earlier history.

The way the wound in her neck was scoured clean, along

with the bloated look of her face and hands, suggested she'd been dead for a couple of days at least. That she was lying here at all meant she'd died after the storm; it would have washed her away, and they never would have found her. That gave them a window to start with, at least. Too big to be really useful, but it was something.

"You've done this before, haven't you?" Teeg asked.

"Done what?"

"A murder investigation. I read the report from that case in Pasadan last year."

"Yes," she said, sighing inwardly. She had done this before.

"So you know what you're doing." He said this hopefully. Needing her to know what she was doing.

She shook her head. "This is nothing like that case." The Pasadan case had essentially been an accident, the result of bad temper and bad feeling—it hadn't been obvious or clear-cut and required some real sleuthing to tease out the situation. This . . . this, on the other hand, signified a great deal of intent, which meant someone in the area was a deliberate murderer.

Teeg said, "You think that Kellan guy might have had something to do with this? You spot that machete on his belt? That could have done this."

"Like maybe he's in shock from having done the thing? So . . . what, he sees a strange woman wandering up the river and he decides to swing a blade at her? And then call for help? Why would he do that?"

"Sometimes people just go crazy, I guess. If he spends a lot of time out here by himself —"

She shook her head. "You're making assumptions. No one goes off like that without some warning. Some other evidence of instability."

"All the crud he runs into, scavenging in this mess—lead,

THE WILD DEAD · 27

mercury, whatever else — that'd be enough to make anyone un-
stable, don't you think?"

"It's too early to talk about such things," she said. "Don't
invent a solution."

Kneeling by the body again, Enid studied it in more detail.
If the woman had been attacked, she might have tried to fend
off the weapon. But there was nothing on her hands or arms:
no cuts or bruises other than those that arose from blood
pooling after death. Enid pointed out the details to Teeg. The
one straight wound and nothing else; this suggested she'd been
attacked suddenly. This hadn't been a fight but a single blow,
finished as quickly as it had begun.

Lifting the woman's hands, Enid studied the fingernails,
and yes, there were bits of blood caked there — dark brown
flecks that hadn't washed away. "She had enough time to put
her hands to the wound, to try to stanch the blood. Not much
more than that, probably. But where did it happen?"

"And did she wash down from upriver, or was she dumped
by whoever did this?"

Enid smiled up at Teeg. "See? You know how to do this.
It's like any other investigation: you ask the right questions until you learn what happened. Here, look at this."

She pulled apart strands of the woman's hair, brushed fingers over a section of the kerchief. Debris had caught on the fi-
bers. Pine needles stuck in knitted loops; dried leaves and even
a few twigs tangled in hair. Bits of forest.

"What's all that?" Teeg asked, leaning in. He tugged a couple of pine needles from the kerchief and spun them between
his fingers.

"Look around," Enid said. "It's not anything that grows
around here. She came from upriver." Up the hill, past the settlement, where scattered trees marked the start of a forest.

"Ah," he sighed. "So we need to go up the river there and look."

Kellan hadn't yet returned with the canvas. Enid glanced back at the crowd, but no one seemed inclined to make their way down into the marsh. The gulls, more accustomed to the presence of people now, grew bolder and began swooping in closer to the body.

"Stay here," she said to Teeg. "Keep those birds away."

This was going to be a really long day, Enid thought, trudging back through the mud. Her boots were already caked with the stuff, and from wiping off her hands, she'd gotten it on her trousers as well.

Back at the road, Enid surveyed the crowd. No one had gone looking for a sheet. Bear the dog was barking at Erik's feet, and the man didn't try to quiet him this time.

"Hola," Enid said. Erik and Kellan looked like they'd been arguing—Kellan pleading with some amount of desperation, clutching his bag to his chest, and Erik shaking his head.

Enid was about to ask them what the problem was when Juni came forward, full of concern. "Kellan says there's a body, that you found a body."

"Yeah, 'fraid so. I sent him to find a sheet or something we can use to carry it up out of the marsh."

Juni shook her head. "That can't be right."

"I think I know a body when I see one."

"But . . . who is it?" Juni looked around at her neighbors, who shook their heads, murmured, confused.

"That's one of the things we'll have to find out. Lucky you've already got investigators here, isn't it?"

Nobody smiled. Enid wondered whether they would have bothered to send for investigators, if she and Teeg hadn't already been here. Or would they have simply burned the woman and pretended she had never washed up at their front door? Enid liked to think they'd tell. You didn't just ignore a murdered body. Maybe this place wasn't missing a young woman, but someplace was. It was no use trying to hide it—such knowledge would fester in a small community like this and come out one way or another.

One of the other women, Anna from Semperfi, said, "I think we've got some canvas up at our place, I'll go get it." She ran off.

"What're you going to do?" Juni asked, her voice gone uncharacteristically small.

"We'll try to find out what happened. Take care of the girl as best we can. Do you have anyone here in charge of pyres, or is that done household by household?"

Another long silence, folk waiting to see if someone else would answer. Finally Erik said, "Last House usually does pyres, since they're closest to the timber."

Most places had a household that did the more difficult jobs, the ones no one else wanted to do. Like tending to funeral pyres. Often, such folk lived on the fringes, didn't fit in anywhere else, like the nervous Kellan. Enid was curious to meet the rest of the folk of Last House. "Kellan, can you go to your folk and see about putting together a pyre?"

He'd pulled off his floppy hat, was kneading it in his hands. The strap of his bag had ended up back over his shoulder. He looked disheveled, mud covering his boots, spattered on his sleeves. Enid was about to repeat the request when Kellan's understanding seemed to settle in, and he mashed the hat back onto his head. "Yeah, okay. I can do that." He raced off, seemingly relieved to get away from the marsh.

Well, that was a couple of things off the list. A good start. There'd be some momentum now, and Enid felt better equipped to start talking to everyone else.

"While you're all here, I'd like to ask a few questions. The body, this young woman, was maybe eighteen or nineteen. She's in a blue skirt and brown tunic, has a knitted kerchief. Brown hair, brown skin, slender, about this tall." She put her hand at the level of her chin, just over five foot. "Does that sound familiar? Any of you recognize anyone fitting that description? Not necessarily from here—maybe someone from down the road. Someone you might have seen at the Everlast market?"

Blank stares answered her. Enid wasn't surprised.

"Any of you who feel up to it, if you could take a look at her and see if you recognize her, I'd appreciate it. Finding out where she came from will be a big step toward learning what happened to her."

"Maybe she drowned in the storm," someone ventured.

"Ah, no," Enid said. "Trust me, she didn't drown."

No one seemed to know what to say to that, resulting in an awkward moment of silence.

"Well then. If anyone thinks of anything, come tell me, yeah?"

## An Unknown Burden

Enid had to do some cajoling, but she got Erik and Jess to help her and Teeg carry the body out of the marsh after Anna returned with a bundle of canvas. One of them on each corner of a makeshift stretcher would make the gruesome task easier.

Bonavista, close to the wetlands as it was, had a house and outbuildings built on pylons, almost as tall as she was, to keep them above the flooding. Enid thought they could temporarily store the body under one of the work houses. Juni, Jess, and their folk wouldn't be happy about it. But this was exactly the sort of situation for which Enid needed the authority of the uniform. They couldn't very well argue with her; it was clear she had jurisdiction over the situation. Somebody had to.

"Oh," Erik breathed, when he saw the dead woman and the gaping wound. Couldn't avoid seeing it. Jess gagged and looked away, hand over his mouth.

"Best if you keep your eyes on the sheet," Enid suggested.

"Sorry to put you through this. But I do have to ask—do you recognize her? Even a little?" If she came from somewhere nearby, Enid would prefer to deliver her back to her household.

Unlike Jess, Erik couldn't seem to look away from her. Slowly, he shook his head. "No," he murmured. "No."

At least this would head off the gossip: the young woman had most definitely not drowned.

Jess asked, "Where could she have come from?"

Teeg said, "We'll do our best to find out."

A body with multiple mysteries. Enid didn't like this at all. "All right. Let's get her out of the mud, yeah?"

The gulls wheeled angrily and scattered, crying, as Enid and Teeg lifted the body onto the spread-out tarp. The body flopped as they moved it, neck twisting awkwardly—far past rigor mortis. The bloodless wound gaped wide. The rank smell might have belonged to the corpse, or might have been the odors of the marsh around them. Enid focused on the task, to avoid thinking too much about who this woman had been a few days ago.

Erik and Jess looked like they wanted to flee, but Enid's authority carried them forward. When Enid gave commands, folk listened. So, on the count of three, the four of them— one at each corner, twisting the canvas in their fists—lifted the body. It sagged in the middle of the fabric, but they were able to keep it taut enough to carry. Teeg tucked his staff under his arm.

The hike back to Bonavista household was a long one, silent and—appropriately, Enid supposed—funereal. A somber procession, as they focused on not dropping the burden. The body wasn't very big, but it pulled at Enid's arms and seemed to grow heavier as they went. Dead bodies were awkward things.

When they arrived at the work house at Bonavista, they settled their load onto the ground, with relief. Erik and Jess backed away quickly, brushing their hands, avoiding looking at what they had just carried. Enid took a moment to straighten the body's limbs, smooth back the hair. She made sure the face and wound were exposed, visible, so there'd be no question what had happened when the rest of the Estuary's residents came to try to identify her.

A few of the crowd found the courage, or maybe the overwhelming curiosity, to follow the impromptu procession up to the work house. Juni was at the front, wringing her hands.

"Juni," Enid called. "You see everyone who comes by on this road. You know most everyone, yeah? Can you come and take a look?"

At the invitation, Juni stepped forward, and the others pressed up behind her. They were curious; they wanted to see. Enid stepped back and let them. Next to her, Teeg gripped his staff and frowned. Being official and intimidating.

One of the women covered her mouth and turned away, eyes closed. There was murmuring. Enid was sure they'd all seen death; you didn't live life in a village like this and avoid it. But they might not have seen violence. Enid didn't have to explain the wound—they saw it, and understood.

"Juni?" Enid prompted. The woman stared at the body, studying its face.

"No, no. I don't know her," Juni said, her hand lingering at her own throat.

"No one knows her?" Enid asked.

No one did. At least, they didn't say they did.

Enid studied those gathered, took note of who was here, which households they came from. Wondered if she'd be able to get all of them down here to look before the body got too decayed to keep. At the same time, though, she wondered if it even mattered: if this group, the ones who most paid attention and who were always at the front when there was something to see, if they didn't know who the girl was, would anyone?

Enid was starting to think that this might be as far as they were going to get at this stage of the investigation. She and Teeg might have to go to Everlast and the surrounding villages to learn where this woman came from. The next question, then. How had this happened? Answering that would mean tracking down the weapon that had inflicted such a wound . . . and finding the person who had wielded it.

"Who would do such a thing?" Jess asked softly.

"Good question," Enid said. "Any ideas on that? Anyone around here with a bad temper?"

"What? No!" he said, shocked. But then he seemed to consider for a moment. He shook his head. "I can't imagine a temper bad as that," he said.

Of them all, only Juni hadn't turned away from the body. She asked, wavering, "What are you going to do?"

"Find who did this. We may have to stay at Bonavista a few days. We'll get supplies and credits up here to compensate."

"It's no trouble. But . . . *how?* How can you possibly find out what happened?"

Teeg spoke up. "Enid's done this before. Solved a murder last year in a town called Pasadan. She's a little bit famous for it."

"Really?" Erik said.

"Did it in just a day, as I understand it," he said, sounding like he was bragging. Or maybe he was reassuring himself.

Enid sighed. "Took three days. With help. And it was a completely different situation." For one thing, they knew who the victim was right from the start in that case. And that death hadn't been so . . . messy.

"But if anyone can do it, you can," Teeg offered.

"We might not learn what happened, but we'll try," she said. It's what investigators did, after all. "Thanks all of you for your help, for taking a look. Teeg and I will be here if you think of anything—any detail at all, no matter what, you come and tell us. Yeah?"

Happy for the dismissal, the crowd dispersed. Even Juni backed away, frowning at the body. An interruption in the normal way of the world.

That left Enid and Teeg alone, with whoever this woman had been.

"No one recognizes her," he said bleakly.

"Makes it hard," she said.

Ridiculously hard. The woman could be from anywhere, washed up on this stretch of coast. Might be their only play would be to make as good a description as they could, then send messages around, asking, Was anyone missing? Were there any runaways?

And along with that, anyone who'd been acting guilty? Anyone with a bloody knife tucked away?

It might not be anyone on the Coast Road who killed her, of course. Who wielded the blade that made that awful wound. If the woman had fled from somewhere, even if she'd just been exploring, she might have run into something—someone —she wasn't prepared to handle. Something in the wild that didn't, on principle, like anything from the Coast Road.

"So, we take her to Everlast?" Teeg asked. "No one around here seems to know anything about her—"

"We haven't talked to everyone yet. We still have more questions."

"Like what? Is one magic question going to reveal all?"

"It might," Enid said, quirking a smile at him. "I want to look her over one more time, now that we're out of the mud."

Enid studied the body again, every inch of skin, pushing aside the tunic and skirt. Looking at every stitch of clothing. Enid took out her notebook, started a catalog, adding every detail. A whole life reduced to a list. She took the kerchief off the body, folded it up. Knitted with a ribbed pattern, distinctive—anyone who knew the dead woman ought to recognize it. They could send it to surrounding communities. The shoes were soft leather, folded over and stitched with sinew; the heel on the right was more worn than the left. Whoever made the garments wouldn't likely have been so helpful as to embroider a name or household inside the collar. But Enid recorded what she could: brown linen overtunic, finely woven gray-blue skirt, and white shirt. No pockets, no lumps or bulges that might be a pouch, a bag, a necklace. No piece of metal or scrap of writing. She found nothing. If the young woman had had anything else on her, any jewelry or a pouch, they'd been washed away.

Enid was replacing the tunic, straightening the sleeves again, when she felt down the body's arms. Felt again, missing something that should have been there. Looked at the skin along the upper arm, where an implant was usually placed. Most medics inserted it in the left arm, but Enid checked both, just in case. Felt, squeezing the skin and muscle, searching for the characteristic lump. Enid had one herself. Every girl got one at puberty. She paused, her mouth open, wondering. She rolled up the sleeve to double-check, searching for the scar, the place where the tiny incision would have been . . . and wasn't. The skin was unblemished.

"What is it?" Teeg asked.

"She doesn't have an implant," Enid said. "Never had one."

Which meant she wasn't from any household on the Coast Road.

She came from the wild.

## Bonavista

This case was supposed to be easy. Enid would be gone only a couple of weeks. Her family— Sam, Olive, Berol, and the soon-to-be-born baby of Serenity household—were waiting for her. She promised them she'd be home in time.

Two years after earning its banner, a year after Olive's miscarriage, Serenity was finally having its baby. Enid wanted to be there, to hold Olive's hand and hear the baby's first cry. To hug Sam and be part of what they'd all worked so hard for.

But her name had come up on the roster, and she'd promised to mentor Teeg, so here she was, a hundred miles from Serenity. Enid was happy enough to do her job and earn her keep. *Someone* had to do the hard work, she was fond of saying. Often as a mantra to herself, reminding her that the job usually went faster when she complained less. But given the circumstances, she couldn't help but complain . . . at least to herself. The problem of Semperfi's house had sounded simple. Wouldn't take long at all.

The morning she left—a whole week ago, she had to count back—Enid had knelt beside Olive, pressed her face to her huge belly, felt a tiny little *something* pushing back. "That's her foot," Olive said.

"How can you tell?" Enid asked wonderingly.

"Because her hands are beating my ribs," she said, shifting position, turning her grimace into a laugh.

"How do you know it's a she?" Everyone had an opinion, and everyone said they had tricks to guess, based on the phase of the moon or the shape of the belly or what a woman had been eating or a hundred other omens that made no sense. People asked Enid if she wanted a girl or a boy, and, baffled, she'd reply that she wanted a baby.

Olive shrugged. "I don't, I guess. I just want to call her something."

"Wait for me," Enid had said to that belly, hands spread over its roundness.

"Don't take too long," Olive said back to her. "I want you here for this."

The whole household had seen Enid off at the door, but Sam had walked with her all the way to the Coast Road. She took hold of his arm—taking in the solidity of him, the comfort, tucking it into her memory—and he kissed the crown of her head.

"How long you think this'll take?" he asked.

"Probably too long," she said. "A week just to get out there. Probably two weeks, there and back, plus investigation time. I wish I'd passed on the case. Told them I couldn't spend that much time away—"

He grinned, amused. "Can't do that if you're going to be the world's best investigator."

"That's not it—"

He laughed then, because he knew her well.

"It should be an easy case," she said. "I'll be back in no time at all. And I'll get to call in favors for making the trek that far out." She was trying to put a good light on it.

"Well. I'd tell you to hurry but I know you will. So—do good work, yeah?"

"Love you," she said.

"I know, love. What happens happens. One way or another we'll all be here when you get back."

"Yeah."

A hundred miles away, Enid's family waited. And now she had a murder to deal with.

"She has to be Coast Road," Teeg argued. "Those clothes are Coast Road–woven. Good quality. She couldn't have come from the wild."

Enid sat on the front steps of Bonavista's work house. Pylons raised it up five or six feet from the mud. Evidence of the recent storm remained, vegetation and debris clinging to the wood and stone. After everyone who'd wanted a look had gotten one, they'd settled the canvas-wrapped body on the ground under the building. Flies had already gathered. Teeg paced nearby, pausing to look down the road, as if someone might arrive to rescue them. The murderer, come to spontaneously confess and save the investigators some trouble. Teeg made Enid feel older than she was. Surely she shouldn't be feeling like such a curmudgeon.

"Apparently she did. Or . . . or I don't know what." The lack of an implant, the telling clothes—this opened a whole new set of possibilities, a whole new set of questions. Enid hardly knew where to start. Getting from what she knew to what she wanted to know seemed an impossible distance.

Teeg said, "If she isn't from the Coast Road, then this isn't our case to solve."

Enid looked sharply at him. "She washed up on our shore, didn't she? What if it was one of ours that did this?"

"You really think that's possible?" Teeg said with such a tone of skepticism, it was clear he didn't believe it.

"Where people are concerned? Almost anything is possible. She was found here, wasn't she? And you wondered about Kellan's machete."

"I was guessing. But if she came from the wild—well, anything could have happened. It's hopeless."

They'd be entirely justified in giving up, wouldn't they? But they hadn't even started yet. One thing at a time. One job at a time.

Teeg was right: these were Coast Road–woven clothes. Find out who made them, find out who was trading with folk in the wild, and they'd start to get an idea where the girl came from.

Enid said, "Records say the road ends here, but you go up the river valley, and who knows what all's up there. Maybe not towns, but there's folk living there."

"You serious?"

"I am," she said. "Remember what Erik said—he wasn't surprised to see a squatter in his house. He's seen wild folk around. She's one of theirs. Maybe she was the one hiding out at Semperfi."

"Then where did she get Coast Road clothes?"

"That's just one of the questions we can ask. Meantime, we send messages. Get the word out to way stations. If someone's missing her—if someone's looking for her—we want to know. And we want to talk to them. She might be from the wild, but that doesn't mean no one's looking for her." Before the woman died she'd been healthy, well fed, well cared for. Must've had a family somewhere.

"Might she have been robbed?" Teeg asked. He was learning to think dark.

"You mean, did someone kill her and take whatever she was carrying?" Enid asked. "Would help if we knew what that might have been. Of if someone around here has something valuable they didn't a week ago."

"We can't exactly ransack everyone's place looking for something that might not belong."

"No, we can't. But we can talk."

"But how do you know if anyone's lying, really? Is it instinct? Can you just tell?"

"You never really know," she said, sounding more tired than she meant to. "That's why you ask a lot of questions, and you ask them over and over again, until someone slips up. And you look for hard evidence." Evidence didn't lie. Cultivated land exceeding quota, a smear of blood on a wall. A body washed up in a river. This was too big. She wanted to go home. "There's a few hours of daylight left. We should get started."

"Where do we even start?"

"We start right here," she said, nodding over at Bonavista's main cottage, close to the road, waiting to greet visitors. The first Estuary people Enid and Teeg had met were Juni and Jess, the heads of the household. They'd been bright and welcoming, offering water and rice bread, inviting them into the shade. And telling them all about Semperfi and how awful the house was and how sorry they were that Erik had caused all this trouble. It had been awkward but understandable.

She had absolutely no idea what to expect from these next interviews.

After the excitement of discovering the body, most members of the house, except Jess and Juni, had returned to the open plot of land behind the buildings, back to work that had to be finished by nightfall. One of the household's main activities was collecting reeds from up the river. They'd been carrying back their harvest when Enid and Teeg arrived earlier in the day, great wrapped bundles balanced on their backs. Now they were spreading the reeds out to dry, separating stalks, turning them. They wove baskets and mats with them, traded them down to the next village for what they didn't grow or make here.

And in a sheath on their belt, each one carried a machete — a stout, foot-long sharpened blade. They used the machetes to harvest the reeds, cut away underbrush, any job too big for a knife. Totally normal, a ubiquitous tool. Everyone around here probably had one. And every single one of them could have made the cut that killed the young woman.

Juni and Jess were sitting on the front porch of the main cottage, waiting. They must have known the investigators would start with them.

Juni immediately stood. "Can I get you anything? Some water? It's been such a long day, please tell me if you need anything."

"Water would be fine, thanks," Enid said. The small woman seemed grateful for the task and bustled inside. Enid could hear dishes clattering and water flowing from a pump.

Enid asked, "You're sure you didn't recognize the young woman?"

Jess shook his head. "No. Not at all. How did she get here? How did this happen?"

Teeg started to say something, but Enid simply said, "We're looking into that."

The door opened, Juni emerged, two mugs in each hand; Jess caught the door, held it for her while she distributed water. "You'll talk to everyone, I suppose?" she asked.

"Yeah." She and Teeg accepted their mugs. Enid drank almost all of hers. She hadn't realized how thirsty she was. Easy to miss, in the exhausting heat. Too exhausted to remember to drink, even.

Teeg asked, "Juni, you didn't recognize the body?"

"No, I never saw her. I don't suppose she had anything that might tell you where she's from —"

"As a matter of fact, we think she might be from outside the Coast Road," Enid said. "Maybe from a settlement upriver."

"Then what was she doing here?" Jess asked, astonished. "Those people never come down this far —"

"Erik says they do," Enid said. "That he's seen them, maybe coming down to the shore to scavenge."

The pair glanced at each other, a worried look passing between them, and Enid waited for the explanation.

"Maybe," Juni said, uncertain. "Sometimes. Not that often."

"Not this far," Jess added.

"What do you mean?" Enid prompted.

Jess sighed. "They trade with Last House," he said finally. "Not much, just a few times a year."

Enid regarded them with interest and waited for more. There was usually more, in a conversation like this.

"I wish they wouldn't," Juni said. "It isn't right."

It wasn't much of a thread, but it was something. "Oh?" Enid prompted noncommittally, hoping she sounded curious and not like an interrogator. Kellan was Last House, and he'd said he didn't know the victim.

Juni continued. "It encourages those folk to come too close. Causes trouble. Look what happened."

Jess grunted in agreement. The work out back had fallen quiet, and the rest of the household's folk had drifted to the front, lurking not-so-unobtrusively by the corner of the house, listening in: four men and women in their twenties who'd joined up over the past ten years or so, and Jess and Juni's teenage kid, Tom. Enid debated—should she ask them to move off, talk to each one separately, or get this all over at once? See if they supported one another or argued.

"You think it's been a problem?" Enid prodded gently. "Folk from outside coming into the settlement? Has anyone made trouble?" She was thinking of the squatter in the Semperfi house. If the young woman had been causing what someone perceived as trouble, there might be a motive there. No one had said anything, but then they'd all been focused on the house at Semperfi.

"Not as such," Jess said, though his gaze went distant, like he was thinking about it.

"Not that we know of," Juni corrected. "What you need to do is talk to Last House. They could be hiding a whole tribe of refugees out there, breaking quotas . . . who knows what else. And the rest of us would never know. You want to know what's wrong around here, ask them." She studied the sky a moment, and sighed. "I'm sorry. We're not usually this out of sorts."

"It's been a hard day," Enid said.

Jess added, "If anyone knows that girl, it'll be someone from Last House."

"Kellan said he didn't know her," Teeg said. "You're saying he might be lying?"

Enid would not have put it so strongly, but she waited for their response with interest.

"Maybe he is," Jess said. "He's a strange one."

"They all are." Juni frowned. "Go talk to them, you'll see."

Enid leaned back. "Are you saying this because of the investigation from twenty years ago?"

The woman from the old household, Juni's former household, who'd cut out her implant had moved to Last House after the investigation. A sort of exile.

"I don't like to talk about that," Juni said. "I wish Erik hadn't brought it up."

"Just go talk to them," Jess said quietly. "If anyone knows anything, they do."

"We will, thanks." Enid looked over; the others from the household had stayed quiet, but still watched, wide-eyed. They were part of a relatively new household, built on the ruins of an earlier one—they might very well be worried. She asked, "Any of you feel like running messages to Everlast?" Everlast was the first town on this section of road that had a committee and the means to pass along messages to regional.

The mood lifted. Giving people concrete jobs to replace vague worries usually did that.

"Tom can run messages," Jess said. "How's that sound? Tom?"

Tom, the youngest of the household at fourteen, perked up, stood at attention. "Yeah, I think so. Late enough I might have to stay the night, but yeah, I can. That okay?" He asked this of Jess.

"Sure, you've done it before."

Enid said, "We just need to let the local committee know this is going to take longer than we expected."

"I can do it," he said, sounding so sure of himself. Like she was sending him on a quest to the other end of the Coast Road.

"Good," Enid said, and he beamed.

The boy added, "Never hurts to earn some favors. Especially from investigators?"

"Sharp kid," Enid said, smiling. "Give us a couple of minutes to get our notes together." Enid and Teeg wrote out a couple of messages, telling about the body, its description in case anyone could identify it, and what they planned on doing. Enid tried to sound positive. They'd follow this investigation as far as they could. Even if it turned out to be not very.

Once Tom had the pages, he put on a hat and grabbed a skin of water and set off at a trot. Kid like that could probably keep up that pace for hours.

And that was another thing on the list done.

"I'm not hopeful," Teeg told Enid, out of earshot of the household.

"Teeg, you're a brand-new investigator. You don't even know what's possible yet. Give it a couple of days. We'll turn something up."

Teeg scowled, and she was determined to smile at him. Wasn't she supposed to be the cynical one?

## Judgment

They'd shifted from investigating one structure at one household to investigating the whole community. This was like expecting a drizzle and getting a typhoon. Enid wasn't ready for it, but if she didn't keep herself steady and moving forward, no one else would. If she let Teeg decide what to do, they'd already be footing it home.

Eight more households stood spaced along the ridge above the river. Bonavista was the only one on this side. After it lay the bridge over the shallow, sluggish San Joe River. Ahead, the next household came into view before they'd entirely left Bonavista behind. The whole settlement was probably arranged that way on purpose—close enough for each household to see the next, far enough apart so they couldn't actually hear their neighbors shout. Close enough to be of help in an emergency, far enough away to avoid idle visiting. It wasn't that they didn't like one another here. They just didn't necessarily want to live in one another's laps.

Enid came from a large household in a bustling town—

Haven, the oldest along the Coast Road, the core of what came after. If she tried, she could understand the isolation here. The quiet, the feeling that all you saw was yours. But she didn't like it herself, and she didn't want to be here.

Next up the road was Pine Grove, which had no evidence of pine trees anywhere near it. Unlike Semperfi's precarious house, these cottages were all well back from the riverbank, away from potential mudslides. Farther up the hill, their pylons were only a foot or so tall. Avery and Lynn were the heads of Pine Grove, which was a couple of generations along, with members who'd joined up, along with the handful of banners of those born here. Had a couple of kids, healthy and cared for. The usual collection of chickens, goats, and pigs, and a big barn cat that bared its teeth at the investigators as if it didn't trust them.

Avery and Lynn had been watching for Enid and Teeg, probably since the body had been carried out of the marsh, and came out to the road to intercept them.

"What's happening? What else have you found? Do you know who she is?" Avery asked, before a greeting even. The whole community had been tipped off balance. Even the air felt heavier, weighed down by the gravity of that body lying shrouded.

Teeg looked to Enid for some hint of how to proceed. One step at a time . . .

"We're just getting started," Enid said. "Can you answer some questions for us?"

Avery pursed his lips, while Lynn, who was thin and dark-skinned, with black hair cropped short, plucked at the fabric of her trousers. Enid took that as a yes.

"You got a look at the body when we brought it up. Did you recognize her? Any idea who she is?"

"No," Avery said quickly. "No idea at all."

Lynn shook her head. "I didn't see her. But if Avery didn't know her, it's not likely I would."

"Any idea where she's from?" Avery said.

Enid said, "We think she's from outside. Not Coast Road."

Avery took a step back at this. Lynn's look hardened.

"They come down this way sometimes," she admitted. "We see them on the shoreline, picking up trash."

Harvesting shellfish more likely, Enid guessed.

"Never so close as to talk to us," Avery added. "And now they're here, killing each other?"

"We don't know who killed her," Enid said evenly. "Not yet."

"If anyone can find out, Enid can," Teeg said, with bravado that came off hollow. She braced for what came next, and he predictably followed up. "Enid's investigated a murder before." The couple regarded her skeptically, and she suppressed a scowl.

"Do we need to worry?" Lynn asked. "If wild folk are coming around here, killing each other—do we need to worry?"

And that was another thing to worry about. Enid didn't expect more violence—this death seemed spontaneous, unplanned, not likely to be repeated. But she hadn't expected people to worry that it might.

"I don't think so," she answered, trying to sound reassuring. "But that's why we're looking into it."

Lynn didn't seem comforted, and Avery put his arm around her shoulder. "We'll keep a watch out. You can handle it, if we find anyone nosing around?"

Enid sighed. "Yes, we'll handle it."

Avery nodded, satisfied, but Lynn still didn't look convinced.

"We're staying down at Bonavista if anyone needs to find us." Enid turned to go, with Teeg at her shoulder, when Avery called out.

"Wait—"

They turned back.

"Can I ask . . . well . . ."

"Yeah?" Enid prompted.

"We were just wondering when you might let everyone know what you've decided about that wreck at Semperfi?"

"You know—I had completely forgotten about that," Enid lied. "I'll have to get back to you." She walked on before the couple could say anything else.

Teeg hesitated before following, and she was afraid he was going to say something to the pair. What, she didn't quite know. She wanted to yell at them about priorities, which was why she walked off. But Teeg waited until they were out of earshot before talking.

"We haven't had a chance to talk about Semperfi, have we? They're the next house on the path. What're we going to tell them? They're going to ask."

She didn't care about the house, the original investigation. If the town had had a formal committee, an investigation never would have been called. It was a nothing problem that would take care of itself in the next storm. Common sense should have solved this weeks ago. She probably shouldn't feel so dismissive, but couldn't really help it. That young woman's face, the gaping wound in her neck and chest, occupied her.

"I have to be honest, I'm not really concerned about the house," she said. "The house will still be there after we've done all we can about that young woman." But not for long, likely . . .

"We were sent about the house, not the body."

Enid stopped, turned to face him. "All right, let's talk about the house. What do you think should be done?"

Teeg drew back, mouth open, ready for more arguing. But Enid—hot, sweaty, bitten up by bugs—wasn't in the mood.

Her partner straightened and marshaled his thoughts. "Erik has to know we're not likely to decide this in his favor."

"Of course he does," she sighed. "But he needed to hear it from someone official. Needed a villain to blame, rather than the folk he has to live with every day. So here we are. *That's* why he called for investigators. Not because he thought he had a chance of saving it."

Teeg's brow creased as he turned over some thought. "Is that our job, then? To be the villain?"

"Sometimes it is." Enid started walking again. They had half a dozen more households to talk to and the sun was sinking.

Teeg kept on. "Did you know it was going to be like that before we saw the house?"

"No. But after I saw it, after he couldn't make a good argument for saving it—we hardly needed to discuss it, did we?"

"Are all your cases like this? Are they all this straightforward?"

"No case is like any other, in my experience. Please remember that."

Semperfi came into view. The horrible wreck of a house was hidden at first—they'd have to take a turn toward the river to reach it. The rest of the holding was entirely normal. Respectable. The paths between cottages were neatly laid out and lined with stones. A row of raised garden beds produced a tangle of herbs and vegetables. A small wind turbine worked, the cisterns seemed well maintained. The place was almost pretty. They didn't need the antique house. Its value was sentimental.

Which wasn't to say that sentiment never had value. But not at such an expense.

Erik, Anna, and a couple of other of their folk were working outside and saw the investigators as soon as they came up the path. Erik strode forward to meet them.

"You found out anything? How that girl got there?"

At least he asked about that first, instead of the house. It improved Enid's mood slightly. "We're still talking to people," she said. "You said you'd never seen her?"

"No, I didn't recognize her at all. And I go to the market at Everlast once a month or so."

"We don't think she's from the Coast Road."

His expression tightened, his jaw clenching. "I told you they'd been coming down here, I *knew* it. You think she was the one sneaking into the house? It was probably her." There was anger in his voice.

Enid tried to steady him. "That's what we're trying to find out. You said you've seen outsider folk around. How often? Would you recognize any if you saw them again?" Maybe the blanket and pouch they'd found belonged to her, which was why they hadn't found anything with the body? It was a possibility.

His mouth worked a moment before he admitted it: "Not often. Every few months. Mostly they go to the coast to scavenge. But if they decided they'd get better pickings from here—"

Enid tilted her head. "If you're sure that girl was here stealing from the households, then it stands to reason someone here at the Estuary was the one who killed her. You know who might do something like that?" She prodded him intentionally, to get a reaction.

"No, nobody here ever would. At least . . . I don't think . . ."

"What?" Teeg demanded. Enid had to put a hand on his arm to hold him back. Pouncing on the guy would only scare him.

"Last House. Talk to Last House. They've been trading with the wild folk. They see them all the time. You want to know what's going on, talk to them. I bet they know."

This was interesting. Lots of fingers pointing at Last House. Didn't necessarily mean anything. Or it meant that no one liked Last House.

Enid asked, "Kellan, the man who found the body—has he been back through here since he went up the hill?"

"No, he hasn't been back."

"All right, thanks. Mind if we talk to your other folk, in case they've seen anything odd?"

He didn't mind—couldn't, really. He stood by as Enid and Teeg asked questions, just as they had at the first two households. Even their child, a nine-year-old named Peety, though his parents bristled at it. Enid was careful, sending Teeg with his staff to stand farther off, kneeling down to Peety's level, and asking gently, "Have you seen anything strange? Have you seen anyone around you didn't recognize?" The boy was wary of her and the uniform, even though he'd likely never seen one before. He'd heard the stories.

She and Teeg finished and set off toward the path again when Erik came up to intercept them, frowning. His face was flushed; he'd calmed down, but some anger lingered. Enid suspected she knew what he wanted, and was feeling contrary enough to make him ask for it.

"Yes?" she prompted.

"I have to know . . . I mean, you have to have decided. I

know you've got other things going on, but you can't leave us hanging. About the house. Do we get to keep it?" He was trying to sound strong, brave. But he couldn't meet their gaze. He kept his eyes on their uniforms.

Enid sighed, annoyed. Time to finish it, then.

"I'm sorry, Erik. You've got to let the place go. You can't ask the others to put time and resources into a thing that isn't doing anyone any good. More, it's a hazard. We don't want anyone to get hurt trying to save it."

Erik listened without reaction, then nodded like he understood. Like he had expected this. He looked away, hiding reddening eyes, and wiped a hand across his nose. He must have known what she was going to say, must have known the whole time. Back toward the main cottage, Anna saw them talking, must have guessed, from Erik's reaction, what about. She came up to him, held his hand, which he squeezed back.

"They're killing the house, Anna," he said quietly.

"It's okay," she murmured.

"Yeah. Okay, okay. I understand."

Enid's shoulders unknotted, and Teeg relaxed the grip on his staff. Enid hoped someday Erik would come to be relieved that he didn't have the maintenance of that wreck hanging over him anymore. She wasn't going to suggest that to him now, however.

"I thought you would," she said. "Thanks for your cooperation; it's been helpful."

"Yeah. Just . . . just one question. This won't hurt our chances for another banner, will it?"

Erik and his household were worried that this—their illogical attachment to a thing that had so little value—proved that they couldn't care for a child. Maybe they were right to worry.

Softer, Erik said, "We just want to know if you're going to impose any other restrictions. You know, for bringing all this up in the first place."

By some arguments, calling for an investigation in a situation like this was itself a waste of resources that ought to be punished. Enid didn't agree with that line of thinking. If people thought that, they'd let arguments stew until they boiled over and people got hurt.

She shook her head. "No. Losing the house is enough, don't you think? As soon as Teeg and I walk out of here, I consider the matter closed."

Erik laughed stiffly. "That's investigators. Coming in, tipping everything over, then walking away."

Enid brightened. "Yeah, that is our job, isn't it?"

Clinging to Anna's hand, Erik looked up the hill, to the ruin behind him. "I guess . . . we should make a plan to start salvaging what we can. Maybe not right away, though."

"You've got time, I imagine," Enid said. "But you might want to get any salvage out of there before the next storm."

"Right," Erik murmured. Enid hoped her smile was comforting, but it felt grim.

There was always another storm, and there never seemed to be enough time between them.

## Last House

They continued their trek up the hill, and once again, Teeg waited until they were out of earshot. "He took it better than I expected," he said.

"I told you—I think he knew it was coming." They went a few more steps, and Enid enjoyed the sound of her boots crunching on dry ground, away from the marsh and mud. "They don't always take it so well."

The next visits went much like the first few. No one who'd seen the body recognized it. Several who hadn't already seen it agreed to go to Bonavista and look, just in case. Enid trusted that they really did want to help, and wouldn't go simply to gawk. No one had noticed anything strange, hadn't seen anyone from outside the settlement wandering around. This was a case with no threads to follow. Enid was afraid they'd have to hold a pyre for the body and walk away with all the questions left unanswered.

At one household, a very old woman sat on a porch under a veil of mosquito net, braiding hemp rope. Even with her stiff, arthritic hands, the movements, over and under, showed evidence of long practice. Enid asked her if she was old enough to remember anything from before the Fall—she looked like she might be—but no, she'd been born right around that time. The woman remembered her parents' stories, but that was all. It had been years now since Enid had met anyone with their own memories of that time. The last was Auntie Kath from back in Haven, who'd died over a dozen years ago now. No, longer than that. Almost eighteen years ago. That last bridge to the old days, to before. Enid likely would never meet another, and the fact felt like loss.

Each visit, right before Enid and Teeg left, folk all asked what she'd decided about Semperfi. Was she going to make them let the house go, or force the rest of them to prop it up? Enid told them it wasn't important, not right now. They'd find out her judgment soon enough. It was like they didn't see the dead body as something that concerned them. Only the house and their neighbors. Enid left them hanging.

As for the identity of the young woman, many of them said to ask at Last House. Last House traded with the wild folk, they might know. Ask them. People seemed relieved to send the investigators on their way with at least that suggestion. As if it helped.

Finally Enid and Teeg arrived at Last House.

The last household on the path was a sprawling, sturdy two-story cottage with rooms added on to the back. Unadorned, maybe even uninviting, though Enid avoided judging the inhabitants. They may have chosen to use their energy and resources on tasks other than making their house pretty for other people. Enid looked for the usual: a cistern full of drinking water, a solar collector for heat and light, a latrine an appropriate distance from living quarters—the essentials. Last House had them all.

They might have tried coming up with a more interesting name.

Piles of salvage were neatly arranged in a clearing on the cottage's south side. Fallen trees and driftwood mostly, but also rusted rebar, flat sheets of weather-stained steel, bins containing broken glass and loops of cable, coils of wire, and broken-up electronics. Clearly a scavenging household. A set of wind chimes made of bits of animal bone and seashells strung on hemp hung silently off the front porch.

"So where'd Kellan go?" Teeg said, looking around.

They hadn't heard from him since Enid sent him off to see about a pyre, and no one seemed to be working on it. Nobody was outside working at all.

Teeg knocked on the door. It felt odd; the grapevine in most villages was such that they rarely had to knock on doors. Folk saw them coming from far off, seemed like. As if their uniforms came with warning bells. Everyone in the Estuary had been watching for them, and Kellan should have already brought them word of the dead woman. Folk usually came out looking for more news after something like that.

They waited. The quiet drew on. Not even footsteps on the other side of the door.

"Maybe nobody's home?" she asked.

"There's four people supposed to live at Last House, from the records, right?" Teeg asked. "If they ran off—what does that say?"

"What do you think it says?"

"That they've got something to hide?"

Enid reached out and knocked again.

"Coming!" a voice inside said.

Enid shrugged, and Teeg seemed almost disappointed. So much for intrigue.

An older man opened the door. He seemed distracted, looking over his shoulder, his soft face flushed. When he saw two investigators on his porch, he stepped back, his mouth open in shock, as if they were monsters. With a deep breath the man managed to settle his expression. He turned stony.

"What's wrong? What's happened?" he asked, with forced disinterest.

Enid's brow furrowed. "Is Kellan here? We sent him back home."

"Yeah, he's here." Then nothing.

Enid paused, waiting for him to fill the silence. But the man didn't fall for the trick. "He didn't tell you what happened?" she asked.

"He's upset, and he doesn't talk much when he's upset. He hasn't been able to get a word out. What's happened?"

She was both surprised that Kellan hadn't said anything, and not. "There's been a murder, down on the mud flats. Kellan found the body. Can we come in and talk?"

He stammered, "Murder? What? Who—"

"Are you Mart? May we come in? It'll only take a moment."

Still, he didn't step back. "This happened just now, yeah? Today? There wouldn't have been time to send for investigators. How . . . we haven't done anything wrong, I don't know what the others told you, but there's nothing wrong here." His wall-like demeanor slipped, and politeness and panic vied for control of his voice. "Why are you here?"

Enid frowned. "I'm sorry—you didn't know? Erik at Semperfi requested an investigation about that old house, the one sitting on top of a mudslide. We were handling that, and then Kellan found the body. We got sidetracked."

"You didn't know that we were here at all?" Teeg asked the man. "That an investigation had been requested?"

Everyone had known, Enid thought. They'd all fallen over themselves to tell Enid and Teeg just what they thought of the house at Semperfi.

The old man gave a quick, wry smile. "We—we don't talk to the others very much."

The time it took for Semperfi to request an investigation, for the message to be delivered—by foot, horse, and solar car— and the time Enid and Teeg took to travel all this way, would have been a couple of weeks at least. In all that time, the area's gossip hadn't reached the Last House folk? They hadn't traveled down the path to Semperfi and Bonavista and the others to hear the news? Had they not even been part of discussions about the dilapidated house?

Not if they wanted nothing to do with it, Enid supposed.

She tried to sound reassuring. "Let's start over, then. I'm Enid, this is Teeg. We're talking to everyone. Originally it was about the old house at Semperfi. But, well, now we're talking about a murdered woman. May we come in?"

Relief softened the man's features. "That explains why Kellan's so upset. Maybe he'll talk to you."

"Thank you," Enid said, still finding her own balance, trying to see where Last House fit in with the rest of the settlement. Maybe it didn't . . . and maybe that was fine. Then again, there was the old investigation from years ago. The finger pointing. Everyone thought the folk at Last House knew something. Did they?

Stepping aside, the man opened the door for them.

Much like the outside, the interior was plain and functional rather than comfortable. The wide space was left open, with a sitting area by a fireplace. A basket of mending sat beside one chair, some carving tools rested on another. Beyond the fireplace was a kitchen—pump and sink, open shelves holding dishes and mugs, pots and pans. And beyond that, a door that led to a screened porch. Wooden steps on one side led upstairs, presumably to bedrooms.

Records from the area, collected and updated by the medics during their semiannual rounds, said four adults belonged to Last House. Enid took the usual quick inventory of the property, glancing over the interior, seeing if what she saw matched the records she and Teeg had reviewed before they came.

"You're Mart, yeah?" Enid asked, moving through the house. Mart was listed as head of house.

"Yeah, I am. Sorry. Was just a shock, seeing you—the uniforms—at the door. Been a while since we saw uniforms around here."

"Almost twenty years, I think. That's a good run without trouble."

He raised an eyebrow. "Without that sort of trouble, at least. Still plenty of the usual kind."

"Oh?" she asked.

"Folk getting into each other's business. You know."

She chuckled, thinking that Mart might end up giving her the best account of the region of them all.

"I don't know what the others told you, but it really doesn't matter what anyone thinks about that Semperfi house. The next storm, that thing'll slide into the river, nothing anyone can say about it."

Enid agreed. "So you didn't know about the request for an investigation. You have an opinion about that?"

"Or about investigators in general?" Teeg added softly, and the man looked sharply at him.

"Don't know that the problem needed investigators at all. But Erik . . . he's stubborn." Mart led them to the back of the house. "Have to warn you, the others won't be happy to see you. Might be twenty years on, but they'll remember."

The other three members of the household were on the back porch, which was set up as a workspace. Screened in, open to the air, the space was cooler than the rest of the house. Kellan sat on a chair. A man knelt by him, holding his hand, murmuring to him. A woman stood holding a large mug, maybe of water. Either Kellan had just drunk something or she was trying to get him to.

The woman would be Neeve, the one who'd cut out her implant twenty years ago. No one would ever know, looking at her now. She wore long sleeves; the scar wasn't visible.

From the doorway, Mart made a curt announcement. "I think I found out what's got into Kellan." Stepping aside, he gestured to Enid and Teeg. The two in their brown uniforms filled the doorway. Even spattered with mud and worn from travel, those uniforms intimidated.

The way those on the porch reacted, the investigators might have walked in swinging axes. Wasn't just shock on their faces as they drew back; it was fear. Enid smiled calmly and turned to murmur to Teeg to maybe put the staff away, but he'd already shifted it behind his shoulder, partly out of sight.

"Hola," she said. "I'm Enid, this is Teeg—"

She was about to ask for their names, but froze when she got a good look at the woman, Neeve.

She looked just like Juni.

A more tired, wary version of her, but still the same: round face, hair in a braid instead of up in a bun, streaked with gray where Juni's wasn't. Frowning and quiet where Juni would be smiling. Nothing in any of the notes Enid had made prior to coming here had mentioned that Juni and the woman at Last House were sisters, much less twins. Yet they clearly were.

"They're Neeve and Telman," Mart said, nodding at the woman, then the man. "You met Kellan already."

Telman — near forty and balding, with brown skin and a long face — looked back and forth between Neeve and the investigators. He would jump in to protect her, if he thought he needed to, Enid suspected. They were wary. They had every right to be. This, not the eager helpfulness they'd seen so far, was the reception investigators usually got.

Enid studied the woman again, getting over the initial surprise of her appearance. Forty or so, with ruddy, sunburned skin, Neeve stood with her gaze downcast, clutching the mug to her chest. She stood like she was bracing for something terrible.

And why shouldn't she? The old investigation had been about her. But this wasn't about her. Enid turned to the man in the chair.

"Kellan. You had a shock. How are you doing?"

The others watched him carefully; they didn't seem to know what to expect from him, either. Kellan straightened, took a deep, unsteady breath, and scrubbed his face with his hands. "There's a body," he said.

"Yes," Enid said. "We're talking to everyone. You said you didn't recognize her."

"No, no, I didn't, no." He shook his head quickly, nervously. Looked at the others, almost pleading, as if he wanted them to confirm.

Mart said softly, "Any idea who it was?"

"She was a young woman, maybe twenty. Brown hair,

about five feet tall or so. We think she's from outside. Not Coast Road."

A silence stretched on, fraught and interesting. The folk of Last House seemed to hold themselves unnaturally still, afraid to speak.

Finally, Neeve said softly, anxiously, "Can we go look? I . . . I'd like to look."

"You think you might know her?" Teeg said, leaning in, maybe a little too excited.

Mart said, "The others probably told you, wild folk come here to trade sometimes. We might recognize her at least."

Finally, something solid. A line of information that didn't end in *I don't know*.

"Do you have a way to get a message to them? Let them know that something's happened to one of their own?"

"No," Mart said, shaking his head quickly. "They come here a few times a year. It's unpredictable. We don't know where they come from. Someplace upriver, that's it."

If they could even get a name to go with the body, Enid would feel they'd accomplished something. "Well. This is a start, at least. It's more than we had before we got here. Yes, please come, we've got her at Bonavista—"

"Why there?" Neeve said.

"It was closest," Enid said. "Juni never said that you were her sister. Are you really twins?"

Neeve folded in on herself and looked away, out the screen to the slope of hill and the distant water. Lost in thought, lost in herself. Enid almost prompted her again, but Mart explained.

"They don't get along. Not since the old investigation."

Juni would blame Neeve for breaking up their old household, Bridge House. Grudge like that would go on forever.

"Understood. But please come and look, if you can tell

us anything. Also, we'll need a pyre for her. I hear you're the house that handles arrangements. That's what I sent Kellan up here for."

Mart nodded. "Yeah, we do. We can do that."

"Thanks. We may have more questions later. The sooner you can come down, the better. We should probably take care of her tomorrow."

Teeg added his thanks, and they turned to go.

"You're not going to say anything else about Neeve?" Telman burst out.

Harsh glares from the others and a spike of tension answered him. The investigators stopped, looked back.

Enid said, "Anything we should say?"

"The medics always check on her. Every time they come through, they check. I just assumed, investigators—"

"Telman," Mart hissed, and the other man looked away.

The folk of Last House would never welcome investigators, and this was why. Even twenty years later, they remembered. As Telman said, the medics still checked her implant, every time, to make sure she hadn't tampered with it. They didn't trust her. Did anyone? It was the reason Neeve lived here, at the edge of civilized territory, without a single banner on the wall.

Because no one else would take her.

Enid said, " Your implant's still in place now, isn't it?"

"I never tried anything like that again," Neeve said softly, putting her hand over the spot on her left upper arm, squeezing idly. Covering the scar that would be under the sleeve, from where she cut herself.

No bannerless pregnancy had resulted from the sabotage. She'd been found out, reported by her own household. In the end, it was always hard to hide a bandaged arm in that dis-

THE WILD DEAD · 67

tinctive spot. Her punishment had been straightforward: no banner for her, nor for whatever household she lived in, ever. She'd left her old home to come here, to a small, scrabbling household that never expected to earn a banner. She'd never made trouble again.

A sad story, some people would say. Olive would say it was a sad story, but she'd spent the past few months being emotional and weepy about any story that had anything to do with banners and babies. Enid was sympathetic to Neeve—one rash action, impacting the whole of her life like this. *That* was hard. But she had no sympathy for the idea that one person could take the fate of an entire community into her own hands. A place like the Estuary settlement couldn't feed an extra, unexpected mouth like that.

"Then there's no reason to say anything," Enid said. "Well then, unless you've got anything else you'd like to talk about, we'll be off. We'll look for you down at Bonavista."

They nodded dutifully, the silence drawing out, cut suddenly by the cries of gulls out on the water. Enid was pretty sure she wouldn't be hearing from them again.

"Afternoon," Teeg said, and left them on the porch. Likely to discuss whether the investigators really were going to let them alone—and if the old trouble really was securely in the past.

Back on the path along the river Teeg asked, "So, Juni and Neeve are sisters? Twins? Did we know that?"

"Must be written down somewhere, but no, I didn't." They'd studied the records. This included a list of every banner awarded to the region, every child born here. Juni and Neeve had been listed as part of the old Bridge House. But not as sisters. When the old household broke down, so did the records. It happened sometimes.

"Juni didn't say anything?" Teeg asked.

Enid thought about it, everything the woman had said about the other households and what they'd find. She'd been quick to talk about Last House, bitter about the old case. But she hadn't mentioned a sister.

"Would you say anything? If you had a twin that did what she did?" Enid said.

They were out of sight of Last House now. Curious, Enid next turned uphill, wanting to see how much farther the path went, what else might be up here.

"What're we looking for now?" Teeg asked, using his staff as a walking stick as the way grew more rocky.

"If I knew that, I wouldn't need to look," she said.

Up the hill, away from the Estuary and the saltwater, trees and scrub got a roothold, and farther up was actual forest. Cottonwood, oak, a few pines. Stumps were in evidence — this was where the settlement harvested lumber. But they weren't clearing the forest, which was good. They kept to the quotas they had for harvesting lumber.

Not more than a hundred yards past Last House, the path narrowed to a dirt track, then trickled out to nothing, overgrown with grasses. It was possible people came up this way, but clearly not often.

"See anything?" Teeg asked, looking around, again with that furrow in his brow like he was searching for something without knowing what it looked like.

"Just trees and wild," she said. They were up in real hills now; the river turned shallow, rushing over rocks, cutting a narrow gulch far below. She could barely hear it from here. "Next I think we should walk up the riverside, see if she left anything behind when she washed down, or if there's any sign of what happened.

"Like maybe a knife someone threw out of sight."

"That would certainly be convenient for us."

Teeg glanced up at the sky and around. "We'll have to wait until morning. We won't find anything in this light."

Dusk was falling. Shadows were long, and the last bit of sunlight filtered strangely through hazy air. Enid didn't want to wait, but he was right. All she saw was shadow.

Nightfall, and the promise of another day in this place. Even the golden light over the wetlands was starting to look ominous. She sighed.

"Right. Let's get back."

## Ruin

By dusk, high tide meant water almost reached the road, shallow waves lapping, receding, and washing smooth the mud flats. The landscape on this stretch must change all the time, especially after a storm. Some of the rusted metal ruins, the pipes and slabs of concrete, were covered up while new ones were revealed. Kellan and other scavengers had their work cut out for them.

If Kellan hadn't gone out on the shore today, he wouldn't have found the body. She'd be covered with water now, and might have washed out to sea when the tide receded. No one ever would have known. And Enid was horrified to find a small part of her thinking that would have been better; there'd be no fuss then, and she'd be on her way home. But no, this was better. The truth was always better.

She still hoped that someone would come looking for the young woman, eventually.

Enid's socks and shoes felt damp. Not wet enough to need

to change. Just *sticky*, like everything else. Made her feel every step of the way. Not painful, but definitely annoying.

Kids were playing out by the water. Peety from Semperfi, a couple of younger girls. Barefoot, they'd run out to where the crawling surf met the draining river, splashing and shrieking with laughter. One of them had a basket, and Enid saw that they were hunting crabs, little skittering things that came out of the sand to pick at what the water washed out. The kids weren't doing it very efficiently, spending as much time chasing and splashing one another as searching out their prey. But every now and then, one of them would shout out and rush over to drop a wriggling thing into the basket. Then they'd go back to running around with far too much energy.

Looked like fun, actually.

Solar lights were on at Bonavista, and they'd hung a lantern with a candle off the front porch. Enid wondered if this was a usual evening habit, or if they'd left the light out for the investigators to find their way. It made the last little bit of their trek easier. They'd been walking all day, with a lot of talking and thinking, and Enid was bone tired.

Juni let them into the main house and enthusiastically offered them dinner—she'd made extra. Clam chowder, which smelled rich and full of herbs. Enid's stomach reminded her she hadn't had anything to eat since the morning. The rest of the household, seated around the kitchen table, invited them in. Tom was missing, still out on messenger duty.

The whole place was clean, well kept, cozy. The kitchen and common area occupied the whole front half of the building. In the back, separated by a short hallway, were bedrooms, with doors on either side. All the doors and windows were open now, letting in air and sun. The kitchen had a sturdy table and chairs, plenty of counter space, pots and pans on a shelf.

Two banners hung on the wall over the front door. Squares of woven cloth, in a checked red and green, a little over a foot on a side. A deep, rich source of color, the brightest things in the room, drawing the gaze right to them. A mark of pride —you had to look at them. Neither of the banners was recent—Tom was a teen, the one before was older still, one of those strong young men collecting reeds from the riverbanks. The household had started up only twenty years before, put together from the pieces of the one that had broken up after Neeve cut out her implant. The old household's banners would have been put away or sent off with the people who left.

Juni collected a pair of bowls from a shelf and began filling them with chowder. "Come and sit. We want to know how everything went. What have you decided about Semperfi? You talked to Erik?"

Enid hesitated, confused for a moment. She hadn't been thinking of Semperfi at all. "We've been a little bit distracted, I'm afraid."

"Oh. Yes. I suppose. I assumed . . . if that poor girl isn't from here, then it can't possibly have anything to do with us. Can it?" She sounded more hopeful than sure.

Teeg's questioning gaze met Enid's. Asking for her lead on how to deal with this. The poor kid still seemed shaken, his grip on his staff a little too tight. He hadn't set it aside all day. Now he took up his role as enforcer, standing at the doorway, keeping watch. Folk kept glancing at the staff he carried.

"That's one of the things we need to find out, isn't it? Mind if I ask a couple of questions?" Enid said, looking around to take in everyone in the room. They stared back at her, and if anyone had a contrary opinion, no one said anything. They could always refuse to answer. And she would note that in her reports, along with the rest.

Weakly, Juni offered the bowls she'd just poured. "But . . . soup'll get cold."

"It'll just take a minute. You said before, you couldn't think of anyone around here that has a temper. That still true? Especially lately, has anyone seemed under a lot of stress?"

Jess said, "If you're thinking of that argument at Semperfi earlier—"

"I wasn't," she said. "But is that kind of thing usual? You do a lot of arguing around here?"

"No," he said. "No, not like that. Not usually. I think everyone's a little on edge. You know. Investigators." He nodded at their uniforms, and Enid smiled wryly. "And no one would be angry at a stranger, an outsider. Not like that."

Leaning against the counter, resigned to the chowder going cold, Juni added, "Erik's been stressed about that house. Nagging at people about it. But I wouldn't say that's unusual. Just now, when it's all come to a head."

Enid was considering that someone who'd just killed a person would show signs of stress, some kind of agitation. But it might also be the case that someone who was already under stress might act out in a way they wouldn't, normally. Erik hadn't been all that surprised to find evidence of a squatter in the house . . .

She'd have to think about this.

Next she asked, "You all have machetes? I saw you working earlier today. Does everyone in the Estuary carry them?"

The silence grew stiff, their stares incredulous.

Finally, Jess said, "You really think someone here could have done it?"

As much as Enid wanted to assure them that all was safe,

that they had nothing to worry about, she wasn't sure. Someone had been sleeping in that house at Semperfi. Maybe it was the dead woman. Or maybe it was whoever had killed her.

"We're just asking questions," Enid said, deflecting him. "We went up to Last House. Juni, you and Neeve really twins?"

The woman seemed taken aback. She turned back to the stove, pausing with a ladle in one hand and a bowl in the other, mouth open like she didn't know what to say. Surely this couldn't be an unexpected question. Finally, she recovered, setting the ladle aside. Talked like nothing was wrong. "Yeah, we are. Two babies with one banner—only time anyone in the Estuary ever exceeded a quota." She chuckled weakly.

Enid smiled at the joke. "Twins—that's something special. You didn't say anything."

"Honestly didn't think about it. Don't think about her if I can help it. I disown her."

"You're the one turned her in, back when this was Bridge House? When you found out what she'd done?" Enid asked.

Juni glared hard. "Thought it might save the household. Didn't do much good, did it? But I got a banner, eventually, didn't I?" Jaw taut, she jabbed a finger at the red-and-green cloth hanging above the doorway. The thing had happened a generation ago, and she was still angry.

Jess came up to stand by Juni. "What's all that got to do with anything?"

Enid shrugged. "Nothing, I suppose. I'm just trying to understand the place."

Juni said, "And what did they say, up at Last House? What did *she* say?"

"That you didn't get along. Really, I get the impression the Last House folk don't talk to anyone much."

"Got that right," Jess muttered.

Juni said, "What did they say about the dead girl? Do they know her? Do they know where she came from?"

"We're still gathering information," Enid said. "It's best we don't discuss it until then. In fact, we should probably take dinner out to the work house." She collected the bowls Juni had poured for them, helped herself to a pair of spoons. Investigators didn't much socialize while in uniform. One of the hardest parts of their training was learning not to apologize for it. Teeg opened the door for her.

"Smells good," he said. "We know you didn't expect to feed a couple of extra mouths. It's appreciated."

Juni's shoulders dropped—she'd wanted to hear it all. "You can stay—it can't hurt anything, can it? Just talking?"

Enid summoned her kindest smile. "It's more the principle of the thing. Thanks very much. We'll leave you folk to it."

BONAVISTA'S WORK SHED was much less cozy than the main cottage. No decoration to speak of, no curtains on the windows, not even a chair for sitting. A work table was set against one wall, and a couple of metal wash basins were shoved in a corner, next to a water pump connected to the cistern outside. They probably did washing here, maybe food prep and preservation. A set of shelves held baskets in various stages of production, waiting to be finished or carried off to market. The place smelled sweetly of dried reeds, tickling the nose. There was a single solar light glaring from a corner. She and Teeg added candles and sat on the floor to eat. The chowder, full of onions and cream, was cooling quickly, but still had enough warmth to melt her limbs and fill her stomach.

They ate in thoughtful silence. Enid's mind kept going to

the body lying just a few feet under them. They didn't even have a name for her.

"Busy day," Teeg said. Maybe unable to contain himself any longer. "All cases go like this?"

"Oh no," Enid said, chuckling. "You don't usually get a case that lands on you before you've even been called out to look at it."

"So if we hadn't been here . . ."

"Yeah, I've been thinking of that."

Spoons scraped against wooden bowls.

"The old case," Teeg said. "Neeve cutting out her implant. Were you around for that one?"

How old did he think she was? "No. Before my time." Her old partner, Tomas—he'd have been around then. He might have heard something. Not that she could ask him. The grief stabbed at her suddenly. It ebbed and flowed like that. Here and now, though, she wondered what he would have done with this, how he would have approached the body, trying to investigate an impossible case. What perspective he'd have offered that would have made it all clear. Or maybe that was wishful thinking.

She was likely doing this all wrong. But she didn't know what else to do. She bowed her head and bit her lip a moment, took a deep breath until the moment of loss and vertigo passed. Teeg never noticed.

"Case like that—it never really goes away, does it?" he said. "Did you see the looks on their faces when we walked into Last House?"

She had—like they'd seen monsters. Like they really thought the investigation might be continuing after so many years, that Neeve would still face consequences for that long-ago infraction. And wasn't that the reputation investigators wanted? That you could never, ever forget what you'd done?

That no one could.

"She seems so quiet. What could she have been thinking, when she did it?" Teeg asked.

Neeve likely asked herself the same thing. It had been so long ago. What could that younger version of her have been thinking? "I don't know. Lots of reasons. They never think they'll get caught until they do."

////////////////////////////////////////////////////////////////

THE NIGHT NEVER really cooled off, and the bedrolls they'd brought with them turned out to be mostly useless. Gave them some padding on the floor, at least. Enid had a restless night, was never able to get comfortable. It wasn't the stark conditions; it was thinking about home . . . and worrying. She didn't like having her attention divided.

Morning came with the call of gulls and buzzing of insects.

She'd fallen asleep and woke back up so many times during the night, that when dawn arrived, light coming in through the shed's uncovered windows, she watched it until her bladder forced her to get up, put on her boots, and visit the latrine. The air turned sticky as the sun warmed it. This early, the haze that hung over the whole of the Estuary felt particularly thick and wet. The air couldn't possibly hold more water without rain falling.

Enid searched the sky out of habit, looking for black walls of clouds on the horizon, the hints of storms building at sea, getting ready to pound the land. They were still in the season for it. She had never before in her life wished for a storm, but that house falling down of its own accord, or being pushed over by an indifferent bit of weather, could resolve a lot of problems and hurt feelings here.

What would happen if Serenity, her own home, collapsed, and no one could help her and the others shore it up? She felt a pang at that. They'd worked so hard on it, building the physical core of their small household. But she'd be more hurt if anything happened to the people. Sam, Berol, Olive. The baby. She'd give up a house in a heartbeat to keep them safe. They could always build something new, as long as they were all together.

A noise caught her attention, a steady pounding, drifting across the Estuary. Because of the distance, it sounded vague and indistinct, but it wasn't natural. It tweaked Enid's instincts.

"What's that?" Teeg asked.

"Don't know. I'll go check it out," she said.

"I'll join you." He checked his belt pouch, where he kept the tranquilizer patches tucked away. Picked up his staff from where it leaned by the steps.

"No need, it's probably nothing," she said.

"You said it yourself — if there's a killer in the area, maybe we shouldn't go off alone."

"There's that," she said, sighing. The shrouded bundle still lay stowed — undisturbed — under the work house. From a distance, it wouldn't look like anything at all. An odd bundle of storage, nothing ominous.

They set off toward the source of the racket.

"Will they hold the pyre for her today?" Teeg asked.

"Likely," Enid answered. "We'll need to find out where they usually do these things, and carry her there." She guessed they held pyres up the hill, closer to the timber, in drier territory where keeping a fire going would be easier. That was going to be a long walk, carrying the body.

The shadows were long, the light glassy. They trekked across the bridge, stopped, and circled, looking out in all directions, and still couldn't make out where the noise came from; it echoed, and the marsh seemed to channel sounds oddly.

"It's up the road, you think?" Enid asked, looking up to the next household. The noise continued, rhythmic and determined.

This was only their second day here, and Enid was already tired of hiking this way. They reached Pine Grove, where everything seemed normal. One of the young women of the household was milking goats in a rough-hewn pen outside, in the shade of a barn. Hearing the footsteps, she looked up, her eyes widening at the sight of the uniforms. Quickly, she shoved away the goat she was milking and stood, brushing her hands on her trousers. The animal bleated loudly and trotted off.

"Hola," Enid said.

"You here about the body? The murdered girl? No one here knows anything, I don't think. None of us knew anything about it—"

Enid was already shaking her head. "No, we're not here for that. You know what's making that noise?" The banging had gotten louder; they were clearly getting closer.

"Oh," she said, relieved. "They're probably doing something up at Semperfi," she answered, matter of fact. Like there was often something up at Semperfi involving loud noises.

"Right. Thanks."

"Should have known," Teeg said as they continued on.

And yes, the sound was coming from the next household. A hammer, if Enid had to guess. A big one.

"What *is* it?" Teeg asked wonderingly. "Erik can't still be trying to put a new roof on that old thing?"

Soon enough they came within sight of the ruined house. The sound of barking broke through the continual pounding. Bear the dog raced at them, tail wagging, bouncing, as he charged down the dirt path. Teeg lowered his staff, but Bear didn't seem to notice and whirled around to run back to the house, then back to them. He made the circuit a couple more times, tongue hanging out of his mouth. Bear was here, so Erik couldn't be too far away. The noise was coming from down in the gulch. She gestured to Teeg, and they continued around, to the edge of the riverbank.

And there was Erik, at the bottom of the muddy slope, slamming away at one of the struts supporting the house — not with a hammer, but with a large ax. Big, angry, impressive swings. He'd taken off his tunic and his back was shining with sweat, his hair soaked flat against his head. She was impressed that even being so angry, even putting all his strength into the blows, he never missed. The strut, which might have been a whole tree trunk in another life, was splintering, pale chips flying off the weathered, varnished surface. He'd done this to a number of the struts, damaging them but not destroying any. The dog was barking at him, as if pleading with him to stop.

"Erik?" she called. He didn't hear her, or maybe was ignoring her. She cupped her hands around her mouth and shouted. "Erik!"

Startled, he spun to face them, gasping for breath.

She said, "Erik. You're chopping at a support while standing under the weight that it's supporting."

He looked up at the porch of the house over his head, snarled a curse. Enid wasn't sure if he was directing his anger at her, or the house. Didn't really matter. He hefted the ax in both hands, as if ready to strike again, but instead growled at the post one last time and marched up the hill to meet her. A shock rattled her—the way he held the ax was the way you'd hold it as a weapon. Was he really going to attack them? Teeg held his staff at the ready, waiting.

Enid tried to gauge his intentions. "What're you doing?"

He stopped, looked at the ax in his hands as if surprised to find it there. Glared back at the investigators, and for a moment Enid believed that yes, the man really did hate them.

Finally, he let the ax hang in one hand and heaved a sigh, caught a breath. "This must look pretty crazy."

"I don't know," Enid said. "I'm waiting for you to tell me what this is about. Then I'll decide if it's crazy."

Shrugging, he looked back at the ruin, sweeping his arm as if to encompass it. "If I can't save it, there's no sense keeping it. Might as well bring the whole thing down. That's what everyone wants."

"Some things take care of themselves," Teeg said.

"And everything dies. I get it. I just . . . I hate seeing it there. If we can't fix it, it's just . . . useless."

Enid said, "I'm not an engineer"—that was Sam, and she thought he would know exactly what to say here, what would put this in the right light for Erik—"but there's got to be a way to get what you can from it. Salvage. Not so violent, yeah?"

"My dad would be so disappointed. I couldn't save it. I should have been able to save it."

Enid glanced back to the beach and the ruins there, the sections of pipes that had washed down and been half-buried in sand, fallen walls and shadows of tall buildings, reduced to scaffolding. The wrecks of another world. Erik didn't want this house to be just another wreck, Enid guessed.

"You can't always save it all," Enid said, sure she was explaining something he already knew. "You can't sacrifice the rest of what you have to save a scrap."

He wiped the back of his hand across his face. "It just . . . I mean . . ." He screwed up his face like he might cry. Sweat, not tears, streamed down his face, but he turned away. "We do everything right. We do our part, and look what happens. And then that body washes up. Somebody knows what happened — Last House, yeah? They see those outsiders all the time, and they've been hiding from the rest of us for years! Who knows what all they're hiding? You know about Neeve, right? What she did?"

"That was a long time ago," Enid said patiently, not liking where this was going and hoping to stifle it. "No one's ever made a complaint about them since."

But Erik wanted to point his anger somewhere, and if he couldn't chop down his house, he'd find another target. He straightened, set his mouth in a line. "I'm telling you, they know what happened to that girl."

"Oh?" Enid asked. Was this bluster, or was there more, and could she draw it out?

Seemingly taken aback, he tried to explain, but there was little to explain. "I told you, we see them sometimes, coming down to scavenge —"

"You see them? Wild folk in general? Or would you recognize them? Do you see the same ones?" Had he been lying about recognizing the young woman?

"I don't know, I didn't pay much attention!"

"Really?"

"I watch them just to make sure they don't get too close. You can't trust them, they might come through, take anything —"

"And how do you make sure they don't get too close?"

Erik looked at the ax in his hand. The blade, with a good solid chop just like the ones he'd made on those supporting logs, could have made that wound. She'd assumed a slicing knife had done it. Maybe not.

"Tell me, Erik—did any of the outside folk ever get too close? You ever have to do more than threaten?"

He shook his head. "No . . . really, no! I couldn't ever. I couldn't." He took a breath. Tried again. "All I'm saying is those people never would come here at all if Last House folk didn't deal with them."

That was another question, wasn't it? Did the folk of Last House invite outsiders to trade with them, or had the outsiders come looking for it? And did it matter?

Erik was pointedly holding the ax at his side now, its head resting on the ground. As nonthreatening as he could be without just dropping it. Pushed hard enough, though, she was pretty sure he could use that ax on someone.

"All right," she said in a neutral tone. "There's still plenty of questions to ask. Thanks for your help." They started off, but Enid looked back to add, "And get some help to take down the house for salvage. Don't let it fall on you."

"Yeah. Okay," he said, and reached down to scratch Bear's ears.

Enid and Teeg headed back down the road. A couple of the folk at Pine Grove paused in their chores to watch them pass.

"Do you believe him?" Teeg asked. "If we're looking for a murder weapon, someone strong enough to actually kill— he fits."

Erik had known investigators were coming. Was already feeling upset because of the house, what everyone was saying about it. He was already angry when the body turned up.

"I don't know," Enid said. "I wouldn't have thought so. But people do strange things when they're angry. We might want to do some defense practice with that staff, if we're spending more time here."

"How long do you think we're going to be here?" She didn't know, and Teeg scowled at her silence. "We've got to get our report in about the house. You know, what we were sent here to do."

"Yeah. Just seems a little pointless right now."

They arrived at the bridge when Enid spotted another group coming down the road, a hundred yards or so behind. She shaded her eyes, made out two men and a woman. Her hair was braided, a kerchief over it. Neeve.

"They coming to look at the body?" Teeg asked.

"I hope so."

"Kellan's not with them."

"I doubt he has any desire to look at it again," Enid stated.

They waited until the Last House folk caught up to them.

"Hola," Enid said. "Thanks for coming down."

"If you think it'll help," Mart said. He stood a little in front of the others, a leader. Or a protector.

"I do. She's up this way."

They started across the bridge.

"Kellan didn't come with you?" Teeg asked.

"Figured he'd already seen it," Mart explained. "I have to tell you, if he didn't recognize her, the rest of us aren't likely to. We all see the wild folk when they come downhill. If she wasn't one of those . . ."

Enid looked over at him. "Even so—we just need to be sure."

## Folk of the Wild

As they came up to Bonavista, Juni watched from the porch of the main cottage. Neeve didn't so much as glance over. They skirted around to the work house.

A couple of the household folk were out back, turning over reeds, drying them. They paused, looked up at the visitors. Stared. All of them had machetes hanging at their belts. Enid wondered, did the outsider folk carry machetes too? If she asked, what would Mart tell her?

She'd worried that they wouldn't be able to find a killer here. But if she tilted her perspective just a little, everyone looked like a killer.

"Ready for this?" Enid asked. "She was in the water for a time, so keep that in mind."

She went under the building first, knelt by the body, carefully folded back the canvas, like the wrapping on some dreadful gift. The hair was tangled, framing an ashen, swollen face. Enid debated about whether to expose the wound, and then decided yes, they needed to see everything.

Stepping back, she brushed her hands on her trousers and gestured to present the body. Watched their reactions closely.

Mart made a noise, a grunt of shock or sympathy. What anyone might do, seeing such a thing. Telman simply stared. He and Mart were both older, gruff. Like nothing ever surprised them. But this shook them.

Neeve's expression didn't change for a long moment, until she put a hand to her mouth and turned away, as if the reality of the image took a long time to sink in, and when it did, it horrified her.

Mart finally shook his head. "Who would do such a thing?"

"That's what I hope to find out," Enid answered. "Have you seen her before? Do you recognize her?"

Enid expected denials. The same head shakes. They were so isolated in their household, of course they wouldn't know anything.

And then, barely loud enough to hear, Neeve said, "Yes, I know her."

From just outside the work house, Teeg leaned in, eager. "You do? How?"

Telman, standing with Neeve now as if ready to hold her up, glanced back. Mart pursed his lips. None of them showed surprise—only resignation. Might the group have discussed denying this, insisting they'd never seen her? Then what would Enid have done? But it was out now.

"You all know her," Enid said, nodding at the body. "You all recognize her. Even Kellan? Did he lie to us this whole time?"

"He was scared," Mart said. "He didn't say anything because he was scared."

"He lied!" Teeg countered.

Neeve had folded in on herself, eyes shut tight, as if holding in tears. Telman put his arm around her shoulders, and Mart moved to stand between the investigators and his folk. Protecting them. Enid must have been glaring harder than she thought.

"I'm not angry," she said, trying to make it sound so. "But you really need to tell us what you know, and you need to be honest. How do you know her? Where is she from? We're only trying to learn what happened to her."

Neeve said, "You know there are folk living up the river. Up in the wild."

Enid nodded. "Yeah. There's more people living out past the roads than some folk realize."

Neeve nodded. "A few of them come down the river to trade sometimes. They bring food, beef, and leather—they hunt feral cattle. And some deer. Bring some pretty good salvage. Still lots of unpicked ruins up north. She's . . . she's one of them. She came down a couple of times a year, with some of the others."

"You traded the cloth with them, then? What she's wearing?"

"Traded the finished clothes. They don't do a lot of weaving, I guess." Her hands clutched at each other; she kept looking back at the body, her face puckering with unshed tears.

That answered that question, and more easily than Enid had expected. "No, a lot of those folk are nomadic. They don't have big looms."

"Neither do we. We trade with Everlast for cloth. But I sew."

Enid smiled kindly. "Everyone's got something to trade, that's what makes it all work. Do you have any idea how she might have ended up in your marsh with her throat cut?"

Mart swore under his breath. Unhappy with her bluntness, maybe.

This required bluntness.

"No," Neeve said softly. "She was a quiet girl. Her name was Ella."

The body had a name now, and that felt like a small victory.

"Everyone around here knows you trade with outside folk," Teeg said. "Did you try to hide it from them? Keep it a secret?"

Enid thought she knew where he was going with this and waited for the answer.

Neeve's hand closed on her collar. "Well, no. I mean, we didn't keep it secret, but we didn't . . . it isn't like they came to the market in Everlast, yeah? They needed things; it felt like helping them to trade. No one much comes up to our end of the road."

"But you had extra to trade with?" Teeg continued. "Surplus?"

Surplus—that was a whole other accusation in itself. If Last House had tried to hide this, what else might they be hiding? Then again, maybe they'd just been keeping to themselves.

"A few things a couple of times a year doesn't usually affect quotas," Enid said. It wasn't like Last House was growing crops that would feed the entire settlement.

"Exactly," Mart said. "It's just odds and ends mostly. Kellan's salvage and the like. There's no quota on salvage."

"Are . . . are you going to find out who did this?" Neeve asked.

"We'll try," Enid said. "Any information you have—anything you can tell us that might help—even if you don't think it's important, I need to hear it."

"It was probably one of them that killed her, wasn't it?" Mart said. "One of the other wild folk. Must have killed her and the body washed down from one of their camps. It couldn't have happened here."

That would be easy to assume . . . and it would absolve Enid and Teeg of any official need to discover what happened. "I don't know," Enid said.

"She wanted to come to the Coast Road," Neeve said. "At least, she talked about it sometimes. She and I did. I tried . . . I knew she'd be safer here." Her gaze turned to Enid, to the uniform, but only for a moment. "I thought she was just about to decide to come live with us. We invited her, and . . ." She shrugged and finally looked away, eyes shut.

It wasn't unheard of. Especially after a year of bad storms or drought, when food wasn't as easy to come by. If someone came stumbling into a town asking for help, people were supposed to help, no matter what. The young woman, Ella, had already established a relationship with Last House folk. Wouldn't have been out of the question to take that a step further. Rare, but not impossible.

"This invitation, it was recent?" Enid asked.

"Just this year, yeah," Neeve said.

Enid's brow furrowed. "Might someone have been angry at her over it? One of the other folk from upriver—might one of them have wanted to stop her from joining your household?"

The folk of Last House exchanged serious looks. Another unspoken conference between them, and there was a story here Enid very much wanted to know.

Mart said, "Don't know. We only ever saw the three or four who came down to trade. They seemed . . . they seemed like family. So I wouldn't have thought they would hurt her. But who knows? Who knows with them?"

"When are you due to see them again? What season do they usually come to trade?"

Neeve said, "They were just here a couple of weeks ago. I wasn't expecting to see them for a few months. Unless . . . unless Ella decided to stay. We told her to come visit any time, that we would work it all out. I'm . . . I'm sorry." Hand over her mouth, she retreated.

Enid watched her a moment, standing in the open, catching her breath. Was never easy, seeing something like this happen to someone you knew. Someone you liked. "Right. If you think of anything else, if anyone stops by looking for Ella—come tell us, yeah?"

"Yeah, yeah," Mart said. "You're going to need that pyre soon, I think." The smell was becoming evident.

"I think we should."

"We can do it today," he said.

"Thank you," Enid said.

The body lay in the shade of the building. Full of silence, full of questions. Enid covered her up again just as gently as she'd uncovered her.

They all came out from under the house, bent over in the shadow and emerging into the glaring light of day.

Juni was waiting there. Not too close, just enough to see. To hear what they said. To pass judgment.

Seeing Juni and Neeve almost side by side, their similarities were eerie. They were the same height, they had the same faces, the same build—were both stout, middle-aged women who rounded their shoulders and crossed their arms, hunching in. But their differences were also stark. Made from the same mold, but used so differently. Neeve looked older; her hair was grayer and the lines around her mouth and eyes cut deeper.

Juni's clothing was haphazard: a tunic and trousers thrown together, wrinkled and splashed with whatever she'd been working on. She was a busy woman who spent time outside, who expected to get dirty. Neeve wore a dress and apron, faded, but neat and carefully mended. Neeve did a lot of handwork—Enid remembered the sewing baskets throughout her house.

The two women didn't look at each other and seemed determined to keep the others—like a wall—standing between them. An old, old bitterness.

"Come on," Mart murmured, and led them away, back to the road leading uphill. He folded an arm around Neeve's shoulder, and she huddled between him and Telman. A close-knit group that looked out for one another. That should have been a good thing.

"Well," Juni declared, once the group had moved on. "Did they recognize her?"

"Yes," Enid said. "Her name was Ella."

"Did one of them do it?"

Enid almost laughed at her. "You were out here listening to everything they said—did you hear a confession?"

She frowned. "I thought you'd have been able to tell. You can't trust any of them. Kellan said he didn't know her at first."

"Juni, I'm very grateful for your hospitality, but please let us do the investigating."

"Right, yes. I'm sorry. I've got some biscuits up at the house if you're ready for breakfast."

"Sounds lovely. We'll take some with us, if that's all right. We have some walking around to do."

Not long after, eating biscuits on the way, Enid and Teeg walked toward the bridge. The sun was high now, a perfect time to examine the riverbanks.

"So Kellan lied," Teeg said.

"He did."

"He had to know we'd find him out."

"I don't imagine he was thinking very clearly at the time."

"Ella," he said, trying out the name. "You think one of them from upriver would really join a household and get an implant and everything?"

"It happens sometimes," Enid said. "Not as much as it used to, thirty or forty years ago. Things have settled down since then. But it happens. She wore Coast Road clothes. Maybe other things about the place looked good to her too."

"Her folk'll never come down the river looking for her," Teeg said. "They'll never talk to us."

Enid looked up to the clear sky, up the river and its muddy, recently flooded banks, and sighed. "We'll see."

///////////////////////////////////////////////////////

ENID CROSSED THE BRIDGE and took the west side. Teeg took the east, and the two of them paralleled each other, traveling up the San Joe. Still swollen from the storm, water lapped over the banks, which were mucky and hard going. Across the water, Teeg used his staff to pick through debris and mud, leaning on it for balance, unsticking his feet when the muck held on too tight. She could have used a walking stick herself, but did her best, looking ahead for footholds and grassy patches.

A rudimentary path wended its way along this side of the river. Or, if not a path per se, there at least were multiple sets of footprints marking the easiest way to go, proof that others had slogged through this route. Enid guessed there was another on the other side, where Juni and the others would come down the hill with their bundles of reeds.

When the water settled they likely fished here as well. The sun beat down; bugs swarmed. A low, constant chirping rose up, faded, then rose again, an undertone to the sound of water—frogs.

She parted waterlogged grasses and drooping willows, searching the edges of the water. Thought briefly about wading in farther, then decided against it. The current was fast, the water chilled, dark with silt. The likelihood that she'd find anything lodged out in the middle of the stream was slim.

She didn't find much of anything washed up on the banks, unfortunately. Finding a bloody machete would be too much to ask for. And even if she had, it wouldn't point to who'd killed Ella—a bloody machete rarely had the owner's name inscribed on the handle. If it were that easy, anyone could be an investigator.

A mile or so up the river, up the steep banks to the west, Enid could just make out the cliff where Semperfi's ruined house teetered, balanced on its forest of flimsy supports. From this vantage, it looked even worse, the steep angle of the eroding cliffside appearing even more severe. The structure seemed to tremble, and she could almost see the mud slipping downward. Maybe Erik would feel better if she brought him here to show him this view.

Around the next bend in the creek's path, along an eroded channel, Enid found a stretch of cut rushes. Willows and cattails, mowed down to stumps. The cut patch went a ways up the slope—the work of a morning, for the folk from Bonavista who must have come up here to harvest. This was where they'd collected the bundles they'd been carrying when Enid and Teeg had arrived yesterday.

Exposed to air and sun and rotting, the spongy ground stank. A blackbird squawked and flapped up and away. For all its unpleasantness, the Estuary was vibrant with life. This mowed patch would grow back even thicker next season. Ruins might litter the coast, but life went on somehow.

Across the river, Teeg whistled to get Enid's attention, then cupped his hand around his mouth. "Nothing here! You?"

"Nothing!"

"Do we keep going?"

Ahead, the channel narrowed, the sides growing steeper. Another hundred yards, climbing farther into the hills, the path dried out and trees took over from cattails and brush. They were running out of a track to follow.

But the reeds were freshly cut; clearly people still came up this way.

"Just a little farther!" she answered. She wanted to get all the way to the trees, to where the wild started.

The households followed the path up the ridge, paralleling the river below. Except for the ruined house, Enid couldn't see any buildings, but she could guess how far along she was, where she'd end up if she could get to the top from here. The farther upriver she went, the more the river narrowed, and the higher it climbed, until it spilled out of the hills and forest above. While it wasn't visible from this spot, Last House would be west of here, just over the edge of the river channel. Just a little climbing would get her there.

She didn't expect to hear voices.

They spoke low and urgently, and though she couldn't make out the words, she recognized the voices of the folk at Last House. Enid held her breath. Neeve said something, too softly for Enid to understand.

Mart answered gruffly. "No, you need to stay clear of those investigators, you hear me?"

THE WILD DEAD · 95

And then they were gone, moving away from the ridge, up the path to their home.

Ella's death had really affected the folk of Last House. Was never easy, seeing violence like that inflicted on someone you knew—someone you'd made plans with . . . whose whole future was suddenly cut off.

Enid continued her trek up the river, along the last little bit before the way became impassable.

And that's when she saw it: a shadow stepping back, rustling a stand of uncut reeds. She almost turned away, thinking it was a deer or raccoon or some other critter. But she squinted, took a few steps closer . . . and a face looked back at her.

Young, maybe early twenties. Male, with the shadow of a dark beard started. Plain clothing.

She couldn't see more details than that, because the figure raced off.

Enid took a couple of running steps, her instincts telling her to go after him. She tried, charging ahead. And immediately got tangled up in the overgrown scrub. Since she might as well try to get out of the mess by moving ahead instead of back, she kept going. Managed to keep her eyes on the guy, who was getting farther ahead. He'd be hidden among the trees in moments. Enid shoved through a willow stand, came out the other side ready to run—and slipped in the mud. Came down hard on her knee and caught her breath.

When she looked again, he'd disappeared into the forest. He knew the territory, she didn't.

But this was new: she and Teeg were being watched. Someone outside the settlement had an interest in the goings-on here.

And likely he'd be back.

She joined Teeg back at the bridge, not limping too badly. She'd have a bruise, but hadn't broken anything.

Teeg asked, "What did you see up there? You were running."

"Not sure," she answered. "But keep your eyes open. I think we may have some interested parties about."

"Someone looking for Ella, you think?"

Enid shook her head; she didn't know. If folk from the hills were looking for Ella—why didn't they just come and ask? Because they didn't trust the Coast Road. That simple. Had Ella really been about to migrate to the Coast Road, become part of Last House? That was Neeve's story. What would Ella say, if she could say anything? What would her people say?

Something about it all didn't feel right.

////////////////////////////////////////////////////////

THEY RETURNED to the outbuilding at Bonavista. Underneath, a figure knelt by the body, a shape that wasn't meant to be there. At first Enid thought it was the man she'd seen hiding in the trees upriver, and this was her chance to talk. But coming closer she recognized the hunched form, the ash-gray hair pulled back over her shoulder.

Neeve.

Enid tapped Teeg's arm and urged him on. They came up to the work house, crouched to look under it. They weren't particularly trying to keep quiet, but the woman didn't seem to sense their approach. She had a bowl and cloth, and had pulled back the tarp wrapping the body. She was washing it. Pulling debris from the hair and clothes, wiping mud from the hands and face.

"Neeve," Enid said. "Can we help you with something?"

Enid might have expected her to jump, to show some surprise at being caught like this—some indication that she felt guilty for being here. But the woman only glanced over her shoulder, a perfunctory movement. She expected to be found, and she didn't care.

"I'm sorry. I just couldn't stop thinking of her."

Giving a signal to Teeg to stay back, Enid joined Neeve, sitting beside her, not close enough to touch, but able to study her face. Her expression was still, and gave nothing back to Enid.

Her washing of the body hadn't accomplished much. Ella's clothing was still caked with dry mud, her hair still tangled. But her hands were folded neatly on her chest now, and Neeve had stitched her tunic shut, covering the wound. She set the cloth and bowl aside, folded her hands in her lap.

"Strange. Cleaning bodies, I mean. We always do it before we set them on the pyre. It's not like they need it. It just seems . . . like the last nice thing we can do for them. When it's too late for anything else."

"What was she like?" Enid asked.

Neeve shrugged. "I couldn't say. They'd bring down hides and salvage out of the hills, and we'd trade them for clothing, knives—"

"Knives?" Enid asked.

"Yes . . . oh. You don't think . . . I never worried about it, they seem nice enough. And everybody needs a knife for cutting. They don't have forges. Our knives are better."

As she said, everyone needed knives. It didn't mean anything.

"Did she ever say anything about anyone hurting her?" The person who killed her had gotten close, likely had been someone she knew. Someone who had hurt her before? Was that why she wanted to come to the Coast Road? "You ever see any odd bruises or cuts that you couldn't explain?"

"Oh no, nothing like that."

"She made eye contact when she spoke?"

"Yes—" Neeve stopped and hugged herself, realizing that she was being interrogated. "When I offered to make clothes for her, her eyes lit up. That was a while back, I guess. They'd been coming to trade for a few years. I knew her, at least a little. I thought I did. They, the ones of them who came to see us, never struck me as violent." She rubbed a tired hand across her eyes. "I'm sorry I can't help. I wish I could."

"If you think of anything else that might help, please let me know," Enid said. Neeve took the implicit command and, giving the body one last look, folded the canvas back over the face. Then she crawled out from under the house and began the long walk home.

## An Impossible Search

Teeg watched Neeve go, shading his eyes from the sun. "Outsider folk will never talk to us—if we could even find them. And assuming we did, and they agreed to talk to us, and we found who did this . . . they don't follow our rules. They don't *care*." He said this offhand, matter of fact. Like he presumed he knew exactly what the wild folk thought.

"You ever talk to an outsider?" Enid asked casually.

He huffed. "No."

"I have. Until we talk to them, we don't know."

Ella had been a healthy, cared-for woman. Someone somewhere—some form of family—loved her and would want to know what happened. Might even now be searching for her.

Teeg paused. "What—that one of them did the deed or that they even care that she was killed?"

Enid glared. Of course they cared. Someone among her people cared. And if not them, then Neeve cared. "We don't know that they won't talk to us. They might want to know what happened just as much as we do. Maybe we just need to walk a couple of days upriver and tell them."

He shook his head. "We'll never get that far."

She refrained from telling him what a terrible attitude that was for an investigator. You couldn't give up before you'd even started. You couldn't assume you would never find out the truth. Instead, she offered a wry smile. "You might be surprised how far we can get. How far you ever traveled? How much of the Coast Road have you seen?"

They moved up the steps into the work house, into the shade of the roof's overhang. Enid offered Teeg a canteen of water, and after he drank, she finished it off.

"A lot of it, I think," he said conversationally. "Down south to the ocean. This is as far north as I've been. I know a lot of investigators say they want to travel the whole road, north to south, but I don't know of anyone who's done it. Do you?"

"Tomas did it," she said, smiling at the memory of her mentor. "He did a lot of it before he was an investigator. He just liked traveling." She was always telling stories about Tomas, passing along what he'd taught her. Seemed like everything useful she knew, she'd gotten from him.

"I wish I could have met him," Teeg said. "What about you—how far have you traveled?"

"Been all the way south to Desolata," she said. It was a brag, and she was secretly pleased that Teeg went open-mouthed with surprise. Desolata was the southernmost household listed in Coast Road records, salt harvesters living at the edge of the desert. It never rained there, and they'd never earned a banner. But somehow people stayed.

"Really?" Teeg breathed. "What was that like?"

She considered. It had been a dozen years since she'd seen the place, but she'd read up on occasional reports from travelers and traders. "It was interesting. Interesting people. Worth visiting. But I wouldn't want to live there. It's flat, far as the eye can see. No trees. No *anything*. I like being in the middle of things too much. As far as north goes, I haven't been to Sierra yet, but I'd like to someday." That was the northernmost household, nested in the mountains to the northeast. A handful of days' travel from Morada, but on a different branch of the crossroads than the one they'd taken to the Estuary. Enid assumed she'd get there someday.

"That's a lot of miles to cover."

"Yes, but that's part of the adventure." The day was already half over, and she didn't feel she had much to show for it. A name, Ella. At least it was something. "I think we should do some sparring. Maybe this evening when it's not so hot out."

"You really think we'll need it?" He glanced at his staff, where he'd propped it on the stairs when they sat down.

"I think someone, somewhere nearby, violently killed a woman with a weapon. Don't know that things will get any more dangerous than that, but we should be ready."

"This turned grim. I didn't expect this to turn so grim," he said.

"No one ever does." Enid leaned back against the workhouse wall and closed her eyes. Just for a moment. If she could just *not think* about it all for a moment, maybe a revelation would come to her. The sooner they solved this, the sooner she could go home.

And if they never solved it?

"Hey, look," Teeg said, touching her shoulder.

Juni was coming over from the main cottage. She had a pitcher and basket. A pretense of bringing food. Trading for gossip, more like.

"Hola," she said, smiling. "Wondered if you might like a bite to eat. They're just sandwich rolls."

"Thanks," Enid said. "Sounds lovely." They took the offered rolls, the mugs of water. Smiled blandly at her. Enid ate because she knew she ought to, because Olive wouldn't put up with her not eating. A slight breeze made being outdoors marginally bearable.

"Was that Neeve I saw walking out a minute ago?"

"It was."

"What did she want?" Juni failed to sound casually curious. Her interest in Neeve was pointed.

"I think she didn't like that the body was here alone."

"I'll never understand her," Juni said bitterly. "What does she care, what happens? Not like she ever cared about anyone before."

It seemed a harsh assessment. Enid suspected that Neeve cared a lot. Just not about the same things.

Juni wasn't finished. "You'd better watch her. Make sure she didn't steal anything from the girl. You sure she wasn't down here taking something—"

Enid sighed. "Juni, please—"

"Is that Kellan out there?" Teeg said suddenly. He was looking out to the mud flats, far past the bridge. Gulls called and wheeled. Not as many as yesterday, when a dead body drew them in. The tide was out now, and had left behind a patchwork of shining pools.

A figure was moving in the distance, splashing in ankle-deep water. Stopping and starting, it crouched over the mud, then trotted on a few steps, erratic, seemingly distressed. Enid recognized the loose tunic, the big floppy hat of the scavenger from Last House.

"What's he doing?" Juni asked. They were all standing now, hands at their brows, looking out.

Enid set down her cup and half-eaten bread and pounded down the steps. Kellan was digging out there, and it seemed to be the spot where he'd found the body.

He was searching for something.

"Teeg, come on." Enid set off, jogging first, then running as much as she could without slipping on the muck. Teeg followed, grabbing his staff.

It seemed to take a long time before Enid was close enough to call out, "Kellan!"

The man didn't look up. He might not have even heard her.

"Kellan!" Even when she was close enough to knock him over with a stone, he didn't acknowledge Enid's presence. Teeg trotted up alongside her, ready to swing the staff, but she held out a hand to stall him.

"What are you doing?" she asked again, and still Kellan didn't answer.

He kicked a couple of lumps of mud out of the way, then fell to his knees and dug with his bare hands. After digging a few scoops out of one spot, he moved to another. There was nothing careful or systematic about what he was doing. He moved back and forth across this patch wildly, his eyes wide, hands shaking.

Enid had been right; this was where the body had been found. Any signs of it, any depression it might have left behind, had been washed away by a cycle of tides. In fact, if Kellan hadn't found the body yesterday, it likely would have disappeared forever. And she and Teeg would be on their way home, instead of standing ankle-deep in muck. She tried not to wish for such a thing. If she could have a wish granted, it would be that the young woman hadn't died at all.

Kellan muttered, his words rushed, sharp, running together. "She had it, then she didn't. It wasn't with her, so she must have dropped it. Unless she lost it, unless she gave it away—"

"Kellan," Enid said sharply. "What are you talking about? What thing?"

Whatever Kellan was looking for, he'd never find it the way he was searching, at random, digging in the same patches of mud and blinking blindly through tears. Cautiously, she stepped closer. She expected him to lash out and prepped for it, ready to grapple with him if need be. He lurched from one spot to the next, dropped to kneel again, and she took this chance to put her hand on his shoulder. "Kellan, stop. You've got to stop!"

Finally he looked up at her, eyes round, and let out a shuddering breath. He slumped, sobbing, inconsolable, hands covering his face, streaking himself with the sticky brown mud. It clotted his hair, matted his clothes. He didn't seem to notice, or maybe he didn't care.

Enid put an arm across his shoulders, trying to comfort him, not knowing why he needed comforting. Maybe he'd known Ella a whole lot better than he'd let on.

"Kellan, hush," she said, to soothe him. Tried not to be impatient, but she really wanted to know what was going on here, and he didn't seem inclined to speak. "What're you looking for?"

He leaned into her, but she still wasn't convinced he was really aware of her, that he recognized exactly who she was. He was responding to the presence of another person, that was all.

"Help me understand," she said. "What are you doing?"

She was about to ask Teeg to run up the hill to get Mart or Neeve. Maybe one of them could calm the man down.

"She wasn't one of us," he said weakly. "Pretended, but she never was. Why did she go? Why did she stay away? She shouldn't have come back."

"Are you talking about Ella?" Enid said. What he said had to mean something; Enid should be able to figure this out. "Did she pretend to be Coast Road? Was there something else going on with her?"

"No, no!" he said, and put his hands over his face again. He acted like someone making a confession. "It's Neeve, I'm talking about Neeve!"

Maybe not a confession, but a betrayal.

Enid glanced at Teeg, confused, seeking the piece of information that was missing. It was like a rock in her shoe, tiny but aggravating. It could ruin a whole trip. Her partner shook his head, just as lost as she was.

"What's this got to do with Neeve?" she said to prod Kellan, desperately trying to keep calm. She wanted to shake him, but then he'd never talk again. Had Neeve, that quiet, unassuming woman, killed Ella? Enid would never have thought so, but *something* had set Kellan off.

"Thought Neeve would want to go back."

"Go back where?"

He pointed up the river, up to the hills. To wherever Ella had come from.

The logic of this belonged to Kellan alone.

"Teeg, we've got to get him out of this muck," Enid said.

"Yeah, yeah," Teeg said. Kellan had cried himself out, and he let them, one at each arm, pull him to his feet. They didn't quite have to carry him, but he hung between them, listless, his feet part walking, part dragging. "What's got him so upset?"

Enid kept trying. "Kellan, what's wrong? Can you tell me?" No, he couldn't, and remained quiet.

Last House was a couple of miles away, so Enid steered Kellan toward Bonavista, to the front steps of the main cottage, where Juni had remained, watching them, worry pinching her face.

"What's wrong, what's happened?" she asked, but Enid didn't have an answer.

"Sit him on the steps there, thank you. Juni, can you go get a cup of water? A big one. And a spare cloth. Thanks." She didn't give Juni a chance to say no. If the household didn't want to take care of everyone, then they shouldn't have parked themselves right here on the front of the road. Juni rushed up the steps to comply.

Enid wasn't a medic—she couldn't diagnose Kellan—but she guessed he was having some kind of anxiety episode, an uncontrollable panic. Speaking softly, she offered to hold his hand, and he clung to it hard, like he was drowning.

"Can't really blame you," she murmured. "Murdered bodies ought to make everyone panic, yeah?"

Kellan let out a sigh that almost had a smile in it. The man was exhausted.

Juni returned with water and a damp cloth; by then Kellan had recovered enough to take a long drink and wash up his own face. His breathing had steadied, though his body was still clenched, like he expected an attack.

The Bonavista woman hovered—loomed, really—regarding Kellan with sharp focus. Waiting for him to blow up, maybe. Kellan wouldn't say anything as long as Juni lurked.

Enid pointed up the hill. "Do me a favor, Juni—can you run and get Mart from Last House?"

Juni hesitated. Likely she didn't want to go all that way to her least favorite place in the settlement to deliver a message. Or maybe she didn't want to miss what was happening here.

Enid continued. "Or maybe you could get Tom to do it? Is he back from Everlast yet?"

"Yes, he's out back—"

"Then send him up to Last House. Kellan needs a friend, and Mart might be able to help. Can you do that? Thanks," Enid said curtly, to dismiss Juni, willing her to leave. Juni trotted to the back of the house to find Tom.

And that was why investigators wore the uniform. So much easier when people just did what you told them to, when there wasn't really time to argue. Still, Enid likely had only a few moments to question Kellan before Juni came back.

Teeg planted his staff. "I'll keep a lookout for her," he said. "Thanks."

Kellan drained the cup of water and continued clutching it with both hands, staring out at the marsh.

"Kellan. Can you tell me what you were looking for out there?"

He shook his head. "It's not important. I just . . . She didn't have it, so I thought it might have got dropped."

"Teeg and I searched that area yesterday. We didn't find anything."

"Yeah. But I just thought . . ."

"What was it? If it turns up someplace else, maybe I'll recognize it."

"That's what I'm afraid of."

This was starting to drive Enid just a little bit crazy. He'd been looking for something—maybe to keep her and Teeg from finding it. Accusing Kellan of hindering an investigation would likely send him into another panic, so she refrained. The next question: Was he trying to protect himself? Or someone else?

"Kellan," she said, as gently as she knew how. "I really want to learn what happened here, and I really need your help. What were you looking for?"

His face screwed up, highlighting lines of mud still caught in the furrows at the corners of his eyes, around his nose. He heaved a shuddering breath, one last sob escaping.

"A knife," he said.

## Just a Knife

Kellan tried to describe the knife—"Just a knife, a normal knife!" he said; Coast Road–made, forged, with a polished bone handle and a carved flower on the end. The blade was old and well sharpened, maybe seven or eight inches long. Exactly the kind of weapon that might have killed Ella. It had belonged to Neeve at one time, Kellan said, but they traded it to Ella for leather a couple of years before.

"An expensive trade," Enid suggested, but Kellan shook his head.

"They don't have blades, not like that. Forged. Right? Them, they grind pieces of salvage for blades. A good knife like that? That's treasure for them. They always have leather. And, well—Neeve . . . Neeve liked her. Ella wouldn't have just left it somewhere; she must have dropped it."

Or her killer had taken it, used it, kept it, Enid thought. The solution still eluded her. Ella could have been killed anywhere, which meant the knife could be anywhere. Assuming it was the knife that killed her, and not an ax, or something else.

"Why didn't you say anything about this yesterday?" Teeg asked.

Kellan sniffed loudly, on the edge of sobbing again. "I barely remember yesterday. Who would do such a thing? Today I remembered, and I thought . . . if I could find the knife, if I knew she had the knife, then I knew . . . I knew that it hadn't . . . that someone hadn't . . ."

"That someone hadn't used it to kill her," Enid said softly. He nodded. "Kellan, why did you say those things about Neeve? About Neeve not belonging?"

"What?"

"When you were digging in the mud, I was asking you why, and you said some things about Neeve."

"I . . . I'm not sure. What did I say? I wouldn't have said anything about Neeve, I wouldn't have!"

"This is useless, Enid," Teeg said, scowling.

Enid frowned. Kellan might have been telling the truth. He might have spoken without even realizing it. But the way he shut down, his stare, his trembling grip on the cup of water — he was hiding something.

Yesterday Enid would have insisted that the old case against Neeve didn't have anything to do with this new, surprise investigation, any more than it had to do with the investigation of the house at Semperfi. Now, everything about this settlement seemed off balance, all tangled up, and Enid found it exhausting.

Movement drew her attention — a young guy with a flop of black hair jogging across the bridge. Tom, off to talk to Last House.

"Kellan," Enid said. "Mart will be here in a little bit to look after you. Can you sit here and rest until then?"

He nodded and let out a sigh. "Yeah. Thanks. Thank you." He still looked grief-stricken.

Teeg continued studying him, with an accusing gaze. "If you remember anything else you forgot to say, you'll tell us, right?"

Kellan just stared back at him.

"It's all right," Enid said gently, and went around the house to look for Juni. She ran into the woman coming the other way. Juni let out a squeak and stepped back.

"You startled me!"

"Sorry," Enid said, smiling blandly.

"I sent Tom off. It'll be a while before Mart gets here. I assume it'll be Mart, he's got the sense out of that bunch."

"Yeah, he seems a bit of a caretaker."

"That bunch needs it."

Enid tilted her head, inquiring, but Juni waved off the unspoken question. "Never mind." She nodded to the front of the house, referring to Kellan. "Is that one going to be okay?"

Honestly, Enid wasn't sure. Kellan was holding something back, and it was making him anxious and scared. But she also had the impression he was often anxious and scared, and she didn't know how far outside normal this was for him. "I think so," she said. "Once all this passes and things get back to normal."

"Normal," Juni said wryly, with a *hmph*. "Though I suppose this is normal for you, all this . . . mess."

"A thing like this is never normal. I know she isn't your favorite person, but can I ask you about Neeve?"

"If it'll help, yeah, sure."

"Thanks. Let's go inside." Enid didn't want anyone eavesdropping.

Enid followed Juni into the house.

"Get you something to drink?" Juni asked brightly, bustling, in her element. A little like Olive in that respect.

"No, thanks," Enid said. "Out on the marsh, Kellan said something odd: that Neeve left, that she should have stayed away. Do you know what he might have been talking about?"

"It just keeps coming back to her, doesn't it?" Juni's mouth twisted.

"What is it?" Enid prompted. The words were there; Juni just wasn't saying them.

"I don't like talking about it. It's embarrassing, I think. What she did was so horrible, I didn't want any of it to rub off on me."

"You don't look *that* much alike," Enid said, and Juni chuckled. Relaxed, just a bit.

"What I didn't say was that the contact went both ways. It isn't just that Neeve was trading with the wild folk, inviting them down, wanting them to stay—she used to go walking up the hill. She'd be away for days at a time. She was going to see them. They'd never have come this far down the river if not for her, if she hadn't found them first."

"So you didn't always have contact with them? They didn't always come looking for trade?"

"Oh no. That was all Neeve. I don't know that she was ever happy here, in the Estuary. Especially after what happened."

"With the investigation, you mean. When she cut out her implant."

"Yeah." Distracted, Juni leaned up against the counter and faced the opposite wall, her gaze turned inward. To memories, maybe. "Just goes to show she's always been a troublemaker. All the Last House folk, that's how they ended up there. Mart wanted to be by himself, and then, well. He kept taking in the strays. What else would you expect?" She turned her crooked smile toward Enid, like an apology.

Grudges over something like banners, and lack of them, could last forever. Enid didn't know what to do with this information, whether it was any more than gossip. But she tucked it away, just in case. This need to assign blame annoyed Enid, because it caused folk to make assumptions—made them think they knew exactly what was what, and that they didn't have to actually look at facts.

Enid masked her frustration. Keep Juni talking, see what fell out. "So Neeve traveled. Made friends with the folk in whatever settlement they have upriver."

"That's right. They started going back and forth, then. She'd go up there, then they'd come here. I could never see why she liked them so much."

"Did she ever talk about leaving for good? Going into the hills and not coming back?"

That happened sometimes. Not very often. Those who didn't want to follow the rules—who didn't care about the Coast Road and banners and the rest—could leave. They rarely did, since it meant being banned from the markets, from everything familiar, from the shelter of the road.

"Oh, not in so many words. But she was never happy, you know? Was a time I assumed she'd go and not come back."

The kind of stigma that came from cutting out one's implant might have had something to do with that, Enid thought. People tended not to forget that kind of thing. *She shouldn't have come back,* Kellan had said.

Juni said, softly, "Not so easy to just walk away, in the end."

Enid needed to talk to Neeve about this. Get some more details, who else might have traveled back and forth regularly, if any of Ella's people might be willing to talk to Enid. Briefly, she wondered if there was a way to deliver Ella's body back to them. But without any of Ella's folk to talk to, she didn't know where to take the body. And even if she did know, without a well-cleared path to whatever distant settlement, several people would need to take time to carry it there. And the body would never last long enough for such a trek.

Juni found something to do, grabbing a pitcher and filling it with water from the pump. "It's not like they even *do* anything, up at Last House. They're all just scavengers. Might as well be wild."

Enid said, "Nothing wrong with scavengers. You all wouldn't have much timber otherwise, I think."

"But they'll never get a banner."

"Not everyone wants one," Enid said. And thought of Olive, and the strange pulsing of her belly when the little one pressed out a hand or a foot. She'd call Enid and the others over to put their hands on her, to feel the movement. For a long time Enid had thought she didn't want a banner. Now that Serenity household had one, she thought of little else.

"I suppose—" Juni started, then paused, like she didn't actually understand at all. "I imagine we're lucky to get any around here. This is a hard place to live. A hard place to raise babies."

"Bonavista earned banners," Enid said.

Juni smiled sadly. "It's like so many other things; you always want more, don't you? But every time we get a new case of malaria, it sets the banners back a couple more years. And I think . . . well."

"Well what?"

"That Bonavista is still being punished for not stopping Neeve from doing what she did."

Interesting, how few people said the words, the details of

Neeve's crime. That she cut out her implant. That she presumably wanted a child without waiting to earn a banner. If Neeve really had walked away from the Estuary, into the wild, would she be spoken of at all back here? Did they wish they could forget her?

"Could you have stopped her, do you think?" Enid asked.

Juni must have thought of that question so many times over the years. Her answer came instantly. "No, I don't think so. I hardly knew her by then, she was gone so much. She'd gotten so quiet. So strange. People say twins are supposed to be magical—they can tell what the other is thinking, sense each other's pain. But I don't think I ever knew her. I hated that we looked alike. I always made sure we dressed different. So people would never mistake us."

Enid took out her notebook and flipped to a dog-eared page, quickly read over it just to be sure she had her details right. "The old household, Bridge House, wasn't dissolved after the investigation." The household wasn't held responsible; the investigators on the case had punished Neeve alone.

"No, but Bridge House folk got discouraged. Weren't many of us to start with. Three transferred out right off."

"But you didn't."

"Oh no—I like it here. This is home. Then I met Jess at the Morada market. And well, seemed a good fit. Starting a brand-new house can be an adventure. Even when you're picking up the pieces of an old one."

Enid nodded. "Oh yes, starting a new household is a challenge. The best kind, though."

"You say that like you know all about it." Juni's smile widened, making for a bright, open expression. She seemed younger. Juni liked talking about families, Enid decided. She clung to families, after what had happened to her first one.

"I do. I helped start a household back in Haven. Serenity." Where Enid's family was right now, where she ought to be too.

"I heard somewhere that investigators don't have households. You just travel up and down the Coast Road looking for trouble."

Truth be told, investigators often cultivated that particular story. It was part of the aura. Made investigators seem even weirder than they were. Like outsiders. Enid wasn't sure it helped.

"Oh, investigators are like anyone else," she said.

"Have you all earned a banner yet?" Juni asked, in that eager, wide-eyed way people did whenever the subject came up.

Enid tried to hide her smile. Couldn't. She grinned just thinking about it. "Our kid's due any day now."

"Oh." Juni sighed with longing. "And you're stuck way out here!"

"Part of the job," she said, shrugging.

"You know that no one would fault you if you let this one be, if you handed it off to someone else. Finding out who did this to that girl . . . it's impossible, isn't it?"

"I have to try," Enid said simply. "Teeg and I will give it a couple more days, then I'll get back to my household. It'll be fine." She kept telling herself that. Kept telling herself that Olive, Sam, and Berol would understand if she wasn't there. They would. "If you don't mind talking about Bridge House just a little more—you decided it was easier to start over, rather than keep on with the old household?"

"I imagine it seems silly now. But it seemed important at the time. To move past it all, to change the name . . . to just change."

Enid suspected that the Estuary's refusal to put together its own committee might have had something to do with it. Med-

ics came through a bit more often, but they didn't have authority to award banners. Estuary folk had to appeal up to regional
for banners, and regional sent someone around these parts only
once or twice a year, to check on quotas and update records. Not
much of a chance to ask for banners, to appeal decisions. Regional would delegate a lot of that work to a local committee—
if there was one. Easy to overlook when there wasn't.

The back door opened, and Jess stomped in, a look of
panic tightening his features. "What's this? What's wrong?" He
was breathing hard, like he'd run from somewhere.

Enid said calmly, "You mean besides obvious recent
events?"

"Jess, what is it?" Juni asked.

"Tom said one of the investigators had taken you inside,
was questioning you." He glared at Enid. "You don't think she
had anything to do with it, do you? She can't have anything to
do with it."

"We were just talking," Enid said.

"It's nothing," Juni added. "Kellan was falling apart out on
the marsh, and I was just helping. Really, she's talking to everyone. Aren't you?"

Enid nodded. "Yes, it was just a few questions."

A knock at the front door made them turn, and Teeg's
voice called, "Enid! Mart's on the way, might want to get out
here."

Out front, two people were trudging over the bridge, toward Bonavista. Enid shaded her eyes: the skinny one was
Tom. The other was larger, his steps deliberate—Mart.

Teeg was still keeping watch at the front steps. Kellan sat
hunched over his mug of water, but he seemed calmer. The
pair might not have said a word to each other while Enid was
inside talking with Juni.

"You ready to go back home, Kellan?" Enid asked.

He said, "I'm sorry, Enid. I didn't mean to cause trouble. I really didn't. We're not in trouble, are we?"

"Not at all," she said. "Just . . . if you think of anything else, anything that might help us find out what happened to Ella—you'll let me know, yeah?"

He nodded sullenly. As much as Enid hoped he would think of something, remember some critical detail after he'd rested and the fear and adrenaline had drained from his system, she didn't think he would. Likely he wanted to forget all this.

Enid waved as Mart approached the house, and he raised a hand back. Tom trotted ahead.

"Thanks again, Tom," Enid said. "Ought to put you on regular messenger duty."

The kid grinned. "I'm earning all kinds of favors!"

"Tom, don't be obnoxious," Juni said, but she was smiling, and her son laughed. His duty discharged, he disappeared around the corner of the house.

"What've you gone and done, Kellan?" Mart asked tiredly, stepping forward to put a hand on Kellan's shoulder.

Kellan's face sunk in a frown. "I got scared. I'm sorry."

"He was looking for something in the mud. A knife Ella might have had with her," Enid added. "You know what he was talking about?"

"Everybody has knives with them," Mart said.

Yeah, that was the problem. Teeg gave Enid a questioning look, and she moved her head in the briefest of shakes. She'd have to explain it later.

"You need to keep better care of your people, Mart," Jess said. He and Juni were looking on from the cottage doorway. He might have meant to sound good-natured, but his glare wasn't, and Mart bristled.

"Kellan hasn't done anything wrong," Mart said. "Nothing's got hurt."

"He's wasted the investigators' time."

Mart flashed a worried glance at Enid, who grew annoyed at Mart and Jess, using her in their argument.

"You said I wasn't in trouble." Kellan's eyes were round again, the panic returning.

"You're not," Enid said. "No one's wasted my time. I've got plenty of time." But she didn't; she was counting every minute, felt like.

"Kellan's always on the flats looking for things, he doesn't need looking after," Mart insisted.

Jess wasn't finished. "I think you all need to decide if you're really part of this community or not."

Mart laughed. "What community? We don't even have a committee! You never care about us until you need a body burned."

"We wouldn't be finding dead bodies on the marsh if not for—"

"Hey—"

*"Quiet,"* Enid said.

Neatly, both she and Teeg stepped between the two antagonists and glared them down. Their anger wilted, and they turned away from each other; folk usually did. Meanwhile, Kellan had curled up on the steps, arms wrapped around his head as if trying to shut out the noise. Or maybe the whole world.

Enid said, "Juni, thanks for your help. And Mart, thanks for coming. We'll let you know if we need anything else, yeah?"

Mart nodded. "The pyre's ready for the girl. We can hold it anytime."

"Thanks," Enid said, nodding.

Kellan leaned into Mart, let the man guide him away.

Enid turned on Jess. "So why don't you all have a committee?"

"What? Well . . . I guess . . . we've never needed one."

"Yeah? Maybe think about that for a minute. Teeg, want to take a walk?"

She marched off, down the road in the direction opposite the bridge, just to get some space. Teeg hurried alongside.

"So," he said. "Kellan's looking for a knife."

"I'm not sure even Kellan knows exactly what he's doing. Ella could have lost it anywhere. She might not even have had it with her when she died."

Teeg stared. "Or it was used to kill her."

"That's the question, isn't it?" she said dryly.

"Do you think Kellan might have done it?"

"He doesn't seem the type." Thoughtfully, she shook her head. The idea was worth considering, however much she hated to admit it. "I don't think he'd be able to keep something that big a secret. He'd have lost it before now."

"You sure about that? He could be losing it now because he's trying to keep a secret that big."

They stopped on the road before they got too far from Bonavista. The main house was well in sight, but out of earshot. Enid did wonder what kind of rumors would start, when folk saw the two investigators off by themselves, having a meeting. Deciding the fate of them all.

Teeg regarded her, downright eager.

"Why? What did you find out?" she asked.

"Kellan said a few more things, about how he's always causing trouble, how the others are always having to look after him. Kellan seems to do this kind of thing a lot, goes off alone, rants about things no one understands. You saw Mart when he got here, like this isn't the first time he's had to come fetch Kellan."

"Yeah," Enid agreed. "I think he might have some kind of undiagnosed anxiety disorder."

Teeg nodded. "It seems to be why he ended up at Last House. No one else wanted to deal with him."

"Like he's a ruined house and not a person," Enid said, frowning. "Last House folk knew Ella pretty well, I gather."

"Yeah, they knew her, so who better to have access to her? To have that kind of opportunity?"

"But why? If it really was one of them, why would Kellan be out there looking for the knife? Wouldn't one of them still have it? To hide it, if nothing else?"

"They probably didn't think they needed to hide it, until the body turned up. With a couple of investigators on hand, no less. If we weren't here, there'd have been no trouble at all. But now they have to cover their tracks." It was an easy answer, and Teeg seemed keen to follow that line of thinking. "Out of them all, don't you think Kellan's the most likely to hurt someone, even by accident?"

"I'm not sure that follows," Enid said. "He's nervous, not murderous. On the other hand, with that ax, Erik looked like he might kill us. If he met Ella up near that house by chance, was startled enough, or angry enough . . ." She shrugged, leaving the implication hanging.

"Everyone around here's got an ax or machete or knife. We have to narrow it down. But Kellan—what if he did do it, and he's hiding behind his reputation of not being all there—"

"That's an awful lot of very good acting for someone who seems so broken up over things."

"We'll just keep an eye on him, yeah?" Teeg paced on the

road, a few steps back and forth, looking back at the settlement like he couldn't wait to dive back into it. "What's that thing you say? Put enough pressure on folk by just hanging around and asking questions, and they'll confess everything."

Enid got a sick feeling in her stomach. It would be so easy to accuse Kellan. He was the one who wandered away from everyone else, he was the one looking for the knife—and then what?

Say he did do it—what then?

"What's the consequence?" Enid said.

"This sounds like a test question."

"You're not in training anymore. This is one investigator to another, talking it out. Say we find who did it, find the evidence, and get a clear-cut confession. Then what?"

Teeg thought a moment, looking out to the hazy coast, squinting. "Exile," he said. "For the worst crime there is, that's the worst thing I can think of."

Sending them into the wild. Barring them from households, from trade. From any care at all, and leaving them to fend for themselves. For someone like Kellan, that might well be a death sentence. Enid didn't like to think of it.

"Though technically," Teeg added, "if Ella isn't part of the Coast Road, do we actually have the authority to do anything about holding her killer accountable?"

"Absolutely," she said. "If someone from the Coast Road did it."

"Ah," Teeg said, his tone uncertain. "But do you think we're obligated? If one of them came into a settlement like this looking for help, would we have to give it?"

"It would be the kind thing to do, wouldn't it?"

"But we're not obligated. They don't follow our rules."

"We all came from the same place a hundred years ago. Keep that in mind."

She glanced up at the sun; it was well past noon now. They still had a lot to do, taking care of the body, following a few more trails of information. She gestured back toward Bonavista.

"Let's get back, take care of Ella's body," Enid said. "Take one more look at that wound." Before they destroyed the only real evidence they had.

The two walked back to Bonavista, went around to the work house in back where they stored the body. It was the middle of the day, and everyone had gone inside, taken a break from work and the sun. The place seemed quiet; even the bugs and seagulls seemed to be resting, and the river's water ran muted.

Enid drew back the cloth, once again confronted by the young face, the tangled hair, and tugged at the collar of the repaired tunic to expose the bloodless wound. It was a gash, maybe six inches long, its edges clean except for where the skin was peeling back, rotting. The flesh underneath was black, oozing. They'd definitely need to burn her this afternoon.

"It could have been anything that did that," Teeg said, frustrated. "Chopped with an ax, slashed down with a knife. Looks like the blow came from someone about her size, maybe a little taller, striking downward."

"She might have been cringing when it happened too. You see someone with a blade coming at you, you try to block —" She shook her head. The Haven archives had books on forensics. She'd read as much as she could, but it was never enough. Some of it was irrelevant — Coast Road investigators didn't have the right tools to do what investigators had done, pre-

Fall. Hard not to feel like she was covering old ground, and doing it blindfolded. "Used to be they could tell exactly what made a wound like this. Use microscopes and match the exact blade to the exact cut."

"That'd sure make this easier. So—do you think it was a knife or an ax?"

"Bone's scored but not broken. I'd think an ax would have cracked bone, just from the force of it." Enid sat back, sighed. "Let's not make that call. Not yet."

## Pyre

In the old days—the pre-Fall days—cities had refrigeration. Morgues and lockers where investigators could store bodies indefinitely. In books Enid had seen pictures of these places, so formal and clean, complicated yet organized. If investigators found a piece of evidence later, they could go back to the body and see if it matched up. Barring that, they had photographs. In either case they didn't have to remember—they could look again.

Enid, however, had to take notes. Pages and pages of notes, hoping she recorded every vital detail, guessing which scrap of information might be important later. In this case, she sketched the wound, measured it, noted every detail, uncertain any of it would be of help.

At the time of the Fall, folk had had to make choices about what to save. Medicine, but not forensics. Windmills and solar collectors, but not photography. Someday, maybe they'd have enough resources and incentive to pick up some of those lost skills again—and a library full of books waited in the cellar archives at Haven whenever they were ready.

But right now, a body was rotting in the heat, and they could keep the flies and scavengers off it only for so long. Gulls had already started perching on the outbuildings, testing the perimeter.

The body had told them everything it was likely to.

Enid thought she would have to order a couple of people to help her and Teeg carry the body up the hill, a trek of a couple of miles. But Jess and others at Bonavista volunteered. Enid was grateful. Again, they used the canvas for a makeshift stretcher, one of them at each corner.

A small, impromptu procession formed behind them. Juni, a couple of the folk from Pine Grove and other households. Enid assumed they followed out of curiosity. Or maybe she ought to give them more credit, and they came because even an unknown stranger, left dead on the marsh, deserved a little respect when being put to rest. No one from Semperfi appeared, and no one was out working at the ruined house. The quiet around the place made it seem abandoned.

Way up the hill, maybe a hundred yards out from the edge of the ravine and just beyond Last House, was a clearing—no trees, no sodden marsh, just a stretch of dirt and rock where a fire could be set without putting any buildings in danger. A low bier of driftwood and deadfall marked the center of the clearing, a lonely, sad mound; knowing its purpose might have made it seem that way. The wood stored under a nearby lean-to looked the same but didn't seem to hold so much somber meaning.

The other folk of Last House, Neeve and Kellan, were there with a lantern and torch to light the pyre, with buckets of water and mud nearby to quench it later. The procession hung back, watching from a distance.

Witnesses. A farewell like this should always have witnesses, Enid believed.

Together, Enid and Teeg worked to arrange Ella's body among the branches. Enid spent a long last moment studying the girl, her clothes, her hair. Imprinting her mind with the sight, wishing that maybe at last some crucial detail would jump out and explain everything. Who Ella really was, why she had ended up like this.

"Enid?" Teeg prompted.

"Yeah. All right."

Neeve lingered over the body for just a moment before lighting the kindling. As the flames rose, she stood back, head bowed, eyes shut. Quietly and respectfully, as if Ella were one of their own, the folk of Last House watched the fire rise up and engulf her.

There was a chance, a small chance, that whoever inflicted that wound was present. To watch the pyre burn, fascinated to see the final result of the death they'd caused. Enid kept a lookout, not really sure what she was searching for. One of the detectives from before the Fall would probably spot something odd right off.

The folk who'd gathered were quiet, somber. No one behaved at all unexpectedly. The vague expectation that one of them would fling themselves on the ground and confess out of sheer oppressive guilt wasn't very realistic.

Enid cast her gaze farther out. The young man she'd seen by the river—if he was interested in Ella, interested in the body, he should be here, watching. Or maybe she'd scared him off, and he'd never come back.

Enid had so many questions for him. So she searched, just in case.

The sun shone down on the sparse trees, not leaving many shadows, at the edge of the wood. But against one of those trees, Enid spotted an anomaly. A shape leaning against a trunk, a figure in hiding. She let her gaze pass over as if she hadn't observed it, and went back to watching the pyre, which was now fully engulfed, whitish ash floating away with the smoke. Enid glanced back and saw that the figure was still there. A young man with the start of a rough beard.

She stepped closer to Teeg. "I'm going to take a walk. Don't look, don't react. Just give me fifteen minutes or so, yeah?"

"What is it?"

"Maybe come running if I shout real loud," she said, grinning wryly, and walked toward Last House's cottage, before curving back up the hill, toward the trees.

///////////////////////////////////////////////////////

ENID FULLY EXPECTED that the man had been watching her closely, saw her leave the pyre, and kept track of where she went next—so there was little point in trying to sneak up on him. What she wanted to avoid was having to chase him down in front of a crowd of witnesses. Maybe he could be persuaded to talk.

Once Enid reached the woods, she angled back toward where she had seen him. And yes, he was clearly watching her approach. His hand rested on a palm-length sheathed knife lashed to his belt.

A knife that could have killed Ella, Enid thought. Maybe she should have brought Teeg along, with his staff.

She moved calmly, arms at her sides, letting her steps make noise. "Hey there," she called out. "Hola."

Back pressed to the tree, the stranger finally caught her gaze.

He couldn't have been more than twenty or so, and still had a wiry adolescent look to him, despite the shadow of beard on his face. His fuzzy black hair was cut short, and his demeanor was hard and wary.

For a moment he just looked back at her. Then he bolted deeper into the forest.

"Oh no, not this time," she muttered, and gave chase.

She thought she'd picked a good route straight through the woods that would cut him off on the arcing path he took, but she quickly got tangled in shrubs and undergrowth, and the stranger pulled ahead.

Enid knew she'd lose to him in a straight-up footrace. Desperate, she slowed, looked around for something, anything, to throw, and found a stick the size of her forearm. Hefted it back over her shoulder and let fly. She wasn't *quite* aiming at him, but if it hit him and got his attention . . . well, that would be okay. It didn't, in fact, hit him, but it flew right past, in front of him—enough to get his attention and make him pull up short, arms flailing as he recovered his balance. That gave Enid time to close the distance between them.

Scrambling, the man made the mistake of looking down at his knife sheath as he reached for the weapon. That gave Enid a window, and she lunged forward, reaching to grab whatever she could. It turned out to be the sleeve of his tunic, which she yanked as hard as she could to try to throw him off balance; it worked—the stranger stumbled . . . and the knife fell from his grip. With a quick twist, she stuck out a foot, pushed him in the direction of his own momentum, and forced him to trip over her outstretched leg. With a frustrated grunt, he fell to the ground.

Teeg had the tranquilizer patches, and she cursed herself for not bringing any. Never mind whether or not she had any real right to use tranquilizers on an outsider.

"Please, I just want to talk! Sit still a minute, would you?"

She loomed over him, and he lay flat on his back, staring up at her, catching his breath. Once he did, he said, with a snarl, "What did you do to Ella!"

"Me? I didn't do anything."

He scrambled to his knees then, and when Enid didn't stop him, he got to his feet. Dead leaves and dirt clung to his clothes. He pointed back toward the pyre. "You're burning her. She's dead, and you people killed her; you must have. She didn't deserve it." He tightened his hands into fists, maybe to start a fight, but he stepped back, instead of toward her. Ready to flee, but his question still hung there.

"You're right," Enid said calmly. "She didn't deserve this. But you and I want the same thing. I want to know what happened to her, how she died. Can you help me?"

"You people killed her!"

Everyone is a suspect when you don't know who the culprit is. He started scanning the ground; jumped toward a spot, reaching, and came back up with his dropped knife. He held it menacingly, the tip pointed in Enid's direction. He left no doubt he knew how to use it. Was it possible he'd used it on Ella?

"The folk down in the Estuary assume one of your folk did it."

"None of us did it. Why would we?"

"I don't know. Maybe someone got mad at her, given how she died."

"What'd you mean, how?"

"So you don't know how she died."

"What're you saying?" He kept the knife between them. Enid was ready to run if he attacked; she was good in a fight, but didn't want to take a chance against his knife. She probably ought to yell for Teeg, but if she did, this young man would definitely flee. She needed him to stay, to talk.

But he didn't flee, and didn't attack.

He backed up until he leaned against a tree trunk, as if to steady himself. His fingers dug into the tree bark, then absently began to peel bits of it off.

"Her throat was cut," Enid said. "Someone attacked her with a blade and cut her throat. Maybe a blade like that."

His face screwed up and he choked, the sound of a stopped sob. "Someone . . . someone cut her throat?"

"Yes, I'm sorry—that's what happened," Enid said softly.

"Folk are afraid of you," he said. "Down on the road, they talk about you. Afraid of the bullies in brown."

Enid had heard the phrase before, but rarely spoken aloud in her presence. "Yes, I know. But we don't kill people. It's our job to investigate when someone does."

"But who would kill her? And why? I . . . I don't . . ." He was stricken; his voice stuck.

"That's what I'd like to find out. Can you help me? Answer a few questions for me?"

The stranger looked uncertain, but he didn't reply one way or another. Enid took it as a good sign and continued.

"Where's she from?" she asked him. "How do you know her?"

He scrubbed his runny nose on his sleeve before answering. "From the camp, up the way." He gestured over his shoulder.

"Up where? How many days' walk?"

He glared. He wasn't going to give away that much.

Fair enough.

"And you—you were in love with her?"

"We were friends, that's all. Just friends."

It was funny. Some on the Coast Road said that the nomads —the wild folk, the ones who lived on the fringes—didn't understand them, could never understand. Were uncivilized and not worth even speaking to. And yet, when this one said "Just friends," the words had exactly the same tone they did when anyone on the Coast Road said it in such circumstances, and Enid could guess the meaning well enough.

"I'm sorry for your loss."

The hard look he gave her suggested that he didn't believe her. The set of his jaw indicated he was grinding his teeth. He rubbed the hilt of his knife, but didn't seem aware he was doing it.

"I hated it when she came down here. I told her not to. Over and over I told her."

"But she came anyway."

"I don't trust these folk. You can't trust them. They give you things and you don't know what they want from you. I *told* her not to trust them!"

"So then she came without you."

"A few mornings ago, yeah. Snuck off. Didn't want to argue with me, I reckon."

"And then?"

"She didn't come back. Days and days, and she didn't come back." He was a young man despairing, the picture of grief, the weight of it anchoring him to the ground, as if he might never move again.

Enid had a sudden thought: Was it possible Ella had been

pregnant? That was usually the first thing an investigator checked for, finding a woman without an implant. But Ella hadn't had to cut out an implant—she'd never had one in the first place. Enid hadn't checked, and Ella's belly seemed normal. They would've had to cut her open to know for sure. And, well . . . it was too late for that now.

But if she had been . . . might someone have wanted to kill her because of it?

More wild speculation. "Someone left a blanket and fire striker down in that wrecked house," Enid said, thumb pointing downriver. "That was you, yeah?"

His eyes widened. Surprised he'd been found out. "I'd meant to go back for 'em. Didn't think anyone would ever go in there."

"You're lucky that wreck didn't slide down the cliff with you in it," she said. "My name is Enid, by the way. And you are?"

He set his jaw, like she had asked him to hand over treasure.

"Please," she said. "I just want to be able to call you something."

He bit out, "I'm Hawk."

"I want to find who killed Ella," Enid said. "You knew her. Do you know who else knew her, who might have been angry with her for some reason? Or how she might have gotten into danger? Had she done anything odd recently? Had she been scared?" Ella might have wanted to live at Last House if someone out in the wild was hurting her. Someone like . . . Hawk? Might all his grief be for show?

He'd started shaking his head before she finished speaking. "I told her not to come here, not by herself. I didn't want her to come here anymore."

Might he have done something to stop her? Might any of the other folk who lived in the hills?

"Where do you come from?" Enid asked.

Hawk's look darkened. What tears there'd been now stopped. "Why you want to know?"

"I just mean: Do you have family? A village? Other people who knew Ella, who I can talk to?"

"Why?"

She'd known this wasn't going to be easy, and reminded herself to be patient. "I want to find out what happened to her, and to do that I need to talk to people. Find out who saw her last, who knows where she might have been right before she died, and why."

"Nobody knows anything," he said, picking at the hem of his shirt. "She's dead and that's it."

He turned nervous — no longer just angry and despondent over the loss of Ella, but nervous — and looked over his shoulder like he was about to bolt. But he didn't; he lingered, however much he didn't want to deal with Enid. Ella was dead. So what was keeping him here?

"What are you looking for?" Enid asked. "It's why you're hanging around. It's not just Ella — there's something else."

His head went up, suspicious. Surprised that she would ask such a thing, maybe.

"It's all right," she said. "I'm like you, I want to know what happened. Any little detail might help."

Nodding, he settled. "She . . . Ella . . . she had a thing with her. Did you find it?"

"A thing? What thing?"

"You'da noticed it if you found it."

"We didn't find anything unusual."

Flustered, he said, "A knife, she should have had a knife."

The back of Enid's neck tickled, and she tilted her head, curious. Carefully she said, "We didn't find a knife, I'm sorry."

"But she had it, about this long"—he held his hands about a foot apart—"and thin, with a bone handle with a flower—"

Enid studied the knife on his belt, the polished antler handle sticking out of the sheath. "Like yours?"

"No. Better than mine. One of *your* knives, not one of ours."

"That the only reason you came looking for her? To get that knife back?"

He didn't answer. Which meant he had expected to come here and find her alive.

"Can I show you something?" She gestured to her pouch, hesitated. "I don't have a weapon. Not like that." She didn't imagine he found her smile all that comforting. "It belonged to her; I think you'll want it." Finally, he nodded, and she drew Ella's knitted kerchief from her pouch. The way Hawk's face screwed up, tears ready to spill over again, he clearly recognized it. Holding it out like a prize, she finally lured him forward. He grabbed it out of her hand, balled it up in his grip, pressed it to his face.

"Smells dead," he said.

"She'd been in the water for a while."

"Someone did this to her. Got to be one of you Road people. She came down here, then she got killed. It had to be one of you all."

"We don't know that she was killed here. We think she might have been killed somewhere else, then washed in on the river."

"How do you know that?"

"She'd been dead for several days, and she'd already bled out."

"Doesn't mean anything."

Enid tried a different tack. "Is there any way I might be

able to talk to anyone else who knew her? Who might know where she'd been, what she was doing?"

"I don't see how anyone will want to talk to you."

"Can I come back with you? Back to your camp?"

His expression locked down. Grief changed to suspicion. All right, then.

"Ella's pyre is still burning," Enid said, gesturing back toward the rising smoke. "Do you want to come and see?"

"Could be she isn't dead. Could be you're lying and it's someone else in that fire."

He'd accepted her word when she first said it. He'd wanted Ella to stay away, he'd warned her away. Enid wanted to know why, but he'd started creeping away, stepping backward, knife still held out as a threat.

"I'm done talking. Don't you follow me," he said.

"I won't."

She watched him go. He followed no path, and she lost sight of him quickly. That was likely her last chance to talk to one of the outsiders, and she couldn't do anything to stop him from leaving.

## Scavengers

Back at the edge of the woods, she found Teeg waiting for her. He'd been savvy enough to keep his distance. Had there been two Coast Road folk bearing down on him — investigators, no less — she was sure Hawk would have fled sooner, or taken to violence.

"Did you get him to talk?" he asked.

"A little. Not much of use."

"And you let him leave?"

"Should I have held a knife to his throat?" she asked, brow raised.

"But what if he's the one that did it?"

"He seems awfully broken up about it."

"Broken up that you found him out, maybe," Teeg shot back.

Enid moved past him, walking back toward the pyre near Last House. "He's looking for a knife she had with her. One with a flower carved in the handle."

Teeg trotted after her, and she shouldn't have been so satisfied, stoking his frustration like that. Petty feeling, there. They were supposed to be partners. Partners didn't often disagree. But they didn't often see a case quite like this.

"The same knife Kellan was looking for?"

"The one that probably killed her, yeah."

"So where is it?"

"That's what that guy wanted to know. I couldn't say."

"Enid," he said, coming up beside her. "We're never going to find the weapon. We're never going to find who did it."

"We don't know that. We've only just started poking at wasp nests."

"It's too . . . it's too . . ." He shrugged expansively, arms raised.

"Too what?" Enid asked.

"It's too much."

She said, "If you had a chance to find the weapon. If you assumed that someone wouldn't throw away a thing as valuable as a good sharp blade, in a settlement that doesn't have a blacksmith, what would you do?"

He thought, staring ahead, steps pounding. "Track down every blade in town. Can't really look for blood—the killer would have washed it, yeah?"

"Likely."

"Then we'd have to follow the body. Track where she was and what she was doing before she died. But that would mean—"

"Yeah. We talk to her people."

"That's not realistic. It's outside our watch."

"That boy might come back."

"Or he might not."

"Then maybe we should wait and see."

"Enid—"

She cut him off with a gesture; they'd arrived back at the clearing and shouldn't be seen arguing in front of the local folk.

The pyre was sinking to ash, and most of the Estuary folk had drifted off. And why should they stay to watch the whole thing burn? The woman wasn't theirs.

Kellan had a length of rusted rebar that he was using to poke at the base of the pyre, collapsing ashes, bringing air to the buried segments of wood, causing flames to rise up again, then subside. The barest shape of Ella was still visible, a shadow buried in light. There were bones, charred, broken. After dark the last of the embers would glow orange, and fade.

Mart had brought out a low stool and sat fireside, whittling on a length of wood. A spoon, looked like. Something with a long handle for stirring. Enid eyed the knife he was using, but it was too small to have made the wound that killed Ella.

Enid came up beside him. "How are things?"

"Calm," Mart said, and Kellan shrugged, seeming to agree. "Sad. She was just a kid, really."

"You knew her well?"

He paused a moment and shook his head. "Not any better than anyone else around here. Just saw her the few times. It's still sad."

"You ever meet an outsider named Hawk?" she asked. "Young man, about this tall?" She gestured to indicate a height close to her own.

The two men looked at each other. Kellan seemed stricken, like she'd just accused him of something. Mart managed to settle his expression and put on a thin smile. "Yeah, sometimes. He'd come with Ella but never stayed long."

Enid pointed a thumb over her shoulder. "I just talked to him. He's been watching from the trees. He seemed angry."

Mart shook his head. "Poor kid. Did you have to tell him what happened?"

"Yeah," she said.

"He liked her," Mart said.

"Did they get along? Did they ever argue?"

"You think he might have hurt her?" Mart asked.

"We're still trying to figure that out," Teeg said.

The head of Last House shrugged. "Yeah, they argued. He didn't like being here, was always trying to get her to leave. She did all the trading; he just kept watch."

"Stood guard?" Enid asked.

"Guard against what?" Mart asked, and Teeg looked at Kellan.

If Teeg was trying to scare the guy, it worked. Kellan dropped his poker, launching a burst of sparks. He had a screwed-up look on his face again, still trying not to cry. Maybe still upset by all that had happened out on the marsh. By their own accounts they hardly knew the dead woman, but grief was strange. Maybe this touched on something else for him. "Leave us alone! It's not our fault, it's not!"

Mart held out a calming hand. "Kellan, it's all right. This isn't about us. Really." Then he raised an eyebrow at Enid. "Right?"

"I don't have it! I looked for it, it wasn't there!" Kellan insisted. And ran off, down the hill.

"Kellan!" Mart stood, stunned for a moment, glancing at the investigators, then at the fleeing Kellan. Then he dropped his knife and carving and ran after him.

"Well, what do you make of that?" Teeg said, seeming a little too smug.

Enid wasn't sure it meant anything, except that Kellan had had more crash in on him than he was capable of dealing with over the past couple of days.

"Let's go find him," Enid said with a sigh, and she and Teeg gave chase. He was younger and faster, so Enid let him get ahead. She'd already chased after one person today.

The young investigator quickly outpaced Mart, but Kellan managed to keep ahead. He was stumbling, though, fighting against the slope of the hill. He'd taken off, paying no attention to the terrain. This side of the hill had no path, was all scrub and rocks. He kept looking back at the threat behind him. Inevitably, his footing slipped, and he went down, this time tumbling, flailing, unable to stop himself.

Mart gasped and called out, "Kellan!"

Teeg got to the fallen man first, grabbing his arm and hauling back like he thought Kellan might still try to get away. But Kellan was finished, sitting with knees pulled up, face pressed to his arms, sobbing. A cut across his temple was bleeding into his hairline.

"I'm sorry, it's my fault. I know what it looks like, but I didn't mean, I shouldn't have—" He cut himself off there, choking on his own breath, hugging himself. He wouldn't look up.

Enid stood back. She hardly knew what to do, how to soften this situation. Mart knelt by his friend, whispering something to soothe him, but Kellan kept repeating the vague apologies.

Teeg looked hard at Enid. "See there? A confession."

"It's not a confession, he hardly knows what he's saying." She knelt by Kellan, held his shoulders. Tried to be gentle, however much she wanted to squeeze an answer out of him. "Kellan. Something happened that you don't want to talk about. I see that. But if we're going to learn how Ella died, you need to tell us what you know."

He shook his head, over and over.

Mart said, "Kellan, I know it's hard, but the only way to make all this better is to talk."

"I don't . . . I can't . . . it's such a blur, it's all a mess—"

Teeg said, "Kellan, did you use a knife on Ella and kill her?"

"I—I didn't want her here, so it must be my fault . . ."

"So you did do it," Teeg insisted, and Enid stood and took his arm.

"Stop it. You're pushing him."

"He did it, Enid. He's all but said so."

"Exactly. He hasn't answered your questions, and it's all tangled in his head. You're not going to get a clear answer from him now."

Mart stared at them, all anguish. "He couldn't have done it! He just . . . he just isn't like that!"

"But what if I did!" Kellan pleaded. As if they could tell him. His eyes held confusion, helplessness.

If he did it and didn't remember, if he'd blacked it out of his memory somehow—what then? A murder always had at least one witness: the person who did the killing. But what if that witness was unreliable?

"I don't believe you," Teeg said accusingly. "This, whatever you're doing here, is an act. Play crazy and no one will believe you. You expect us to just walk away?"

"But . . . I don't think I did it . . ."

"You don't *think?* But you're not sure?"

Enid stepped in. "Teeg—"

"I don't remember!" Kellan insisted. Kellan, huddling on

the ground, was surrounded now, the others looming over him. The man was frozen; he wasn't going to say a word.

Teeg was practically spitting. "I think you do remember, and it'll go easier if you just *tell us*—"

Enid grabbed Teeg's arm and hauled him back.

"Hey!" He tried to yank out of her grip, but she was ready for him. For a moment, he looked like he was going to take a swing at her. Part of her wanted him to, just to see what would happen next. Instead, she shoved him, putting some space between them, glaring.

"The man isn't stable and you're pressuring him," she said. "You need to stop it."

"But what if he did it? What if he's a murderer?" Teeg pointed. So sure of himself.

"I don't trust his testimony. We find evidence. Where's the evidence?"

"We'll never find any evidence; all we have is instinct!"

"And you trust your instincts, do you? Think it's infallible, that gut feeling?"

"It's all we have," he said, but weakly now.

"I would rather walk away than punish someone who can confess only while sobbing on a hillside with two investigators looming over him!"

By the hard look in his eyes, the tension in his expression, Enid guessed that Teeg felt differently. Right, so they wouldn't be able to walk away from this.

Mart was staring at them. Investigators were supposed to present a united front. So much for that.

Enid said, "Mart, we're going to take a bit of a walk. See if you can calm him down. If he tells you anything, let us know, yeah?"

He nodded quickly, reaching for Kellan and urging him

to his feet. The man was weak, shaking. His hair had fallen to cover his face. As Enid took a last glimpse of him, he seemed to stop crying. That was something, at least.

Meanwhile, she marched Teeg away, back toward the path. But he was insistent. "Kellan did it, I'm sure of it."

"What's your evidence?" she asked tiredly.

He counted off on his fingers. Didn't take many of them. "He found the body. If she was scavenging, he might have seen her as competition. He might have been unhappy with how friendly the household was being toward her."

"Then why not bring it up with the rest of the household?" Every single person within a fifty-mile radius might have done it, she thought. She could make up a story for any one of them.

"I didn't say it would make sense. There's something clearly wrong with the guy."

That didn't make him a murderer. "Teeg, all you have is speculation."

"Speculation is all we have! *Somebody* killed her."

"And Kellan's the easiest one to point the finger at, isn't he?"

"What if it's easy because it's true?"

Their instincts were at battle. Enid's gut told her they were still missing something, that none of this fit together. Teeg's gut wanted to solve the case, right now.

She said, "The last murder I investigated, the one in Pasadan—you know what the easiest solution to that one was? The simplest? That the victim just fell. Tripped and fell in his own workshop. Easiest thing there would have been to say it was an accident and walk away."

Teeg had read the report. He knew this. "So you're saying the simple solution isn't ever the right one."

"I'm saying, be suspicious of anything that comes easy. It

makes you blind. At Pasadan, one more walk around the scene showed the smear of blood on the wall that meant someone else had been there, that someone had witnessed what happened. And we almost didn't find it."

He frowned. "What if it's impossible? What if there's no possible way to find out what happened? We can never really know, can we? Without witnessing a thing ourselves."

"Hmm, wouldn't that be something? Be omniscient? Able to witness everything we ever wanted? Get the answers to just about anything, then, couldn't we?" She'd been born long after the Fall, but what if, somehow, she could see what the world was like before. The way it *really* was, and not the way they all thought it was from the stories, the cautionary tales handed down about waste and corruption. Despite how much she'd read—and she'd read so much in the Haven archives—she always wanted to know more.

"I'm serious, Enid."

"We're not omniscient. We can't do it all. Maybe we just walk away." It wouldn't be the simplest decision in this case. No, walking away might be the hardest thing to do here. But they might not have a choice.

Pointing back at Last House, Teeg said, "Mart won't tell us anything he finds out. He'll protect Kellan; that's what households do."

"We'll just have to risk it." She spit out the words. Part of her thought walking away might be the best thing. But no— they'd already picked out too many threads. Had to clean up at least some of their mess. Enid straightened, rearranged her mental to-do list, and readied herself to go back into the fray. She nodded down the road. "You go. I'll see what else I can do here, if anything."

Teeg glared hard at her, but did as she asked.

CHAPTER THIRTEEN · **THE ESTUARY**

# Evidence

Enid met Teeg for the first time at the start of the Semperfi case. She'd known his name; investigators sent one another updates about who was in training, who was thinking of training, and who was almost finished training, and shared advice. Their little cohort was close-knit; that helped with the job. Enid hadn't been paired with a new partner since Tomas died. Instead, she'd been picking up nearby cases as she was needed. If she and Teeg worked well together, he might become her new partner. She'd been looking forward to working with him. It was part of why she took the case when she might have bowed out to stay home with Olive.

When Enid had arrived at the committee house and investigator station in Morada, the young man was already there, going over records and prepping for the case—his first. He'd spread out ledgers and notebooks across the whole length of a table by a window, sunlight illuminating his work. She'd pulled up a chair next to him, and he'd immediately started talking.

"I think I've got everything," he said, showing her both

his notes and all the records he'd reviewed. "Do I have every-thing?" He'd seemed like a kid, and she wondered if that meant she was getting old, if he looked too baby-faced and optimistic to be doing the job.

She went over it all again and didn't find anything wrong with his work. "Been six months since anyone's been out there, so we might need to update some of this. We'll see how it looks when we get there." He eagerly added that to his long list of notes.

"What about the old case, with the implant? That going to have a bearing on this one? If so, how do we handle it?" He pointed to the page in his notes that discussed Bridge House, Neeve cutting out her implant, the whole distant mess of it.

"Ideally we won't mention it at all. Happened a generation ago, shouldn't be relevant to a construction mediation."

That was the first time he'd frowned. "But the woman cut out her implant. Doesn't that mean something? About what she's like, what the whole place is like?"

"Not if she hasn't done anything wrong since, so unless someone brings it up, it's done. One case at a time, Teeg." Enid tried to be gentle and mentor-like. Who was she, to be offering advice on anything? She'd barely gotten out of training herself, felt like. Some days she still felt off balance, especially without Tomas there to steady her. She didn't feel ready to do that for someone else.

At least this case was supposed to be easy, a simple media-tion. A good one for a newly minted investigator to partner on.

They finished their research, headed outside to a small yard at the front of the building. Noontime, the crossroads town was bustling with work and traffic.

"We leave in the morning, yeah?" Teeg asked.

Enid shook her head. "No reason we can't leave in an

hour. There's a way station just a couple of hours out; we can get there by nightfall. The sooner we start, the sooner we can wrap it all up." And the sooner she could get home to Serenity and the expected baby.

Teeg ran off to finish his preparations. She was already packed from the trip up from Haven, and so had a few moments to herself.

A man in a brown tunic joined her in the yard — another investigator, Teeg's mentor. Enid didn't know Patel well, but had crossed paths with him a few times. A big man, serious and thoughtful.

"What d'you think?" he asked her, nodding after his student.

"He reminds me of me ten years ago. Exhausting."

Patel chuckled, but didn't really smile. "Just do me a favor and keep an eye on him, yeah? He may need a bit of reining in."

She raised a brow, studied her colleague, the set of his frown. It wasn't just what he said, but the careful way he said it that raised an alarm. "You sure he's ready for this?"

"Yeah, yeah," he said quickly. "He's got to start somewhere. We all do."

This would be an easy case, she reminded herself. Wasn't a whole lot that could go wrong. "I'm sure it'll be fine," she assured Patel. "We'll get along great and be back before you know it with the report."

"Exactly," Patel said. "I look forward to hearing all about it."

///////////////////////////////////////////////////////

AT THE TIME, Enid thought maybe Patel was just nervous. How Teeg did on the case would reflect on him, after all. It was the worry of a parent watching a fledging leave the nest — or tumble from it. Now she was trying to figure out exactly what she would tell Teeg's mentor about how his trainee was doing on the case. She wasn't looking forward to that conversation, not anymore. Patel had told her Teeg was brave. Headstrong. He thought this was one of his student's better qualities.

Headstrong in the wrong direction was something else entirely. Reining in, Patel had said. Right.

Kellan was far more likely to say something helpful if he wasn't being directly accused. Anyone would, really. Enid turned back to Last House to try to clean up the aftermath of Kellan's breakdown.

The household came back into view, its lone cottage tucked in at the edge of the sparse woods. She tried to look at it without all the assumptions, the judgments imposed on it—that its folk were strange, isolated, antisocial, and that this must mean something was wrong with them.

Easy to see the house itself as rundown, lacking in charm. Too far out of the way to bother with. In truth, it was a nice spot. Higher up the hill meant cooler air, away from the muggy haze hanging over the marsh. Farther away from the fishing and such, but closer to the trees. Protected from flooding.

The house was simple. Usually, Enid liked to see a home with at least some decoration. A well-marked path, flowers in flower boxes, maybe even some painted trim. It showed pride in a place, a willingness to put in extra effort. This was a plain house, not even a kitchen garden to add some green. But the pile of driftwood and rusted salvage was organized, neatly corralled and sorted, not scattered about haphazardly. The roof was in good repair. The front steps weathered but not warped. The bone wind chimes on the front porch knocked hollowly, like someone was tapping a drum.

You could look at a house like this and see anything you wanted. She was pretty sure Teeg didn't see anything good.

Enid heard voices around back. In the direction of the pyre. She held her breath. A group spoke quietly, two voices, low, male, and the tone of the conversation had an urgency to it. She thought one of them was Mart. Enid looked around for a way to keep hidden, maybe eavesdrop. Stepping softly, she circled around the house, moving along the wall until the words came through.

"She came here, now she's dead, and you can't explain it?" A husky, angry voice — the outsider, Hawk.

"We don't know what happened, honest." That was Mart, sounding weary.

"She's dead and it's your fault!"

"Hawk. Please. You should be looking at your own folk; they didn't want her here any more than we did —"

"Mart!" Neeve hissed. So the woman was with them, part of this discussion.

More calmly, Mart said, "If we all just keep quiet, the investigators'll be gone in a day —"

Hawk said, "You don't know that."

Silence answered this.

Then, Neeve said softly, "It happened, it just happened. Something bad was bound to happen —"

"It should have been you," Hawk shot at her.

Enid was baffled. Teeg might not have been far off after all. Not about who had killed Ella, but that people were keeping secrets. Lots of secrets.

The question was, how might some of those secrets be cracked open?

Enid left the cottage, running to the path so she could

approach by the usual way. No one had to be startled by her arrival.

"Hola," Enid called, still some distance back, and waved.

The whole household was indeed there, behind the house. Mart stood, facing down Hawk. After Hawk's confrontation with Enid, the guy must have come back around to interrogate the folk at Last House. He might have done so earlier, if Enid hadn't ambushed him. Telman was off to the side, pacing, glancing up at the trees, uncomfortable and avoiding the discussion. Neeve and Kellan, unhappy-looking, were sitting on a set of steps leading down from the back porch. Kellan had quieted, but his face was still red and puffy.

They all froze, looking back at the investigator. No hope of Enid appearing nonthreatening here. Best she could do was smile and hope they didn't freeze up.

"Investigator Enid. There's nothing else come up. I don't know how else we can help," Mart said cautiously. He seemed to roll his shoulders and straighten his back. Preparing. The others watched him for cues. Mart, the protector of strays.

"My partner was out of line earlier," Enid said. "I'm sorry for that. But I think he's right, that there's a lot around here that isn't being said. You want to help me out with that?"

The group stared back, seeming particularly guilty. Neeve had knitting in her lap, paused between stitches. Like Kellan's, her eyes were red from crying. The scene stuttered like that, just for a moment, as everyone waited for someone else to speak first.

Hawk ran, straight for the trees. Predictably, Enid reflected. She thought about chasing after him yet again, but only for a moment. Three pursuits in one afternoon were just too much, and she suspected she was already looking foolish.

She turned back to the folk of Last House and crossed her arms. "Well? What did our friend here have to say?"

The expected silent conference ensued, the four of them trying to nominate with glances and earnest looks who would speak and what they would say. Neeve turned back to her knitting, hunched over it as if the stitches were the most important thing in the world.

Mart said softly to Enid, "You mind walking with me a bit?"

She had a sudden thought: that Mart was the killer, and he was now trying to get her alone to finish her off next. But no, he was smart enough to realize the kind of trouble the murdered body of an investigator would bring down on him. Besides, he wasn't wearing any kind of knife or other weapon. He'd left his pocketknife behind.

With a nod, Enid let him lead her off, away from Last House.

"I know everyone's gone all quiet," he said, when they'd walked a dozen or so yards, out of earshot. The others lingered, watching. "But all this—it's got them rattled. Ever since Ella turned up like she did. And, well. Folk don't end up at Last House because they're good with a crisis, you know?"

Enid smiled with sympathy. "So how did you end up here?"

"Came to the Estuary when I was young 'cause I liked the salvage. The ruins spoke to me. Thought I'd be the one to make some great discovery. Bring back something lost. A working engine, a radio. Something like that." He shrugged, a fatalistic gesture. "I did all right. Found a bicycle once, the whole thing. Got it working again, and traded it down at Everlast. Mostly it's just parts, though. We store them up, waiting till we can put a whole one together. Anyway, I came up here to get away from the heat. And, well. I like the quiet. Quiet's what folk like Kellan and Neeve need, really."

A local murder wasn't likely to grant anyone peace and quiet. Especially when they seemed to keep ending up at the center of so many questions.

"Hawk seems very interested," she said, hoping to lead Mart to reveal some useful bit of information.

"He's distraught. He wants someone to blame. To punish. Anyone'll do, I think. He . . . he thought she had come to stay, was coming to talk her into going back with him. Then he found out she was dead. He'd just found out."

"Can you tell me—did Ella really seem like she wanted to stay, or was that Neeve's wishful thinking?"

He chuckled. "Neeve liked the girl, I won't argue that. I think she wanted a friend. As for the girl . . . I don't know what she was thinking. Can't even guess."

"Could Hawk have done this to her? Or one of the other outsiders?"

"No, no, I wouldn't think so. She'd just show up sometimes, along with a couple of others, when they had hides to trade. Ella liked the clothes Neeve made. Didn't talk much about where they came from, but they seemed normal enough, even if they were wild. It's . . . it's hard to think of them doing something like what was done to that girl. Didn't think they had it in them."

"Even though they're hunters? They hunt to get the hides they bring you, yeah? Whoever made that wound knew how to use a blade."

"I guess I never thought of that."

"When they came, did they bring weapons with them? Did you ever notice?" Enid tried to keep her voice from sounding so eager, but wasn't sure she was succeeding.

"Hawk was asking about a knife, you said."

She nodded. "Yeah, same one Kellan was looking for."

"They all have knives," Mart added. "Mostly salvaged metal, I think. Old signs make good spear tips and arrowheads, if you can cut the shapes and grind the edges."

She imagined the vicious wound a length of ground-down steel could make. This was frustrating—the more questions she asked, the more possibilities presented themselves. Possible weapons were ample, common. Everyone had access to blades, salvaged or otherwise. She couldn't figure out what motive might drive someone to use such a weapon, and on someone like Ella. Jealousy was a possibility—her last investigation, the one Teeg was so proud of on her behalf, had been about jealousy. Hawk loved Ella, though Enid was unclear as to whether or not they were a couple. But Ella kept coming here, and he didn't like it. Had she been visiting someone in particular?

Enid said, "You traded with them, the folk from upriver—you have any way to get a message to them? Anything like a regular line of communication?"

"No," he said. "They always come down here."

"Neeve used to go up to their settlement, years ago. Does she travel there anymore? Ever disappear for days at a time?"

"That all ended with the last investigation. She's stayed here ever since."

"Right." Enid squinted uphill, to the woods, and all the answers that seemed to lie in that direction. "Thanks again for putting the pyre together for Ella. If I have any more questions I'll let you know. Have a better afternoon."

She started to walk off, when Mart called after her. "You really think you can find out what happened to her?"

Enid said, "We'll try."

And Mart nodded with such confidence, such assurance

that she could really do this thing, that Enid was sure she'd undermine the uniform, damage the entire authority of investigators if she failed to catch Ella's killer.

The thought made her weary.

////////////////////////////////////////////////////////////////

THE TREK BACK DOWN the hill to the marsh and the bridge seemed to get longer every time she made it.

They'd taken care of the body as respectfully as was possible. Enid had spoken to someone who'd known Ella, who knew where she came from, however unsatisfying the talk was. The questions she'd been asking locally hadn't led to any real answers. How much more time was reasonable to spend on this before it made sense to give up?

When she arrived at Semperfi, Teeg was waiting for her, leaning on his staff, scowling.

"What is it?" she asked.

"They tell you anything new? Did Kellan confess? In a way you'll listen to?" He spoke lightly, like he was trying to make it sound like a joke, but he bit the words off.

"If Kellan had done it, he never would have told anyone about her body."

"Then who do you think did it? Erik?"

"Possible." Or it was someone they hadn't talked to yet. Someone they wouldn't expect. "I'm most interested in talking to Hawk, I think."

"He didn't even know she was dead."

"True. But maybe it's someone like Hawk. Someone from upriver."

"Would they kill one of their own?"

"People do it all the time; that's what murder is," Enid said.

She glanced around at the windblown slope where the hill had started climbing from the marsh. The ruined house was just visible. She imagined she could hear the boards creaking ominously. "Why'd you stop here?"

"Anna was waiting for us. Wants to talk to us."

"Oh?"

"They're up this way." He set off for the ruin. Enid had hoped she wouldn't need to look at it ever again.

They met Anna, who stood off a bit from the front door, wringing her hands, brow creased with worry.

"Anna, hola," Enid said. "What is it?"

"Can you talk to him? I can't get him to leave it alone. Please, talk to him."

Then she noticed Erik seated on the ground, slumped against the wall, almost to the edge overlooking the river. If the building collapsed now, it'd pull him down along with it. He was staring out, like he wanted to make sure he saw the moment the whole thing tumbled down the ravine. He held that ax across his lap, gripping it with both hands.

"He's just been sitting there?" Enid asked. "How long?"

"All day. He won't let it go," Anna said. "When he asked for the investigation, I couldn't sleep; I thought you'd take one look at the place and break up the whole household for letting it get so bad. For trying to keep that thing going. When all you did was tell him to let it go . . . I was so relieved. I just kept thinking, we won't have to fix it anymore. We won't have to think about it. But I think you've made it worse."

And this was supposed to be a simple case. "I'm not sure I can say anything to help. I'm the bad guy here."

"Well, he hasn't listened to me," Anna said, glaring out at the man.

Enid looked at Teeg. "Have you tried?"

"Not me," he said. "What am I supposed to say?" He had a look on his face, the one most people around here were wearing, that said they thought Erik must be crazy.

She walked over, stood between Erik and the sun, catching his attention by putting him in her shade. "Erik. Anna's worried about you."

He sighed. "Yeah, I know."

"You want to maybe go home so she can look after you?"

"This is home."

"A household's generally made up of people, not buildings. You've got a good household here, Erik. Don't blow it."

He squeezed his eyes shut and bowed his head. "My father kept this place up. Decades, he kept it up. Then he dies, and . . . it falls apart. Why can't I keep the place up like he did? What's wrong with me?"

"I think we've had this conversation already," she said. "You know this place is no reflection on you? If it had been wiped away all at once by a massive typhoon, would you be so torn up?"

"It would have been like someone dying—that's what you don't understand."

She did understand. But he wasn't going to listen to her. "Erik—"

"It's not that. It's not *just* that. You know I've seen them. I've sat right here and watched them come down the river, doing who-knows-what."

She shook her head. "What are you talking about?"

"Wild folk. Like that girl." His hands closed on the ax handle.

Her name was Ella, Enid almost murmured at him. "Oh?"

"You can tell they're not like us because they keep to the river, not the road. Normal folk would come down the road."

Outsiders were perfectly normal, of course; they just weren't from the Coast Road. "Erik, out with it."

He looked hard at her. "One of them could be hiding in this house, just waiting for their chance. I won't let that happen. I'm standing guard."

Enid said, "You know, I got a good look at that wound. It's a good sharp blade that made it. Mart tells me the folk upriver don't have very good knives, that they do what they can with scrap metal. To get good forged blades they come down to the Estuary to trade for them. I'm sure it's a Coast Road blade that killed Ella. Maybe something like that ax. Are you sure you didn't see anyone around here, five or six days ago? Someone who you decided didn't belong? What were you doing, right after that storm? If I asked Anna, would she say you were here the whole time?"

Enid expected denials, assurances that he could never do such a thing. They didn't come. His expression didn't change. He said, "One of them could have stolen a blade. That's why we have to keep watch. There's no one else looking out for us."

"Would someone like Ella really be a threat to you?"

Erik pursed his lips, shook his head. But it didn't seem like a denial so much as a refusal to think of it at all. The man wasn't any easier to talk to than Kellan. "Erik, go back home so Anna can stop worrying about you."

Enid turned and marched back downhill.

## Small Debates

A flat sandy spot behind the shed offered as good a place as any to practice, later that afternoon.

Enid rushed Teeg like someone in a rage would do, unthinking and without tactics. He stepped out of the way, pivoting, and brought his staff down on her back. Feigning a stumble, she went to one knee and imagined sprawling. The staff pressed down on her back; in a real attack, it would come down with force, and it would stay there, confounding an assailant.

Tom came out to feed Bonavista's handful of hens, and stopped to stare open-mouthed at the two investigators, his basket wrapped in his arms. Enid didn't mind the audience. News of their sparring certainly couldn't hurt their reputation.

"Again," Teeg said, and Enid straightened and prepared to rush him again.

Lunge, pivot, smack, fall.

And again, he wasn't hitting hard—he knew how to pull punches—but she was going to have a bruise on the small of her back. A hard *thwack* in the kidneys would floor someone in a real fight.

He expected her attacks, but the idea was that the repetition, driving the pattern into his body's memory, would make the movements come instantly when they were needed. Tomas could make these moves look like dancing, with a twist of an arm and a right turn of his body redirecting the force of his assailants' attack and sending them to the ground. Tomas didn't need to practice often, but Enid always appreciated observing. She never worried with him watching her back.

Teeg still needed some practice. This wasn't natural for him yet. Enid attributed the problem to a lack of confidence rather than skill. If he was like her, then in the back of his mind he was imagining a knife or machete in his opponent's hands, wondering what he would do if an enemy were armed.

"Again," she ordered.

She got back to her feet, and this time lunged at him before he was quite ready, his staff still loose at his side and out of position. He stumbled back, swung the staff up, and she went low to avoid the coming strike. Fell forward, grabbed his calf, and pulled, throwing him off balance. With a shout of surprise, Teeg toppled, and Enid tumbled to the ground after him.

They both lay sprawled, breathing hard. He'd dropped his staff, and he groaned as he pushed himself up on his side. For a moment she worried that he might have gotten hurt in the fall, but then he said, "Not fair."

Chuckling, she sat up. "I know! But you're awake now."

"I was awake before!" He glared at her, planting the staff to help him stand. "You trying to teach me some kind of lesson? Put me in my place?"

"And what place is that?"

"You think I don't know what I'm doing."

Not that, precisely. But she had to consider how to explain what she really thought. "I think you're not thinking things through. You're too worried about winning, and this isn't a game."

Enid sat, legs out, taking the moment to rest. She was tired and she had to acknowledge how long the past couple of days had been and how much they'd taken out of her. If not for Ella's body and its wound, they wouldn't be here practicing at all.

Their uniforms were grubby, stained with dried mud and sweat. They'd each brought only one change of clothes; they weren't supposed to be here this long. They could wash, but nothing ever seemed to dry out in this humidity. Well, maybe she could scrub out some of the stains and hang the clothes to let the wrinkles fall out overnight.

"I think I'm done," she said, sighing.

"No. One more. I want to end with a win. You can't quit after shoving me over like that." He stood and held the staff in both hands like he was going to charge her with it. Strike her in the gut and shove her over, just like he'd been trained.

She could have told him that this was exactly his problem: he wanted to win, no matter what. But he had a point; if this was training, might as well let him feel good about himself. A boost of confidence. Or he'd pout the rest of the evening.

In the end, the fact remained that someone out there in the world had killed a woman with a blade. Maybe the killer had fled. Maybe had run for a hundred miles and would never be found, and would never do another horrible thing again.

Or maybe the person was nearby and ready to strike at any moment, should anyone discover the truth.

No, they had to be on guard.

"Right," she said, heaving herself to her feet, brushing off the dirt she'd collected on her tunic. "Again."

///////////////////////////////////////////////////////////////

ENID AND TEEG accepted yet another supper from the folk at Bonavista—clam chowder again. Enid would be sure to send back a large stash of supplies in repayment. But they'd already settled the case they'd come here to investigate. So what were they still doing here?

They weren't solving a murder; they were smashing pottery.

"Kellan confessed!" Teeg declared, yet again. He was sure they'd solved both cases. Again they'd taken their supper and retreated to the work house, eating on the front porch to take in what fresh air there was. Enid couldn't get him to see that what Kellan had said wasn't a confession, but blind panic. She'd stopped trying, so they ate the rest of their meal sullenly, in silence.

It was Enid's turn to deliver their dishes back to the main cottage. Doors and windows were open to let in air, screened over to keep out bugs, and after dark things turned pleasant. A cool breeze came in from the ocean, and the front room was comfortable. The household gathered here, under solar lighting, to work on projects, mending and knitting and the like. The kind of pleasant domestic scene Enid always appreciated, which meant everything was working the way it should.

Enid set the dishes next to the sink and pump. "Already washed, thanks."

"Oh, you didn't have to do that, it's no trouble," Juni said, rushing over, domestic and attentive. If Enid didn't know better, she might think the woman didn't trust her definition of clean. She recognized the type.

Enid leaned against the counter and looked over the gathering. A woman stitching a shirt, a couple of men, maybe ten years younger than Jess, whittling and catching the shavings in a bucket at their feet. Seemed to be pieces of driftwood, like what Kellan collected. Jess sat in a chair, sharpening machetes with a handheld whetstone. The scraping noise had been innocuous, like the background calls of birds, until Enid focused on it. Then it grated loudly, making her teeth ache.

"I'm so relieved that we were able to take care of that poor girl's body. Feels like closure," Juni said, fidgeting with the bowls, stacking them one way, reversing them, then finally setting them with their fellows on a shelf over the counter. "I suppose you'll be off soon, then?"

Juni sounded a little more hopeful than she should have. Enid was amused. "I have a few more rocks I'd like to turn over."

There was a hitch in the metallic scraping. Stitching and whittling paused. Everyone listened close.

Juni said, "I didn't think . . . that is, it seems like it would be very hard to know what happened."

"Oh yes," Enid said. "I'd still like to talk to her people. Neeve's had the most contact with Ella's folk but doesn't seem able to get them a message. If I wait, maybe one will come looking for Ella." Another one besides Hawk . . .

Jess muttered, "That woman won't help you at all."

"And yet," Enid said, "I'm still looking for a possible murder weapon. Like those, for example." She nodded at Jess and the handful of blades sitting on the floor by his chair. "Everyone around here uses those, yeah? To cut back vegetation or harvest reeds and things? Like you all were doing the other day when we got here."

Jess said, "You don't think any of us did it? We couldn't have."

"You saw the body," Enid said. "You saw the wound. You tell me — you think one of those machetes could have done it?"

Silence answered her, because they had to admit that yes, a blade as long as a forearm could very well have killed the woman.

"Why would we? We didn't even know her," Juni said, her voice almost a whisper.

"Maybe someone thought she was sneaking around, that she was a danger somehow, taking something that wasn't hers. Erik thinks folk from upriver have been coming down here more than anyone knows. Taking things. If one of you saw one of them, got angry — well then, who knows." She shrugged. "That's one of the things I have to figure out — why someone would hurt her, when she seemed so harmless. Usually folk hurt each other when they get angry, and if I ask enough questions I might find out why someone was angry at her."

"It wasn't us," Jess said starkly. "I can tell you, it wasn't us."

"I'm not accusing. Just thinking out loud. Sorry. I'll leave you to it —"

Juni said, "It's Last House. It must be someone at Last House. They knew her, if anyone had cause to be angry —"

"Juni — let it go," Jess said.

"Yes, right, sorry." Juni finally finished with the dishes and stepped away from the counter.

Enid smiled thinly. "Sorry to disturb you all this evening. Thank you again for the meal."

Back at the work house, Teeg was sitting on the steps of

the porch, notebook in his lap, writing by the light of the overhead solar lamp. Enid slowed her approach, watching, wondering at her instant suspicion of him. What, exactly, was he writing? Shouldn't matter, should it?

"Making notes?" Enid asked.

He glanced up. "Starting our report. The one on Semperfi, at least. Might as well. And I suppose we'll have to say *something* about the murder, however it works out."

Sighing, she joined him. Night had fallen, and tiny bugs swarmed, attracted by the light. The gulls were gone, but the frogs at the river seemed even louder. The air was still sticky.

"I still think Last House folk know more than they're telling," Teeg threw out.

"All right. Doesn't mean they're all murderers."

"Not all. Just Kellan."

"Teeg, stop—"

His gaze flared again. He was so sure. "There's something not right there." He tapped his pencil on the page, like he wanted to drill a hole in it.

Teeg wasn't wrong. Kellan was so jumpy, and all of them so wary . . . was it just the usual anxiety at seeing brown uniforms show up at their door, or something more? Then again, just because someone acted guilty didn't mean they were. At least, not about *that*.

Teeg added, "I just don't know how to get at them."

"We need more evidence," Enid said. "A better lever to pry with. We need to talk to Hawk again."

"And how're you going to do that?"

That was a good question, and she didn't know the answer. Well, maybe she did. She just wasn't sure it was a good idea. "I'll go talk to him."

"You'll go talk to him," Teeg answered flatly.

"They've got to have a settlement or camp or something not too far away. He didn't have a pack or travel supplies with him. I'll follow his trail and go find him."

"That's crazy, Enid."

"Or we wait. He came down to harass Last House once, maybe he'll do it again. We wait for him."

"You really want to wait around for that? I'd have thought you'd be ready to go home, no matter what."

"Not until we ask a few more questions," she said.

"The longer we stay here, the less happy folk'll be about it," Teeg said. "I haven't been doing this that long, but I've learned that much about the job."

This used to come so naturally with her last partner, the wise and unflappable Tomas. They would toss ideas back and forth, and she never felt that she was being silly, or that the ideas were outrageous. Teeg, though—he was judging her.

"Really," Teeg said, offhand. "You have to wonder why anyone would live that far out of the way, and care so little about what goes on in the rest of place."

That was the wrong answer. That was the quick answer, the suspicious answer.

"And yet," Enid said, "they pull their weight, don't they? How much of the driftwood that Kellan finds is worked into bowls and spoons and furniture for the rest of the settlement? How much mending does Neeve do for the lot? And they tend the pyres for everyone, don't they?"

Teeg turned back to his journal, frowning.

She tested her next thought, the next obvious step on this case. "We should go upriver to find Hawk. Anyone else from their folk, if we can. Get their side of it."

He set down the pencil and glared at her. "That guy won't

talk to us. And if one of them did it—" He was scowling as his words broke off.

"If one of them did it, then what?" Enid pressed him.

"Then it's not our business, is it? It's not like they'll take our judgment."

That was a philosophical question that could occupy a room full of investigators for hours. Strictly speaking, no. If an outsider killed one of their own, it was none of the investigators' business. But Enid wanted the answer. She wanted to know, even if she couldn't do anything about it once she did. If she believed Kellan didn't do it, then she needed to know who did, and why.

"There's a settlement of them somewhere upriver. We go there, ask a few questions. It'll take some effort but we can do it."

Teeg drew back. "Seriously?"

"What's the matter?"

"It's too far. It's not our job."

"Scared?" she said, grinning, aware she was prodding him and not caring.

"It's not necessary," he said.

As they talked, Enid made plans. They'd need at least a couple of days' worth of food. The weather wasn't likely to turn bad, but they should bring an oiled tarp or something just in case. Staff and tranquilizers, of course.

She said, "If we leave first thing in the morning we can make good time, maybe even find Hawk and his folk before nightfall. Come back the next day."

Teeg said, "Wouldn't you rather go back home? Aren't your people waiting for you? Your baby might be on the way right now."

She promised Olive she'd be back as soon as she could.

There'd be no shame in leaving all this, no shame at all. No one would judge her.

"It'll only be a couple more days," she said. "We can do this."

"I won't go, Enid. I won't." His mouth twisted in horror. She might as well have asked him to slit his wrists. He was scared. Nothing she could say would convince him.

"Then I'll go alone," she said.

Investigators worked in pairs for situations just like this one. So they could tell each other when they were off base. So they could check on each other. Suggest, gently, when the other might be wrong. What now, then? Was she wrong?

"But you can't," he said, with the certainty of a child who didn't know any better.

She smiled wryly. "Where's your sense of adventure?"

"I don't think we're supposed to have a sense of adventure," he answered.

"Oh no, you have to have a sense of adventure to put on that uniform." You had to have a spine to wear the brown uniform that made you an outsider, that made people afraid of you. Maybe Enid had too much of a spine, was what Teeg was saying.

"What happens if you go and don't come back? What am I supposed to tell regional then?"

"Tell them it's my fault," she said. "I thought it was a good risk, and I was wrong. It's not on you."

"But it will be! I'll be the only investigator in history to lose a partner!"

"No, you won't," she said softly, thinking of Tomas dying in her arms last year. Teeg looked away; he knew the story.

"You can't go, Enid."

She stopped arguing. Teeg went back to writing. She wondered how much he could possibly have to say about the Sem-perfi house. "Maybe if I sleep on it, I'll come up with another idea. Good night, then."

"Good night," Teeg said, not looking up from his work.

///////////////////////////////////////////////////////////////

ENID WENT TO BED without drawing any interesting conclu-sions, then restlessly tossed and turned on the thin blankets and hard wood. Missed Sam's arms around her. Thought of everyone back home, her folk at Serenity, wondering what was happening there. Would be very easy, to just drop it all and go back home where she belonged.

But she would always, always wonder. She wasn't finished following this thread.

The sound of water moving, both in the river and on the coast, were unfamiliar and made Enid feel like something was sneaking up on her. Maybe something with a knife.

What had Ella been doing, the moment before she was killed? Had she known what was about to happen or had it been a shock? Had she trusted the person who did it, or had it been a stranger?

In some books about crime and investigations in the old world, from before the Fall—the handful that had survived—experts stated that murders were usually committed by folk who knew the victim. Rarely were they random. The reason might be simple and unsatisfying—long-simmering anger and a burst of temper. But there had to be a reason for this.

There *had* to be.

///////////////////////////////////////////////////////////////

ENID LAY AWAKE on her bedroll and heard Teeg come in and settle into sleep.

Before dawn, she got up—very quietly—and put together a pack of supplies. Enough for a day or two of travel, bread and beef jerky, dried fruit, a blanket. Her own knife. She'd find a staff of her own once she got to the woods; she wouldn't ask Teeg to give up his. She took some tranquilizer patches out of Teeg's pack.

When the sun rose, she was on the road, walking up the hill, and beyond.

## The Last Bit of Path

Serenity's banner, when it came, came quietly—almost anti-climactically. No fanfare, no grand announcement. In fact, Enid had been mostly drunk at the time.

Haven's committee met in conjunction with the big mid-summer market, and the whole town turned the event into a party, with music and booze and folk traveling in from households twenty miles around. People ate too much and didn't even feel bad about it.

Olive was dancing in a crowd to a fiddle and drums, Sam and Berol were off finding food, and Enid was on the ground, on a blanket, back propped against a tree. She'd lost track of how much cider she'd drunk. People kept refilling her mug, and she kept not stopping them. Things had gotten loud, and rather than try to find out what was taking Sam so long, she stayed put so he could find her.

When one of the town's teenagers stumbled to the ground next to her and tugged on her sleeve, she thought there must be a mistake. She couldn't make out the words.

"I'm saying you've got to come, Enid, committee wants to see you!" the kid said breathlessly.

"Now?"

"Yes, now!"

"But I haven't done anything wrong," she mumbled back, and he rolled his eyes at her.

So she'd clung to the bark of the tree and managed to haul herself to her feet. Left her mug nestled in the roots, not really trusting that it would still be there when she got back. But she didn't think it would be entirely proper to appear before the committee with a mug of booze in hand.

Buzzed, not paying attention, she still managed to arrive directly at the committee house. The way there was so familiar, after all. Could be a dozen reasons the committee wanted to see her in the middle of a big meeting like this. Probably it was investigator business. Someone had a question about an old case, or maybe a new one had come up.

Enid still wasn't entirely sensible when she stood blinking at the three committee members across the desk, and they smiled happily back at her like she should be pleased.

Finally, she realized they were holding out a square of green-and-red cloth. She might have wished to be less tipsy at such a profound moment. Then again, maybe it was for the best that she wasn't able to speak.

"Congratulations, Enid. It's well deserved; Serenity house does good work," said Otto, the committee chair, a medic who'd run Haven's clinic for a decade now. He was normally serious, but now he positively grinned, and Enid just gaped at him—and she never gaped. She always knew exactly what to say.

"You might go tell the rest of your house now, hmm?" came the gentle suggestion from Clare, the town's gray-haired matriarch.

"Yes. Thanks, thank you," Enid finally stammered. She might have bowed a few times on her way out; she couldn't really remember.

And then she stood in the clearing in front of the clinic for a long time, staring at the cloth in her hands, rubbing it between her fingers. The texture was rough, tightly woven with a kind of rustic handspun yarn. Of course they wouldn't use good soft fiber on something that wouldn't be worn. The tactile reality of the cloth fascinated her. The green was dark, like the forest. The red was like bricks.

Word got out. Someone spotted her there with the banner, staring at it as if under some kind of spell, and there was shouting, and Olive, Berol, and Sam managed to find her soon enough, and all of them together began screaming and laughing. Enid clutched the cloth while they hugged her, and all four of them clung to one another, beaming, while happily accepting congratulations from everyone else at the market festival.

They'd had no hint that they were about to receive a banner. Something like that ought to come with some kind of warning, a chance to prepare, Enid thought later. She had the vague thought that she hadn't handled the announcement very well. When she said this out loud, Sam laughed at her, insisting that there was no way she could prepare for everything.

Back at home an hour or so later, the four of them kept drinking. A celebration, just for them, with a bottle of brandy Berol coaxed out of someone back at the market. They collapsed in front of their fireplace, which was unlit in the middle of summer, but still served as the cottage's focal point.

Sam took a swig straight from the bottle, handed it to Enid, who took a long drink, and then passed it to Olive. "We have to get as much drinking in as we can now, since Olive won't be drinking for a while," Enid said, her usual cheerfulness turned brilliant.

"What?" Olive blinked back at her, startled, gripping the neck of the bottle.

"If you're going to be pregnant, you shouldn't drink. Not like this, at least," Enid said happily.

"She's right," Berol said, taking the bottle from Olive in turn. "You have to take care of yourself."

"But . . . we haven't talked about it. I assumed . . . I mean . . . I thought we would talk about it, that we'd decide if Enid or I would be the one . . ."

"You want it, though, right?" Enid said. "You really want to be a mom, yeah?"

And Olive started crying, right there, hand over her mouth and eyes squinched up. Berol set the bottle aside and folded her in his arms, chuckling quietly while comforting her. Drunk, Sam buried his face in Enid's lap to hide his laughter, and Enid kissed his shoulder out of sheer good feeling.

"You mean you all just decided, without even talking . . ." Olive sputtered, when she was able to catch her breath.

"It just seems obvious," Enid said.

Olive seemed to need a moment, a few breaths to steady herself, but finally she smiled and reached for Enid's hand, which Enid grasped tight. "Okay," Olive said. "But Enid pins the banner to the wall."

"Yes, of course," Enid said, and did so right then and there, climbing up on a chair while Sam held her steady and Berol handed her a nail and hammer. Between the three of them they managed to do the work of one sober person.

Olive got her implant removed the very next day. She'd wanted it out that night, but the others talked her out of it, mostly by convincing her that drunkenly waking up a medic in the middle of the night couldn't possibly end well. The next day would be soon enough.

The actual removal felt anticlimactic. There should have been witnesses. There should have been a ritual. It should have been . . . more difficult.

But no, the clinic had already gotten word of the banner from the committee. Enid, Sam, and Berol waited outside. Olive emerged from the back exam room ten minutes later, with a bandage on her upper arm and a startled look on her face, like she couldn't believe it. Girls got their implants as soon as they started menstruating, and some women never had them removed, only replaced, their whole lives. It was a part of you. Unless you earned a banner, and then you became something else.

"How does it feel?" Enid asked.

"I don't know," Olive answered. "I'm afraid to look."

"I'll look," Berol said, picking at the edge of the bandage, and Olive slapped his hand, pulled away, and then hugged him.

"Let's go home. Right now."

"What? I thought we were going to go find some brandy, celebrate some more—"

"No, we are going home right now," Olive said, grabbing his hand and pulling. Her face was flushed.

Enid and Sam stayed out of the house for the rest of the day. Got sandwiches and had an impromptu picnic out by the duck pond, snugged up under a tree. Sam even fell asleep, his breathing turning deep and steady. Enid kept waking him.

"Are you sad? That it'll be theirs and not ours?"

"Hmm?" he shifted, securing his grip around her. "It'll be all of ours."

"You know what I mean."

"Well. I do think you'd have a beautiful baby."

"So would you. We both would." And yet, somehow, she couldn't quite picture what this imaginary baby would actually look like. Would it have light hair or dark? Her round features or Sam's square ones?

Enid also couldn't imagine herself pregnant. But Olive—she could absolutely imagine Olive pregnant and glowing from it, the way some women got. In fact, she couldn't wait to see it.

Sam murmured, "If it happens, it happens. No reason it shouldn't."

"But what if we never earn another banner?"

"That's too far ahead to think about."

"But—"

"Enid. You're overthinking it." He tipped her face up and kissed her, and she melted, grateful to do so.

That was how it worked. Your household earned a banner, one of you had your implant removed, and every child was wanted and cared for.

But no one had cared enough to come looking for Ella. This had kept Enid awake. Why did no one want to learn what had happened to her?

It was like her people already knew she was gone.

ENID CROSSED THE BRIDGE and continued up the hill with purpose, just as the Estuary's inhabitants were waking up and starting morning chores, collecting eggs, milking goats. She had no interest in talking to anyone; they'd told her everything they were going to. Time to move on.

But when she got to Last House, to where the road ended, she stopped. Mart watched her from the front steps. He was just going out the front door; might have seen her coming up the path.

She paused to ask, "How's Kellan?"

He shrugged. "This whole business has wrecked him." They had to raise their voices, to hear each other across the distance between them.

"I'm sorry for that."

"Kellan didn't do it. You told your partner, yeah?"

"It would help if we had some evidence that he wasn't involved."

Mart scowled. "He's usually off by himself, scavenging on the shore. Alone."

"Yeah," she said, looking away. That was what she had assumed. Evidence would have to come from someplace else. "Right. Well. I'm going after Hawk to see if there's anything he can tell me. I don't suppose you know exactly where he's run off to?"

Folding his arms, holding himself close in, Mart shook his head. "He said we must have done it. That we may not have held the knife, but we drove Ella out and got her killed. Offered her a place, then didn't protect her. He just . . . I think he just wanted us to say it was our fault. He wants to blame someone."

"Everybody does. You think he's trying to blame someone else because maybe it was him that did it?"

"What? No—at least, I hadn't thought so." His gaze turned inward. He was thinking about it now.

"You know anything about that knife Kellan was looking for?"

"Yeah—Hawk was looking for it too."

"You saw it, before it disappeared."

"Neeve gave it to her," he said.

"Gave—not traded?"

He chuckled. "Maybe it was a bribe. But I haven't seen it since the last time Ella was down this way. Month or so ago, I guess. She had it then."

"And the next time you saw her was after Kellan found the body, and there was no knife."

Mart shrugged, a noncommittal gesture. He seemed to be trying to put together the same broken pieces she was.

"Any idea where it could have ended up?" asked Enid.

"With whoever killed her, I guess. They likely buried it somewhere."

"Even though a blade like that would be valuable to outsider folk?"

"I don't know; you're the investigator, you tell me."

She suppressed a smile. "Right, then. I should be back in a couple of days. Maybe I'll have it all figured out by then."

She started walking, and Mart called after her. "They're violent out there. Wouldn't put it past them. If it wasn't Hawk that killed her, it was likely one of the others, one of his kin."

"That's what I'm going to try to find out."

"Enid, wait." He trotted down the stairs, came close enough that he didn't need to raise his voice. "With you gone, your partner'll be back up here. He'll lay this on Kellan. What're we supposed to do then?"

"I'll be back to clear everything up."

"But what if you aren't?"

They were so sure she wouldn't be back.

"How about we figure all this out then?"

She walked on.

///////////////////////////////////////////////////////

ENID HAD DONE THIS BEFORE—walked into the wilderness. She'd met outsiders there, spoken to them. They hadn't been dangerous, not obviously. But that had been a couple hundred miles south, hadn't it? These were different folk.

She wasn't worried. Couldn't be. Half of her job was acting like she absolutely knew what she was doing.

The final bit of path, the very last remnant of the Coast Road in this part of the world, dissipated to grass, then forest soil, as trees grew up and closed in around her. After that she was on her own, following her sense of direction northward, orienting to the sun, which was arcing west in a hazy sky, and to the San Joe, now a fast-running creek a quarter-mile to the east, cutting through a steep gully. No clear path cut through the woods here. She'd almost expected to find one, given how often Hawk, Ella, and others traveled back and forth to Last House. But they must have hidden their routes, taking different ways through the forest each time. Being careful. They didn't want to be found, which discouraged Enid. With a million places to hide out here, she might never find them.

A dozen years ago—before becoming an investigator, before Serenity, before practically her whole life—walking into the wild was easier. She didn't have much to lose. Now she felt the pull of what she left behind. This was dangerous. She shouldn't be doing this. Olive would be horrified if she knew what Enid had planned. Sam would be concerned. But he wouldn't tell her not to do it. Just to be careful.

Enid needed to know.

Just like she'd done the last time she trekked off the road, she found a fallen branch. She pounded it on the ground a couple of times to test its sturdiness. With its twigs and leaves stripped off, she could use it as a makeshift staff. Both for walking, and for just in case. Probably wouldn't need it, but didn't want to be without it if she did. Made sure the tranq patches were in her belt pouch, within reach. Continued on, and hoped for the best.

On that first excursion into the wild, she'd been traveling the Coast Road with Dak, her former lover, and trekking overland to the ruined city had been an adventure, a lark. They'd stood on the western hills and looked out at the tangle of shadows, lost in haze, its own sub-climate of rusted steel and decaying concrete. Folk thought steel and concrete lasted forever, but they didn't. In a hundred years even a city could be overrun with trees and swamp. People still lived there, Dak had warned her. He insisted that they were dangerous, wild, threatening. But they hadn't been. She had met them, sat with them at their campfires. Like anyone, they were mostly concerned with getting enough to eat.

Now she walked into wild territory not with a noble sense of exploration, but with grim purpose. A quest, but she wasn't sure she knew what she was looking for. An answer must be somewhere; she might as well look.

Those overriding questions remained: Were the people she looked for dangerous? Had one of them killed Ella? And if they had, could she expect them to tell her what had happened? What if one of them admitted to it?

Then she realized that if one of them had done it, Enid would have to be satisfied with turning around and walking home, learning the truth her only outcome. It would have to be enough. She prepared herself for that.

This might be a stupid thing she was doing. She promised Olive she'd be back home soon, and this seemed like a good path to maybe breaking that promise. Enid stopped and almost turned around right then. She would never find what she was looking for. And she was endangering herself unnecessarily.

Instead, she took a deep breath. Noticed how different the air smelled, even this little ways away from the settlement. The briny, muddy reek of the Estuary was gone. Here, the muggy thickness gave way to air that was almost cool. The cleanness of it stung her nose, and she filled her lungs. Pine trees grew straight, their branches reaching. She looked up at a washed-out sky, crisscrossed with branches. It was beautiful. Nothing like this back home. Flickers of movement caught her attention. Birds, she decided, but they never stayed still long enough for her to get a good look at them. Their calls were staccato, muffled.

Ahead a great cracked slab of concrete blocked her way. Beyond it, a fallen steel pole. Could have been a lamppost, could have been part of a building. Hard to tell now, out of all context. She couldn't resist poking around, kicking away dirt where ruins met the ground, looking for clues as to what had been here a hundred years ago. Even in what looked like untouched woodland, the earth held remnants of what had once been towns, before almost everything had washed away. Bits and pieces left, like shells on a beach. When she got back to Haven, she could check old maps, find the names of what had once been here. But right now, she had to focus not on history but on what had happened to Ella just a few days ago.

"Sam, what am I doing?" Enid murmured. As if he would tell her anything but to follow her instinct. Trust herself.

So on she walked.

Dusk fell; she was still heading north and hadn't seen any sign of people. She passed more concrete slabs that had once served as foundations for buildings, and evidence of a road—a strip of rotted asphalt under a series of fallen trees. The people in the ruins she'd explored a dozen years ago had used broken walls for shelter and navigated via old roads. But here, no one.

Hawk had to live somewhere. He hadn't been carrying enough with him to suggest he was nomadic, though he might have stashed his pack nearby rather than bring it down into the Estuary with him. Maybe she should backtrack, head out through the woods in another direction.

Enid hadn't particularly wanted to spend the night in the wild—the idea wasn't as romantic as it had been when she was younger. But she was frustrated. Her instinct told her Hawk was out here.

Somewhere.

She followed the trail of ruins, hoping. If there were people here, they'd be living on the bones of what came before. The woods had become very quiet, the shadows long.

She felt a prickling on the back of her neck and looked around, thinking there must be something here, someone watching, but she just couldn't see it.

This wasn't home; she didn't know this area. Her attackers did.

And knew just the right moment to strike.

She was in a spot where the ruins had more substance, where walls still stood, though they were stripped down, windows missing, roofs gone. A charred layer suggested a fire had come through at some point, leveling most of what had been here—a street in some hillside town. The handful of walls formed an aisle.

A trap.

She should have recognized it; instead, she'd walked right up that aisle until she had nowhere to run.

She heard a rustling through dead vegetation, something passing through air, shifting the whole atmosphere of the forest. Then the steps, a pounding on soft forest earth. She turned as he raced toward her through skeletal dead buildings. Enid planted her feet and braced her staff in front of her.

The second one came at her from behind.

His sharp inhale told her he was there. She twisted to look over her shoulder, quelled the spike of panic. He had a club, raised and ready to strike.

The first, a slim young man, bare-armed, growling, was there as a distraction. The second, bigger and quieter, moved decisively toward her.

Ducking, Enid evaded the striking club, but the move wasn't graceful or stylish and didn't put her in a good spot. Off balance, she stumbled back, and they closed on her. They had all the momentum, all the advantage. She had no time to go for the tranqs in her pouch; the men would just knock the patches out of her hand even if she had. She'd be able to use that trick only once, at any rate.

The second attacker raised his club again—she got a better look at it this time. It was wood, the stout end of a branch, stripped of bark and polished smooth. When he swung, she got her staff in the way to block. Wood striking wood made a sickly crack.

The first guy lunged to grab the end of the staff, and yanked.

At first she held on, got into a brief tug of war that she knew she would lose. Recovering enough to let go at just the right time, she sent him flailing backward. Then the second one got a grip on her arm. And he just held on. He was a full head taller than she was, and he came in close, ready to knock her over. She had to get away—if she could just get away and run.

She would not scream, and she would not panic.

Enid slammed her foot on the attacker's instep; her boots were much tougher and better made than his soft leather ones. Her boot had a heel. A scream of pain would have satisfied her, but his gasp and stifled groan were good enough, and she wrenched free as he dropped his club.

Nursing no illusions of her chances in a fight with these two hardened outsiders, she ran.

Enid wasn't sure she'd be faster than them both. The bigger guy, yes, but his wiry accomplice, maybe not.

Didn't matter. She had to try.

Not five strides on, she came up against a half dozen more wild folk, fanned out before her, waiting. She had no place to go. No chance of escape.

She bent over her knees and caught a breath that came out as a chuckle. Straightened and studied her assailants, now her captors. And yes, one of these new ones was Hawk. He glared at her with satisfaction.

Enid was the only one smiling. She looked at each of them, marking, remembering. Two were women, scrappy like the rest. They ranged in age from twenty to maybe forty.

"Well then. Isn't this lucky? I've been wanting to talk to you all."

Silence. Not even a touch of wind to creak through branches. The light was fading, the forest turning dark.

"I have a few questions about Ella," she said. "You all knew her, yeah?" She caught Hawk's gaze, but he ducked away, scowling.

"No talk here," said the large man, still standing uncomfortably close. He'd picked up the club again and now held it at his side.

"All right. Where should we talk?" Maybe they had a camp

THE WILD DEAD · 185

somewhere. A fire might be nice right about now. Everyone felt better around a campfire. With night coming on, the air was definitely chilled. This was nothing like the sticky heat of the marshes.

"Let's go," the man repeated.

"I'd be glad to. Where?"

They closed on her, quick and smooth, the wiry guy grabbing her pack off her shoulders, the pouch at her belt, another one gripping her arms and wrenching them back, yet another dropping a sack over her head, forcing her into darkness.

Her breath came fast and hot, too close to her ears, held in by felted wool. A coil of rope went around her wrists and tightened. She couldn't move her arms at all now. Hands held her shoulders, clutching the fabric of her tunic.

They weren't going to kill her, she reassured herself. If they meant to kill her, they'd have just done it. Could have put an arrow in her from fifty paces away and not gone through all this trouble.

So they weren't going to kill her.

Probably not.

Not yet.

Another loop went around her neck, and she gasped. They didn't pull this one taut. Instead, they used it like a leash, tugging her forward.

"This way. Go on," one of them said. Not Hawk, not the burly guy. She didn't know who was speaking.

Her feet remained free, for all the good it did her. She stepped forward because she didn't have a choice, feeling for the ground in front of her, her senses stretched to breaking. Hunched over, moving carefully as she could, she stayed quiet, didn't struggle. The troop moved around her, setting a pace that was just a little too fast, but not so fast she couldn't keep up. She was irrevocably off balance.

Well.

She'd wanted to talk to them. Now, it seemed, she'd get her chance.

## Darkness

Enid grew exhausted from working at not falling. She stumbled on what she assumed were tree roots, random stones, pre-Fall bits of road. But she would not allow herself to trip and give her captors an excuse to manhandle her back to her feet. From inside the hood she shifted her head, trying to adjust the fabric so she could maybe glimpse something past the bottom edge, to at least see her feet. Didn't work, and the air only got heavier and stuffier.

They marched for what felt like hours. Endless hours.

Eventually, the rope tugged at Enid's neck, bringing her to a halt, and a hand on her shoulder steadied her.

"Sit here," said a voice, a new one, and directed her to a hard perch. Concrete, likely. It felt too smooth and flat for stone. Enid sat still and listened hard, but the troop of wild folk did no more than murmur among themselves. She didn't pick up any of their plans. Someone started a fire; Enid heard the crackling of wood, caught the orange glow through the hood's fabric.

They'd been settled for a while when someone yanked off the hood, and Enid blinked, disoriented. Night had fallen, and the light from the fire hurt her eyes.

One of the wild folk—she didn't get a good look at which one—held a skin of water to Enid's mouth, and water splashed down the sides of her face as she drank as much as she could. Then they took the skin away and put the hood back over her head.

Enid didn't say anything. She didn't complain. She could be patient as stone.

They stayed here for the night. She assumed that some of them slept, while others kept watch. Assumed that someone was guarding her. They left her seated, her stomach growing hollow with hunger—she hadn't eaten since noon. Her hands tingled, grew numb. She stretched and clenched her fingers as much as she could, trying to avoid cramping up.

Though she listened, she didn't hear anyone say anything about Ella. Whether by inclination or intent, they were keeping quiet on the subject.

She must have slept a little, propped up against the ruin. Her head would nod, and she'd jerk awake, over and over. In a half-daze, she felt someone tug at her arm, urging her to her feet. Sudden wakefulness jolted her, and she wrenched her arm back, out of her captor's grip. Noises around her—low voices still scratchy with sleep, quick commands to quench the fire, to gather close—suggested they were about to march on.

"I need to go behind a tree for a minute," she muttered. "Can I do that?"

A whispered conference ensued. Enid spent it considering if she could just piss where she stood and let them deal with the mess of it, however uncomfortable it would be for her.

She'd rather not, and decided she could maintain her dignity in either case. This was on them, not her.

Listening for footsteps, for voices, she heard when they approached and steeled herself not to flinch when one of them took hold of her wrists and pulled at the knots in the rope that bound her. So they were reasonable . . . at least to a point.

As soon as her hands were free, she stepped away and yanked off the hood. Again, they surrounded her. One of them was even holding her staff. Nice, in a way, that they'd think she was so dangerous. She held her palms out and moved slowly.

"It's all right. I won't fight, I won't run. I told you, I want to talk to you. There's no need for all this mess." She tossed the hood at Hawk's feet. "I'm just going to step over here for a moment, yeah?"

They were treating her like some kind of weapon, like she might destroy them with a look. What stories did these people tell each other about the Coast Road, about people like her?

The forest here was much the same as where she had been last evening, when they'd captured her. Not so many signs of ruins. A wide track traveled through where the trees were just saplings, and a strip of sky was clear overhead. A remnant of yet another old road. They were everywhere, if you knew what to look for. The group seemed to be following it.

She didn't go far to relieve herself, and was aware that the whole troop of them were watching her. The tree she'd chosen wasn't quite wide enough to hide behind, but it would have to do. When she emerged, the troop's leader, the burly man, waited with the length of rope in one hand and the hood in the other.

"Really?" Enid said. "Don't you think we've had enough of that?"

"You want to talk or not?" he said.

She nodded at the hood. "You think that's going to hide

where your camp is, or are you just trying to be cruel? I promise, I won't cause trouble."

Unless they started it first.

Around her, some of the wild folk—most of them were really just kids, weren't they?— fidgeted, tightening grips on spears, darting glances at their leader. She was making them nervous. Yet they could kill her easily. They could swarm her and beat her to death with their bare hands if they decided to.

She knew it was dangerous to keep poking at them, but she had to keep on like she knew something they didn't. Like, even now, she was stronger. She wasn't afraid; she was curious.

"Let's go," the burly man said finally. "But go slow and quiet. No trouble."

"No, of course not. What's your name?"

He didn't answer. Gesturing up the road, he urged her forward, and fell in behind her.

Surrounded by wary fighters, Enid walked carefully, her gaze ahead, not wanting to rile them by staring and making them any more jittery than they already were. But she kept watch out of the corner of her eye.

///////////////////////////////////////////////////////////

AFTER WALKING ANOTHER HOUR or so, the smell of wood smoke tickled Enid's nose. Someone had a campfire up ahead. They'd passed more and more cut stumps—a lot of wood harvesting went on here. The road opened to a clearing with blue sky overhead. Voices traveled, the familiar sounds of people living their lives, focused on food and shelter and shouting after children.

This wasn't just a camp, as she'd seen before among outsider settlements—temporary arrangements made by folk who traveled, following good weather. This was a village. Permanent structures made of split logs, neatly stacked firewood stored under shelter. Cabins that used the walls of pre-Fall buildings and had substantial roofs. Worn paths and well-used fire pits between them all, a web of connections. The central clearing had the look of a market square in a decent-sized town.

No livestock that she could see, not so much as a chicken. No goats, which meant no milk. No sources of wool, at least not right here. Everything they ate, they foraged. She saw no blacksmith's forge. Nothing that looked like complex metal-working. As she'd been told, all their metal was salvaged scrap. Anything else, they'd have to trade for.

A dog bounded out, barking at Enid. Rangy and scrappy, with short brown-and-cream fur and pointed ears, it might have been a hybrid coyote, or something that had been feral for a few generations before being re-tamed. More bristly and alert than Bear back at the Estuary. This one didn't assume everyone was a friend. Spotting Enid, a stranger, it looked like it might charge. She stood her ground, wished for her staff. But the burly man waved the animal off, hissing a couple of words. The dog tucked its tail and slinked away to watch from farther off.

"Over here," her captor said, pointing to an open-walled shelter on the far side of the clearing. A sturdy roof on steel supports covered a concrete slab. The concrete was cracked and repaired with multicolored clay patches that had been smoothed down, then patched and smoothed again. The beams supporting the roof were riveted and painted. This was a pre-Fall structure. Not a whole building—likely it had never had walls. But it seemed the village had turned the old shelter into a community space. A couple of teens were inside, twisting hemp, making rope. A woman was pounding something between stones. Nuts, looked like, making paste.

Activity stopped when Enid arrived, and people stared. She was clearly a stranger: taller, more muscular. Better fed. Dressed in linen cloth, not leather, hemp, and felt. Enid left her hands at her sides, trying to appear friendly and harmless.

"Wait," the burly man ordered, pointing to a wooden bench. "El Juez'll come look at you."

The troop gathered in the shelter, hemming Enid in. More spectators emerged, coming from sheds and cottages, from farther out around the clearing, to see what this was about. To look at *her*. Wasn't much different than when an investigator arrived in any town: cautious curiosity. No one wanted to get too close, but everyone wanted to see.

A dozen adults, plus as many kids. Too many kids, she thought. She made calculations that were second nature to her —how much did they grow, how much could they forage, how much did they hunt, and was that enough to feed everyone? Probably yes, if they spent all their time on it. They likely all helped, even the little ones. She thought that most of the adult women here had had more than one child each.

A set of bone wind chimes hung from one of the beams. Just like those at Last House, ribs and vertebrae on twine, with a few rough wood beads in between. They'd clack together in a breeze, but at the moment the air was still.

"Did Ella make this?" Enid asked, pointing. "Or maybe Neeve?" No one answered. Not even any nodding. She wasn't really surprised. She glared out, a thin wry smile on her lips, and studied the faces around her, as carefully as she had done when they first captured her. Let them believe they hadn't rattled her.

These folk might decide to kill Enid as some kind of exchange for Ella. One of theirs for one of ours, that sort of thing. Enid hadn't been thinking in those terms, and for the first time regretted coming here. She had been considering higher notions, like truth and justice. Impractical notions that didn't put food in anyone's mouth.

She had to give them a stake in talking to her.

"Hawk," she said, and the young man flinched. "Did Ella live in the camp here?" He pressed his lips shut, seemed determined not to speak. "Did you all know Ella?" she said to the rest of them. "Were any of you close?"

For a moment, she wondered if they even spoke the same language.

"What is it?" said a booming voice with a clipped accent.

The speaker emerged from one of the cabins. The man was big, tough. Brown hands used to gripping, legs used to walking for miles, all wrapped in leather and felted cloth. His unruly beard was going gray, his thick hair tied back in a tail. He glared, full of iron and suspicion. This must be El Juez.

Enid slowed her breathing and looked on, calm as she could make herself. The people seemed to expect her to panic, so she didn't.

"Hola," she said. "I'm Enid."

He looked her up and down, studying her just as closely as she studied him. She wondered what he saw.

To the head of the small band he said, "Why did you bring this here?"

"She can tell about Ella, Hawk says." The burly man spoke carefully, hands folded before him, deferential.

"Hawk said that already. Didn't you, Hawk?" said El Juez.

"Yeah," Hawk said, softly, his gazed lowered.

It wasn't that the folk seemed scared of El Juez, exactly. But they offered a great deal of respect. They kept a physical space around him.

"So that's enough. Don't need more," he said.

The tough guy said, "But—"

The leader waved him off. "Ella made her choice. You." He pointed a callused finger at Enid. She met his gaze squarely. "You can go. We don't want you here."

She imagined he didn't. Part of her thought she'd be better off walking away. Safer, certainly. But then she'd have made this difficult trip for nothing.

"El Juez, yes?" The judge. Name and title. "I'd like to ask you a few questions." This was all part of the investigation.

He studied her, and she bore it quietly. "About what? Ella?"

"What her life was like here. It's not enough to know what happened to her. I want to know why."

Oddly, counterintuitively, the longer he studied her, the calmer she grew. He didn't seem to have a bad temper. He didn't seem likely to kill her out of hand. She could deal with him, she thought. And if she could get him on her side, the community would follow.

He waved a hand at the surroundings, the structures, campfires, the work going on.

"You ever seen a place like this?" he asked.

"Yeah, I have."

"Then you know what you need. Best foot it back to your people."

"Ella was going to leave here, wasn't she? She was going to settle on the Coast Road. Live with Last House and get an implant. You all couldn't stand that, could you? Losing one of your own, a strong young person at that. You need all the help you can get, in a place like this."

"She was free to go if she wanted," the man said.

"You sure about that? Did everyone feel that way?" And El Juez looked at Hawk, who flinched as if the look was a blow. Enid could see there were suspicions. She prodded them to say more. "Did you send Hawk to kill her, or did he do that on his own?"

"I didn't!" the boy shouted, and lunged at her. It happened so fast, she didn't have time to react. But El Juez stepped between them, and both he and the burly guy from his troop grabbed the young man and held on as he thrashed, hollering. "It wasn't me, I didn't do it, I didn't do anything, she's lying!"

El Juez looked back at Enid, and she stayed calm. Hoped her lack of reaction looked like some kind of supreme confidence and self-control. Their leader's gaze was appraising.

"He says one of you did it," El Juez said. Prodding her, just like she prodded him.

"A lot of folk running around with good sharp blades. Any of them could have cut her," Enid said. "I'm looking for evidence. Ella was down in the Estuary for a reason, and I think that reason got her killed."

"Why do you even care?" El Juez said, his voice tired and sad. There it was, her hook.

"Because it's right to care."

The man's stare was dark, penetrating. He intimidated by staring, and she made the effort not to wilt before his gaze. This felt like some kind of test.

"I don't believe you," he said.

"Can you tell me how many days ago Ella left? When was the last time you saw her?"

El Juez turned his back on Enid. The rest of his folk did likewise. Even Hawk, moving off from the shelter with a determined gait.

Ignoring her. Driving her away by sheer indifference.

She looked around, searching for another way in.

## A Way In

El Juez and his enforcers scattered to their own business, as if Enid's arrival hadn't caused any stir. The work of the camp, the work of any camp—food, shelter, cleaning, mending—went on. The storm from a couple of weeks before had left its mark here too, in different ways. Fallen branches had been dragged into piles, the rivulets of temporary creeks had cut through the dirt. An older boy and girl were up on a cabin roof, patching it. Clothing and hides hung on lines to dry.

Enid stood for a moment as the life of the camp went on around her. Folk stared, glanced away, looked again, but no one engaged with her. This was as pointed a request to just leave as was possible without physically tying her up and dragging her back down to the Estuary. That they didn't go that far encouraged Enid to stay. They could ignore her for only so long, and she was here to learn. About Ella's life, and about Neeve's connection to these people.

Hawk watched Enid, his gaze hard and glaring. She made

sure not to turn her back on him, keeping him in the corner of her vision at least. Keeping other people between them.

No one stopped her from wandering. No one challenged her, no one threatened her. They certainly didn't seem worried that she would capture everyone and force them back to the Coast Road for implants and whatever other horribleness these people imagined awaited them there. That said something about them, and what they might have thought about Ella. Ella leaving here wasn't seen as threatening or dangerous. When El Juez said it was her choice, he wasn't blustering.

The camp—more than a camp, if less than a town— seemed to be arranged in a series of family units, lean-tos and sheds clustered around maybe a dozen cook fires. A couple of areas for messier work lay farther out. Drying meat was arranged on a rack. At the very edge of the settlement, a tannery. Latrine pits almost out of sight—and out of smell, downwind. The arrangement of it all was familiar. Roof and food and clothing. Only so many ways to keep a settlement alive.

Enid wandered over to have a look at the tannery, because she didn't have a lot of experience with the process of making leather. A woman in her thirties, hair tied back, wearing a belted tunic and skirt, was working alone, pulling what looked like a whole deerskin out of a wide aluminum vat a couple of feet wide and deep. Pitted and beat-up, but clean and polished smooth, the vat must have been salvage from before the Fall. A thing like that, rare and useful, was always well taken care of. The hides had been soaking in muddy-looking liquid. Some kind of solution, Enid couldn't guess what, but it smelled acrid. After letting the skin drip a moment, the woman lay the hide on the ground, staked it taut, and on her knees started scraping hair off with a dull-looking metal spatula. She'd scrape, shake hair off into a pile, scrape again, wipe off the spatula, over and over. It seemed tedious and awkward, the kind of work you had to get right, or else it could ruin all your previous effort. But the woman was clearly well practiced at it. The bare leather emerged in moments, clean and smooth.

"Hola," Enid said, and the woman flinched, dropping the scraper. She glared. "Sorry. Didn't mean to startle you. Can I help?"

The woman frowned. "Think you can stake the next one like this?" She gestured to the vat, and to a clear spot on the ground.

Enid wasn't sure, but she would certainly try. Gingerly, she reached into the vat, grabbed hold of what looked like the edge of a skin, held it up. Took a couple of tries. Soaking wet, the thing was heavy. She expected it to stink, but it had the nose-tickling scent of a dying fire. As the woman had done, Enid let the hide drip, then laid it out as best she could, taking small wooden stakes from a nearby pile, punching them through the edges and into the ground. This took Enid much longer to accomplish than it did when the woman had done it. But she managed it on her own, and by the time she finished, the woman was done scraping the first hide and ready to move to the next. She didn't offer to let Enid try scraping, which was just as well. That looked like it required some real finesse.

"I'm Enid."

The woman took a long time to answer. She had hair the color of rich brown earth, a tan face marked with soot and fatigue. Lines pulled at her mouth. "Creek," she said finally. She never stopped scraping. The messy pile of byproduct was growing.

"These are deer hides, yeah?"

"Yeah."

"We don't see a lot of deer down south. I understand you hunt cattle as well? Folk say the leather's better here."

"The best. We trade with you folk sometimes."

"You ever go that way? South to the Estuary?"

"No need to."

"Did you ever meet Neeve?" Creek seemed the right age to have known Neeve.

A pause, as the woman glanced up. She said, "When she used to foot it up here."

"I heard she spent quite a bit of time up here."

"Long time ago."

A third skin was soaking in the tub, so Enid went to stake that one onto the ground too. She wasn't helping much, not really, but Creek was polite about it. She moved straight to the third skin as soon as she'd finished with the second.

Enid asked, "You want to talk at all? About Ella? What you think might have happened?"

"She died. It's what happens when folk leave, she knew that."

"I'm not sure that follows," Enid said.

Creek sighed. "No one trusts a person wandering on their own. You don't trust us, we don't trust you. Doesn't end well."

"And Neeve? Did you trust her?"

"Was never like us. She couldn't stay, no matter how much she wanted to. And Ella . . . well, Ella was Ella. They were a lot alike."

Enid waited, but Creek didn't offer more.

"Can I ask some advice?" Enid asked. "What's the best way to get El Juez to talk to me?"

At that, a corner of Creek's lip went up, and Enid was hopeful. But she said, "You don't. He comes to you if he wants."

"Ah." Well, at least that was something of a guideline. "Thanks. Take care."

Creek remained bent to her work, scraping the last of the hides, not looking up to watch her go.

After that, Enid found a couple of guys chopping wood and offered to help. They let her, mostly because they couldn't seem to figure out how to tell her no. Their axes were made from the salvaged, ground-down steel Mart had talked about. Not very good, making the work slow, even dangerous. The salvaged blades were unpredictable. But Enid knew how to chop wood, and the guys seemed impressed. She asked about Ella when they paused for a rest. They'd known her, but had little interest in the Estuary settlement and questioned whether Hawk was even telling the truth.

"Maybe she ain't dead," one of them said. "She decided to stay down there, it'd be just the same. We'd never see her again."

"I miss her," said the other, frowning.

They couldn't say why she'd left, and if she was really dead, they were sure one of Enid's folk must have killed her. None of the people at the camp would ever do such a thing. Exactly what the Estuary folk said about themselves.

"Thanks," Enid said, and went in search of her next interview.

She caught sight of an altercation: way off, out of earshot, El Juez chastising Hawk. Pointing at him, flicking his collar, then pointing away. Ordering him off, to stay away from Enid maybe. That was what it looked like, but it was just Enid's guess. Hawk stomped off. After that, El Juez was the one watching her.

The man was a patriarch, in the best sense of the word that she could think of. He had his people; he cared for them,

looked after them, and kept them close. In turn they were de-
voted. They looked on him with admiration, with love. Some
fear, but nothing like the cringing terror she might have expected. Which, oddly, made her trust him—he wasn't one to
lash out, she suspected.

By evening Enid knew she was being tested. If these folk
ignored her long enough, would she just go away? How long
could they make her wait? Enid knew there were answers
here. The connection between Last House and the camp went
deeper than trading deerskins and knife blades. She could go
back and dig harder at Last House, and they'd say the same
things they'd been saying all along.

This was the other side of it.

The gang had left her pack and belt pouch under the shelter, making it clear she could pick them up and leave whenever
she liked. She was able to get some of her travel food from it. A
couple of people offered her bites to eat, dried meat with a kind
of flatbread made from ground nuts, and she accepted. Over
the course of the day, she had spoken to almost all the adults
and a few of the teens—they hadn't known Neeve at all, which
meant the woman had stopped traveling this way some time ago,
just as Enid had heard. Enid got some stories, some corrobora-
tion. Ella was a picky eater. Was proud of the Coast Road–made
clothes that Neeve gave her and wanted to learn to make such
things herself. Thought following Coast Road rules for a few
years in exchange for learning to make good cloth would be
worth it. Some folk thought she was going to stay away just long
enough to learn to make good woven cloth, then she'd be back.

But Hawk, they said, hadn't thought the trade was a
good one.

"You think Hawk might have hurt her?"

"Oh no, never." They all said that, with an air of astonishment. They didn't want to think ill of their own. No one ever did.

Which brought Enid back to thinking of who at the Estuary might have done this. Erik, who was so suspicious of intruders. If he'd chanced on Ella in the dark, he might not have even known what he was doing. Then there was Kellan, who couldn't talk about the incident without melting down.

Everyone who agreed to talk to her didn't say much, but they were usually specific. Eight or nine days ago Ella was still at the camp. She'd helped butcher rabbits, and she'd watched the kids. She was usually the one to fetch water every morning, and now someone else had to do that job. When she left, she let folk know. They all knew she'd gone.

Enid asked, "Did she seem normal? Was she acting strangely? Did she talk about anything odd?"

Now that Enid mentioned it, yes, a couple of folk answered. They noticed that Ella was restless. She rushed through work. She seemed distracted, maybe even sad. "She and her boy had a fight maybe, yeah?" one older woman said.

Enid suspected this was true, and that Hawk didn't want to talk about it. Or Ella might have just been nervous about the big change she was embarking on. A kid like that, setting off to travel the wider world—Enid understood that restlessness well.

It may have seemed like small talk, but it was something of a relief. It felt like a real investigation—solid questions and solid answers. Enid made notes in her book. Folk looked at her writing with curiosity. They knew about reading and writing, but none of them knew how.

Everyone had knives. Everyone used them, on food and rope and daily chores. Some of the knives even had decorations, carved pieces of wood and bone, like what Hawk had described. But most of the blades weren't ones traded from the Coast Road. Likely, they wouldn't have been sharp or long enough to make the cut that had killed Ella. But that nice forged blade that Ella had gotten from Last House . . .

Enid asked more than one person, "Your knife . . . I hear that Ella had a nice one that went missing."

The answers she got back were variations of "Whoever hurt her probably took it." Thinking just like the Estuary folk did.

"So her knife—you haven't seen it recently, have you?"

"Not since she left."

And so on. Everyone made that obvious assumption, the same one Enid and Teeg had: whoever had that knife now had probably killed Ella. So no one was just going to show it to Enid when she asked.

Dusk fell. Fires were banked, until just one was left burning, and much of the camp gathered around it. Enid held back, nibbled on some of the beef jerky she'd brought in her pack. And yes, El Juez still watched her from across the way. She gave him a friendly smile.

She spent the night wrapped in a blanket, shored up against a tree trunk. Chilled, uncomfortable. Uncertain this was doing much good. She supposed she could have asked for shelter, for food. But if they gave her that much, would they feel the need to give her answers as well?

She could wait.

///////////////////////////////////////////////////////

HER SECOND DAY at the camp was a lot like the first. Folk didn't go out of their way to be friendly, but they didn't turn her away. She was like a dog who'd wandered in and didn't make trouble, and might get a couple of scraps if she behaved herself.

She acquired a flock of children, following her at what they probably thought was a safe distance. Giggling, they'd whisper and dare one another to approach, then run away if Enid looked at them. Eventually, she settled on a slab of concrete, tore a page out of her notebook, and started drawing. She wasn't very good at it, but the couple of round shapes for body and head and the long slender ears she made were plainly a rabbit. The kids were intrigued. They came closer, to see better.

"What should I try next?"

"Make one of Bill," a small girl said. Bill was the not-feral dog that had kept an eye on Enid but stuck close to the people it knew. Enid did her best, and the kids *ooh*ed and *aah*ed. Enid gave the picture to the girl, and the children ran off.

The pattern of the day was similar enough everywhere to be familiar. This place might even seem pleasant, if it was what you were used to. But Enid couldn't help but sense a faint background tension of desperation. So many kids, and so little food. Every inch of work mattered here. They didn't have quotas because there was simply never enough to go around. The quotas were "as much as we can."

In the old world, that attitude had remained in place even in times of plenty. "As much as we can" meant everything, until it was all gone.

For a second night, Enid watched the campfire, put up with surreptitious stares—not as many as during the night before—they were getting used to her, if not comfortable with her. She slept tucked up by a tree.

She decided she'd learned all she could here and would go back down to the Estuary tomorrow. Leave these people alone. She needed her own family.

The next morning, Enid was wakened by a hand touching her shoulder. El Juez knelt beside her and offered a clay bowl filled with something pudding-like and steaming hot, and a flat wooden spoon. Her stomach growled for it.

"Thanks," she said. Tried to eat slowly and politely rather than shovel it in. It tasted nutty and smelled a bit like the pine forest around them.

"So," El Juez said, settling in to sit cross-legged beside her. "What have you learned?"

"Folk miss her. But no one's surprised she left."

"No. Did they tell you she was mine? My girl."

Enid paused, spoon half-raised, and looked at him. She saw it then, in the slope of his jaw, the brown of his skin. The rangy frame. But their faces were different. "Your daughter?" He nodded slowly. Sadly.

No one had said a word about either of Ella's parents, but people's reticence fit the general mood. They were letting Ella go, putting her in the past. Pushing all thought and knowledge of her away.

"I'm sorry. It's a hard loss. I really am trying to find out what happened."

"She wasn't killed here," El Juez said. "She left camp ten days ago. Next we hear of her, Hawk comes back saying she's dead and that you burned her."

"We held a pyre for her. It's what we do."

He nodded. "It's what we do too. But she shouldn't have died at all, not like that."

"I agree."

"Isn't that a wonder, us agreeing?"

Her smile only flickered. This was hard. "Folk down in the Estuary think one of you did it. Maybe Hawk, in a fit of rage. Folk do crazy things when they're angry." The young man was up and poking at the fire near the main shelter, bringing it back to life. Pointedly not looking over at them.

"He says he didn't. He says a guy from down your way did. Kellan?"

"Maybe he's accusing someone else to turn attention from himself?"

El Juez grinned. "You think that one's got the brains for that?"

Yes, he knew his people. Enid chuckled.

He said, "Even if you get the truth, it won't bring the girl back."

"That's not the point," she said. "Figure out what happened, stop it from happening again."

"Still gotta eat."

"Yeah." The nut porridge was good; she finished it all.

"Come, there's sage brewing at the fire." He gestured toward the shelter, and she hauled her stiff body upright and followed him over.

The sage was dried sagebrush and mint steeped in hot water. Hot and astringent—it woke her up. Cleared her sinuses enough to make her eyes water.

He said to her, "Another question, since you seem chatty enough."

"I've been completely open with you all."

He nodded in acknowledgment. "Why do you keep asking about the knife she had?" So he really had been watching her.

"I think it might have been used to kill her."

"It wasn't." Declarative. He was very sure.

"How do you know that?"

He held up a finger. "Wait."

He went up the path a ways to his cabin and returned with an object in hand. Long, narrow. A knife in a leather sheath. He offered it to her. Enid took it carefully, like it was precious and fragile, and drew the knife partway out of the sheath. It was exactly what Kellan and Hawk had both described. A polished, cared-for blade, a stained leather grip, a carved flower at the end. It was personalized, distinctive. No mistaking it at all.

And if it was here, had been here the whole time, it probably hadn't been used to kill her. Enid grit her teeth in frustration.

El Juez said, "She gave this to me because she said she could get another. Said we had more need of it here than she did, where she was going. Though now I can't bring myself to use it."

Enid handed the knife back to him, and he took it gently. Cradled it before him, very like how one would hold a newborn, cupped in both hands, gazing on it with love. This knife was all he had left of her. With a clenched heart, Enid thought of Olive and Serenity. She so wanted to be there now, but was so far away.

She arranged her words carefully and said, "Last House said they invited her to live with them."

"I guess she was going to do it."

"I thought if we found the knife, we'd find the murderer."

"It was one of you, I'm sure of it," he said.

This put her right back at the start, with no evidence but what people told her. She glanced around the camp, where women were working with fires and minding children. The middle-aged ones old enough to have grown children.

"What's Ella's mother say about it all? Is she here?"

He cocked his head, confused, and she wondered what mistake she'd made. "You don't know?"

"Know what?"

El Juez said, "Her mother is Neeve."

## Bannerless Child

Enid paced, too full of sudden energy to stay seated, her skin buzzing with it. Every scrap of information she'd learned, the whole timeline and all the details, crowded in her mind at once, arranging themselves in a new shape. It was too much; she needed to think.

"Wait a sec," Enid said, as the air seemed to fall still, voices around her suddenly muffled. "What're you saying?"

"Neeve's her mother. Didn't they tell you?"

No, they didn't. Because no one in the Estuary knew. Neeve had kept it secret; all this time she hadn't told anyone. No, that wasn't true: Kellan knew. *That* was what he wouldn't tell anyone. That was what drove him to fits every time the topic got close. Keeping the secret was breaking the man.

El Juez started to say more, but Enid held up a hand, shushing him. She needed quiet, space to piece it all together, because this one scrap of information kept skittering away from her. It wasn't possible.

And it explained everything.

She sank back onto the concrete slab and got out her notebook, going over the timeline again, reviewing everything folk had told her about Neeve. Twenty years ago, she'd cut out her implant. She'd been caught, reported by her own household—namely her twin sister, Juni—and after that had become a recluse. She wandered, spent weeks away from the settlement. During that time, could Neeve have hidden a pregnancy? Had there been enough time for her to go upriver, give birth, and leave the baby with the outsiders—

Maybe.

But would she have done that?

Turning to the detailed description and inventory of the dead body, Enid recalled the girl—her hair, the shape of her face, the color of her clouded dead eyes. Compared that image to Neeve. And yes, there it was. The round face, the thick texture of the hair—it was the same, though Neeve's own hair was going gray. The similarities had never occurred to her before—and why should they have? No one had ever had a bannerless pregnancy without being discovered. Investigators always found out, everyone knew that.

Took twenty years this time.

Amazed, unable to hide her shock, she turned back to El Juez. "Why didn't Neeve stay? She spent so much time here, went through all that trouble to have a child—to have a child with you—why didn't she stay? Why did she leave the baby behind? She could have stayed!" When Neeve returned to the Estuary, when her cut-out implant was discovered—she must have already given birth. And she'd hid it all this time.

"Don't know," El Juez said, shrugging. Tension pulled at his shoulders. "Not sure she ever meant to stay. When she left the last time, I thought she'd be back. She left Ella here because she said you folk would take the baby away from her."

That was true. Someone who so egregiously stepped out of bounds, as Neeve had done, couldn't be trusted to care for a child. The baby would have been fostered out. But no one on the Coast Road had even known there was a baby.

"You never went to find her?"

"No, wouldn't go down there. Didn't need to. She knew where to find us."

Neeve had tried to stay in the camp with her child, but couldn't. It wasn't home, and for all that she was a recluse, she was still Coast Road. Electricity was a hard thing to give up. But she couldn't just return with a baby; she'd never have been allowed to keep it.

Maybe . . . maybe . . . Enid hadn't been the only one to suddenly recognize similarities between Neeve and Ella, mother and daughter. Maybe someone had seen her, made the leap. Someone in the Estuary found out, and was furious. Even after all this time. Someone met Ella by chance and recognized the resemblance instantly.

"I have to go," Enid said, slipping her notebook in her pouch, marching to the tree roots where she'd stashed her pack. "I need to get back."

"You know who did it? What happened?"

"You were right, it's nothing to do with your people here."

"Ella was our people."

Except she wasn't. Or rather, was only half. But that other half meant Enid *did* have jurisdiction in this. The right—the duty—to make a judgment.

She hesitated, studying the man one last time. Wondering how much to tell. "You didn't have to raise her. You could have . . . I don't know. Taken her back. Demanded . . . some responsibility." Enid suspected many folk would consider abandoning a baby a worse crime than cutting out one's implant.

But Neeve had left the child with its father. She must have trusted El Juez to raise her.

And then, years later . . . Neeve wanted her daughter back.

The man scowled. "Nobody just lets a baby die. Unless . . . do you people?"

"No. Never. At least, we try not to. But Ella . . ." Enid shook her head.

"What's the punishment for this?"

"They'll be dealt with."

"We would kill them. Crime for crime."

"They'll be dealt with," she repeated, though she couldn't say exactly how. Murder didn't happen enough for there to be a standard procedure in place. She'd have to figure it out as she went along. It would depend on how this played out. How her suspect reacted. How Neeve reacted.

Enid didn't know what she was going to do about Neeve. She'd kept insisting the old case involving Neeve's implant and the new one investigating Ella's death weren't related. Oh, but they were so tightly woven together.

"Why you? Why are you the one to judge?" El Juez asked. His name meant "judge"—she wondered if it was a title, like investigator, rather than a name. He was used to having the last word.

She considered her uniform. The brown fabric hid the grime and stress of the past few days pretty well, but it was rumpled and ripe. And here, it didn't mean anything. All she could say was "Because my people trust me."

He seemed to be debating whether he did. She'd come here, made demands. However useful her visit had been for her and the investigation, what had it done for El Juez and his people? She swooped in, rushed back out again—and then what? She didn't know.

"Is there anything you'd like to tell Neeve?" she asked.

"Nothing," he said curtly. Didn't even have to think about it. "But you can't leave."

"What?"

"You don't know how to get back."

She'd been blindfolded for half the trek. Still, she blithely pointed down the mostly visible roadway. "It's that way."

"You won't make it without help."

"Well then. Will one of you help me?"

A long silence. Some of El Juez's enforcers had gathered to watch the exchange. Enid caught the gaze of a few folk, who quickly glanced away. She wondered if any of them would step forward to help. Maybe Hawk? Oddly, he was nowhere in sight.

El Juez let the silence draw on. Waiting to see if any of his people would act. Would disobey him. No one did.

"Looks like you're on your own," he said. He seemed pleased. They didn't owe her any help.

Enid wasn't sure what they expected. For her to show fear? Beg? Weep? If they thought this was some kind of revenge? In truth, she hadn't expected help. She trusted herself to figure out the way.

"Right. Well. That's that. Thanks for all your help, it's been useful. And again, I'm very sorry for your loss."

She gave a nod and marched off, back to the Coast Road and the end of this investigation.

////////////////////////////////////////////////////////

THE SILENCE OF THE WOODS fell around Enid quickly. Noises of children, the underlying sounds of the camp at work, faded, then vanished. The smell of campfires lingered, then cleared, and she might as well have been in the middle of a vast forest wilderness.

She tried to pace herself: moved steadily, not quickly. But she wanted to run. She wanted to confront Neeve. She wanted to tell Teeg what she'd learned. This information would blow up a whole community, but they needed to know. An old wound had festered until it had killed. The Estuary folk may not have wanted to know why Ella had died like she did, but they needed to.

Suddenly, Enid pulled up short. Stopped, studied the quiet forest around her. She didn't know why, just that the prickling on her skin had started up, and a sudden jump in her heart had her body tingling. She'd felt constantly watched all week—it wasn't just paranoia, she was sure of it.

Scouts from the camp had tracked her coming up the hill. No reason they shouldn't track her going back down. But it wasn't a whole troop of them, like before. This time, it was just Hawk, charging straight at her with a club, screaming in rage. He must have been holding that primal scream in for days, the way it twisted his face and tore out of his throat.

In a way, his weapon confirmed her suspicions. A knife wasn't his preferred weapon; if he'd been the one to kill Ella, he would have beaten, not stabbed her. Now he wanted to beat Enid to death. Just as well—Enid thought she could do a little better against a club than a knife. Even after leaving her makeshift staff behind so she could move faster.

Hawk was furious, uncontrolled, charging with the quickly hewn, arm-length branch cocked up behind his shoulder. Like he expected her to just stand there while he took her head off.

Enid dodged, ducking so that she ended up behind him while he ran on ahead. He spun around, faced her again, panted for breath.

"Hawk, stop," she said. "I haven't done anything."

"Then tell me who did—I'll kill 'em!" He rearranged his grip, squeezing the wood again and again, nervously.

"Not your job. I'll take care of it."

"You won't! You bullies in brown just make everything worse."

He might not be wrong there, though she tried her best. People might not feel good about her efforts, but at least they'd know the truth.

"Tell me!" he demanded again.

"No. I'm not going to open the door to another murder." Carefully, slowly, she let her hand creep near her belt pouch, hoping he wouldn't notice.

He shouted and charged, perfectly willing to enact a new murder, it seemed.

She ducked out of the way again; he was ready for her this time, but his own rowdy movements made pivoting after her difficult. Once again she was able to get up behind him, grab the sleeve of his shirt, and yank, pulling him off balance. He stumbled, his knees hitting the forest floor. But he didn't drop the club, and instead swung at her from the ground, aiming for her knees. Enid scuttled backward.

This gave her enough time to draw one of the tranquilizer patches from the pouch and tuck it into her hand.

To give Hawk credit, he didn't repeat his mistakes. He didn't charge her again. Now he kept his distance, lunging in to swing with the club, then holding back, then trying again. He wouldn't let her get behind him this time, which narrowed her options.

She was going to have to tackle him head on.

Meeting his gaze, Enid stepped back, just a little. Inviting him closer. And closer. Making herself look like an easy target.

At last, he took the bait and jumped toward her, swinging hard.

She intended to step out of the way, to grab his arm and use his momentum to haul him to the ground. She made it as far as stepping out of the way, but she underestimated his ferocity, and he got in a blow. She blocked, arm raised to protect her face, and Hawk's club came down on her shoulder. Wood against bone sent a shock down her arm, across her back. The limb went numb. She didn't think about it, couldn't, because Hawk stepped back and lowered the club. Expecting her to fall. Waiting for her to curl up, helpless and injured.

She didn't.

Bending low, she leapt forward, tackled his legs. He had no choice but to fall, and this time he dropped the club, then scrabbled after it in the dirt. She pinned him with her knees, reached forward as far as she could, and slapped the patch onto his neck. Pressed hard, holding it there. The drug would work faster when applied to the neck than if she'd put it on his arm.

Screaming, he thrashed, shoved at her; Enid jumped away and waited.

Hawk sat up, reached for the club. Enid had a brief panic, thinking the patch had failed, that it was from an old batch or that she had applied it wrong. But though he reached for the club, he wasn't able to get a hold of it. For a moment he wobbled. Looked back at her, his head tilted in confusion.

Then he collapsed.

She rushed to kneel by his side, to speak urgently before he fell entirely unconscious, "Don't follow me, don't come back to the Estuary, nothing good will come of it. I'll see justice done for Ella, I promise. I promise."

And then he was asleep, breathing steadily.

Enid sat back and sighed. Rubbed her shoulder, which

hurt, a throbbing all the way to the bone. She finally could check the extent of the injury. That whole half of her body ached, but she could rotate the joint and move her arm, wiggle every finger. Nothing was broken. The bruise was going to be beautiful, she guessed. She really ought to get some ice on it, but there was no ice for fifty miles.

Hawk had a coil of rope on him, hanging off his belt. She used this to tie his wrists together, loosely. He'd be able to work his way out of it easily enough, once he came to. But it would slow him down, and maybe make him think twice about coming after her. Still, she'd be looking over her shoulder the whole rest of the walk back to the Estuary. She'd have to warn the settlement too. She hated making Erik right about that, at least. That the folk in the hills might be a danger.

Down to her bones, she wanted to lie here and sleep for a week. This had all been so *exhausting*.

But she had a lot of miles to go before she was done.

///////////////////////////////////////////////////////////////

KEEPING TRACK OF TIME, of landmarks, the ruins of this old road, Enid recognized the clearing with the slabs of broken concrete where she'd convinced her captors to take off the hood. Beyond this point, she was walking blind. She knew the general direction she should go—downhill, and south. But she didn't know the way.

She didn't pause to worry about it. She didn't have time. Kept going in what she hoped was the right direction. Listening for the sound of the creek that would flow into the river that became the Estuary.

Enid thought she made better time coming down from the hills than she had going up, blindfolded and arguing with her captors. It had taken half a day to get to the camp. But she thought she could be back at the Estuary by midafternoon. Assuming she was going the right way.

At noon, with the sun high overhead, the trees were all wrong, the hill was too rocky, and she was a long way from the river, she sensed. She thought she was generally headed in the right direction, that she was a little off. Trying to encourage optimism to overcome the sinking feeling in her gut, she decided not to backtrack and try again—that would just send her in circles. She needed to go south . . . and keep going.

Finally, hours later, trees gave way to open country, out of the woods and down the hill. But there was no sign of settlement, of people.

She came out of the woods far north and west of the Estuary. She'd been traveling at the wrong angle, and this had carried her up the coast. Past a vast field of mud and wetlands, the edge of the ocean shone. It would take an hour of slogging through muck to get to the waves.

Southward, a ridge of land bulged up from the mud flats. From here, it was little more than a smudge of gray, indistinct in the boiling haze. She was pretty sure that was the hill the Estuary settlement was built on. She hadn't realized she'd traveled so far from the river.

It would take a long, hot trek to get there, and she didn't have much choice but to get started. Sooner she got back, sooner she could clean all this up. Seemed impossible and amazing, that she might actually get to *leave* this place.

Distance on these mud flats was deceptive. The ridge she aimed for somehow kept receding. Or her steps were getting slower. Distinct possibility there. She hadn't brought water with her from the camp, hadn't had a drink since leaving the stream's track, and her mouth had become swollen and sticky.

The problem grew worse in the heat of the lowlands. Her shirt and tunic stuck to her, and mud had splashed her trousers up to her knees. Her head pounded from the sun's glare. She wasn't sure when the headache had started, but it was getting worse. She wanted her hat.

Would have been better to come down from the hills and find that nice path that led straight to Last House. Of course it would have. But she was probably lucky she'd left the hills in anywhere near the right place. Stubborn as she was, she'd have made it back one way or another. Some days, seemed like being stubborn was all she had.

Well then, she'd have to use it.

But she was tired and thirsty, and this was turning into a hard march. She never seemed to get any closer to that hazy ridge and the settlement. Or she was walking in circles. She was sure it couldn't have been that, though; the ocean stayed to her right. That should have kept her going in a straight line. Suddenly she couldn't be sure anything she did was right. The air kept growing hotter, her feet kept sticking to the ground.

She stopped a moment to catch her breath but had trouble pulling air into her lungs. Realized with a shock that if she didn't keep moving, she might not survive. As long as she was walking, she'd be fine.

But a blackness, full of exhaustion, was collapsing around her vision.

She had trouble seeing the ridge at all anymore, and she definitely couldn't make out the shape of the bridge over the river, the edges of those houses on the road.

Maybe if she squinted.

Then, she knew she was falling but couldn't do anything to stop it.

## Mother

Olive's first pregnancy ended almost before it had begun. She'd been pregnant long enough to know that she was, to confirm the news, to begin planning, celebrating, settling into the new condition. And then it was over, in pain and mess. Enid's mother, Peri, was the medic who treated her. Her gray hair pushed back with a headband, Peri was vibrant, had a kind smile and gentle hands. Olive was fine, she determined. Or would be. She insisted this wasn't unusual.

"I know it's small comfort, but this is common. This is normal. You're healthy, you'll get pregnant again, you'll have plenty of chances. Rest for now, think about the rest of it later."

Peri kissed the top of Enid's head, squeezed her shoulder, and left them at home. Enid heard her speak to Sam and Berol out in the front room, but didn't hear exactly what they said. She focused on Olive, who'd cried herself out long ago, exhausted but still shuddering with grief.

Miscarriage might be common, but Olive said she could feel the loss inside her, that something had been there and was now gone. Through most of the night they sat in bed, Enid propped against the wall, Olive clinging to her. Enid held her, not really understanding but still aching for her. Aching for the missed chance, and from witnessing a process she couldn't comprehend.

Enid looked up once to see Sam standing at the doorway, his expression drawn, concerned. Their gazes met—was there anything he could do? She shook her head. No, not at the moment. Sam went to the front room to sit with Berol, who must have been feeling wretched. Berol would take the next shift with Olive, but for now Olive wanted Enid to sit with her, so here she was.

Enid's arms circled Olive, blanketing her. "You want something to drink? You should drink some water," Enid said. "Want me to make some tea?"

Olive shook her head, tightened her grip.

"I must be broken," she choked out. "Am I broken?"

"No, didn't you hear Peri? She said you're fine, everything's going to be fine."

"Doesn't feel fine."

"I know, love. I know."

"Maybe . . . maybe . . . you should try. Maybe I wasn't meant to—"

Over the next few weeks, she'd repeat that. *Maybe it should be you,* she'd tell Enid, who hushed her fast every time. There'd be plenty of chances. Olive had no business giving up so soon. Besides, her implant was out; it would be wasteful to put in a new one so soon.

Enid leaned in close and squeezed her eyes shut to keep tears from falling. "It's too early for that. You'll try again. It'll be fine."

She could only keep saying that. Nothing else she could

do. Was like sitting in a cellar, waiting for a storm to pass while wind beat at the doors.

Enid had felt so much anger at the unfairness of it. Olive had wanted the baby so badly. And now here was Neeve, who'd given up the Coast Road for a child. And that was fine, that was fair. But then she'd changed her mind. Like you could just change your mind about something like a baby. By Coast Road rules, Ella was bannerless. And now she was dead, which was the greater tragedy.

At least Olive had gotten a second chance. Just six months later, she was pregnant again, though they spoke in whispers about it and walked softly until the first trimester was done, then the second, and finally when she couldn't hide her belly anymore, they announced it officially—Serenity's baby was on the way.

They'd have their baby, very much wanted. And part of Enid knew she would be desperately afraid for that child's safety her whole life. She'd seen firsthand how brutally, terribly wrong things could turn out. The four of them at Serenity might not be enough to stop it. But they would try, with every drop of their blood and every spark of their souls.

///////////////////////////////////////////////////////////

ENID HAD COLLAPSED in mud only a few dozen yards from the bridge near Bonavista household. As two sets of hands worked to haul her upright, she came back to awareness, battling her queasy stomach. A dog was barking. Bear, dancing toward her, then bounding in place, as if he couldn't figure out whether she was friendly or dangerous.

"I'm fine, just a little tired." Her voice came out a whisper. She couldn't make herself heard, which was frustrating.

"No, you're not." That was Jess, she thought, surprised. What was he doing here?

She blinked, squinted to focus. Both Erik and Jess were here. The two were helping her walk toward the buildings at Bonavista. Well, at least she'd made it back. Barely. Jess, on her left, tried to pull her arm over his shoulder, and she gasped. Her whole arm ached, but his grasp made it scream with pain. She'd really need to get a look at that bruise.

"It's okay," she managed to say. "Just got hit a little." She tried to walk with more vigor, so they wouldn't hold her so tightly.

"Get something to drink, then talk," Erik said. Apparently, she'd been trying to speak. She wanted to shake her head, but it hurt too much.

Next thing she knew, she was on the front porch of the main house at Bonavista, with a whole swarm of folk fussing around her. Jess folded her hands around a mug of water. The kid, Tom, lurked nearby. Enid looked around for Mart, for anyone from Last House. Didn't see them.

Another face she expected to see was missing.

"Slow," Jess ordered. "Not all at once."

Enid sipped. The wetness filled her mouth and woke her up. Steadied her.

She'd survive.

Faces surrounded her, but not the one she was looking for. "Where's Teeg?"

"Drink some more, Enid. Then we can talk."

"No, where is he?" She set the mug aside, tried to stand. Erik and Jess urged her back down.

"Well . . . he left," Erik said.

A fury growing in her, Enid tried to swear, and the heat pressed down on her again.

Just then, Juni came around the corner, a bundle of reeds slung over her shoulder like the ones she'd carried the day Enid and Teeg first arrived. In her hand, her machete, her grip on the handle sure. Enid focused on that blade until she couldn't see anything else.

Enid had so much to do. She had to talk to Teeg. And Neeve, where was Neeve? She'd meant to stop at Last House first, so she could talk to the woman.

But then Enid fainted again.

////////////////////////////////////////////////////

JESS PUT HER TO BED, and Enid agreed to stay there only because lying down felt so blissful. She could think better when horizontal, propped on pillows. At least for the moment. Her injured shoulder felt better when she kept it still, and she wondered if it was more damaged than she first thought. But she decided to keep quiet about it until she could get back to Everlast, to have a medic look at it. After a couple of hours lying down and sipping water, she felt her dehydrated mind slowly becoming alert. After taking in soup as well as water, she was able to read her notebook. She wanted to be very sure she remembered everything that had happened to her in the hills. That the connections she'd made hadn't vanished.

But Enid had a more pressing issue. "When did Teeg leave?"

"Just this morning," Juni explained, taking away the cool cloth that had been pressed to Enid's forehead.

Enid watched the woman closely, wondering how much she knew and when she had found out. She was being so *helpful*.

"Someone has to go after him," Enid said.

Juni exchanged a glance with Jess, who was standing in the doorway. The man's brow furrowed. Clearly uncomfortable.

Enid scowled. "What's the matter?"

"Them," Jess said. "Someone has to go after them."

This gave Enid a sinking feeling. If she had just come back a day earlier, if she had just given up . . .

"Them?" Enid prompted.

"He took Kellan with him," Juni said, and she had the gall to sound pleased. "Said the case was finished and he had to close it out. When you didn't come back, he said he had to let someone know what happened to you."

Nothing had happened to her. She glared, and they looked away. "I'm not missing and the case isn't closed." She studied the room, found Tom slouched up in the doorway next to his father, watching. She pointed at him. "He should only be a few hours down the road, yeah? Can you go after him, Tom? Take a hat and a bottle of water with you."

"Tom, maybe instead you should get word to Everlast and bring a medic back?" Juni ventured.

"I don't need a medic." But when Enid tried to sit up, blackness crept around the edges of her vision again, and she felt suddenly nauseated. With Juni's hand on her shoulder, she eased back down on the cot. Enid didn't want this woman looming over her. "Tom, go now. Bring Teeg and Kellan back, that's it."

He nodded and rushed out.

Jess stared at Enid. "You know what happened. You figured it out."

Suddenly frowning, Juni said, "Kellan did it. I thought the investigator decided that."

"I won't talk about it till Teeg is back." Enid sank back against the pillow, pretending to be more calm than she was.

And now she had to wait for Teeg to return. Enid supposed she could do this all on her own, but she wanted witnesses. She wanted backup. If she rested now, maybe she'd be on her feet by the time Tom brought them back. She'd need to be strong.

She was annoyed with herself for ever thinking she could just walk away from this, from Ella's body. Give up, like Teeg wanted her to. She'd have never been able to live with that. Not ever. She'd hold Serenity's new baby and think about the girl who died. That someone else's child had died, badly.

This case wasn't impossible; it had just taken work. She was almost to the end of this one. Tomorrow. She could go home tomorrow.

By suppertime she was able to sit upright without wanting to throw up, but the washed-out feeling, like her lungs had been turned inside-out and shoved back down her throat, continued. She ignored it as best she could. Carefully managed her intake of water and Juni's salty clam soup, and waited for Teeg to return. Assuming he agreed to come back.

She almost would rather that he stayed away.

Someone was always sitting with her, Jess or Juni. Erik and Anna stopped by. Folk from other households drifted in, gawked at her, asked questions in hushed tones. Enid said as little as possible, enjoying stringing everyone along more than she should have.

No one from Last House came, though. What had the folk there said, when Teeg ordered Kellan away? The investigator would have threatened the household with dissolution, to get Kellan to cooperate. The whole scene must have been ugly.

Had word gotten to Last House yet that Enid had returned? What would they think?

Erik had asked a lot of questions during the Semperfi

folk's visit. "How far did you get? Did you see the outsiders? Where they live?"

"I did," she said coolly.

"And they didn't kill you?" Peety, the kid from Semperfi, asked.

"Apparently not," she answered. Peety gasped, all amazement.

The stories the kids at the camp believed about the Coast Road hadn't been so outrageous.

Later, she moved from the bedroom to the front stairs. Enid making herself visible. But she still didn't say a whole lot. The sun sank, casting that strange late-day light across the marsh, a golden sheen that made the water flash. Gulls and shorebirds were specks, soaring in and out of the gleam. It was hypnotic. She tried to memorize the image, so she'd have something good to say about this place when she got home to Sam.

Jess shaded his eyes, studied the road out of the Estuary. He pointed. "There."

Enid couldn't see them at first, in the haze and slanting sunlight. When one of the three approaching figures set off in a run, the motion clarified their forms. Tom ran to the house. Didn't seem at all exhausted. That was why she'd sent him.

The next two figures followed, one more briskly, and this one paused every few strides to look back at his charge. Maybe shout at him to hurry up. But Kellan kept the same plodding gait.

The impatient one, Teeg of course, still in uniform, held his staff balanced over his shoulder. He looked up, saw the gathering on the steps, and stopped.

Enid said to Jess, Erik, and the several others gathered

around, drinking and making small talk, "Would you mind giving Teeg and me a few minutes? I promise, you'll learn all you need to soon enough."

They did so, reluctantly. And she made sure they didn't just to retreat to the house to eavesdrop.

Tom trotted up, sweaty and glowing. Enid thanked him, and he beamed. Then she sent him away too, so when Teeg and Kellan arrived, they stood before Enid alone.

Kellan was drenched with sweat, his brown face flushed, his eyes red and puffy. The man looked wilted, his arms hanging limp at his sides.

Still guarding him, Teeg looked tough, his expression set. But when he finally looked at Enid, he seemed confused.

She said, "Kellan, go inside where it's cool, and rest. Tell Jess I said to give you water."

"But . . ." His sigh was a half-sob.

"It's all right. I know you didn't do anything wrong. You didn't kill Ella."

Kellan tried a smile. Nodded solemnly and wiped a sleeve across his nose. She'd expected weeping, but he was already cried out. He climbed the steps and went inside.

"What are you doing?" Teeg demanded. Enid was aware of the staff across his shoulders, perfectly balanced to grab by the end and swing straight at her. Didn't expect him to really try something like that, but she hadn't expected a lot of things with this case.

"Hola, Teeg," she said. Thought about standing, which would be more polite. But she didn't want to risk falling over if another dizzy spell hit her. She wasn't completely well. "So, what do you think?"

He exclaimed, "You're all right!"

"Told you I would be." She stared hard at him. "So you went to make your report to regional. Brought Kellan along to prove you solved the case, with or without me. Yeah?"

"He confessed, you were right there, you heard him—"

"That wasn't a confession. He panicked because you threatened him. How many times did I tell you?" Teeg clamped his mouth shut. She continued. "What were you going to tell them about what happened here? About me?"

He shifted his weight, set his staff on the ground. Picked at it. "Exactly what happened. That you couldn't let an impossible case go, and you wandered off into the wilderness. Took your life in your hands, nothing anyone could do about it."

"So if something went wrong, it was my own fault. You weren't curious? Had no interest in figuring out what happened? In maybe following me, when you saw that I'd gone?"

"I tried to argue with you. You wouldn't listen."

And clearly he felt that was the extent of his responsibility. There were plenty who'd agree with him.

"It's good I didn't."

His eyes widened. "You found something. You actually found something. What—what was it?" He leaned in, eager. Like she was telling some campfire story.

"I'll tell you when I tell everyone else."

"Enid, I'm your partner."

Her lips curled, and she ducked to hide that wry smile. "Right."

"Enid."

"This'll be over soon. Then we can get out of here." She couldn't tell what he was thinking. The kid who couldn't shut up was just staring at her. "Well, let's get this finished." She stood, then paused a moment, feeling flushed again, waiting for the moment to pass. She was still wobbly, and didn't like it.

"You okay?" he asked.

"Little bit of heat stroke," she said. "Too much walking in the sun. I'm fine."

"Enid. Maybe you should rest. I can handle this. Or we can handle it later. If you just tell me what happened—"

"I'm fine. I want the head of each household to meet us . . . let's say by the ruin at Semperfi. Nice and desolate. I also want Kellan and Neeve, Mart and Telman. Everyone from Last House. Got it? Can you get everyone there in an hour?"

He was off balance, unsteady. His expression showed that he remained unconvinced. "Yeah, I think so. Or close enough to it. Yeah." He nodded with enough decisiveness that she believed him. Yes, he could do this task. "If Kellan didn't do it, what do you want him for?"

"So everyone knows he didn't do it. Including him. Especially after you dragged him off like that. We have to clean up your mistake."

"But then who did it? Tell me."

"Go, get everyone. Then we'll talk."

## Last Threads

This was both her most and least favorite part of a case. Enid loved the finish, the conclusion, the revelation. Pull all the threads together and weave the story. It was vanity, making these people wait for her to speak, knowing her words would change them. Holding them in suspense. That was a bit of power, and she confessed to enjoying it.

She didn't like to see herself as destroying lives here. That had already happened, and she had to try to make repairs, somehow. That part she didn't like—feeling that no matter what she did, cracks would remain. Sometimes, nothing could be done to fix the breaks.

The ruined house wasn't looking any better. In fact, it might have been her imagination, but the structure seemed to be listing toward the ravine at a discernibly more acute angle. In the quiet, she thought she could hear wood groaning, almost at the point of cracking.

No, she wouldn't go inside that building again for anything.

Teeg was already there, supervising. Making a statement,

leaning on his staff, and watching the people gather. Fulfilling his role as enforcer, as if nothing was wrong. As if he hadn't walked off with the wrong suspect just this morning. Most of the audience had already appeared, half a dozen folk waiting in the clearing before what had once been the front yard of the crumbling building.

Enid came with Jess, who carried a candle in a lantern; she hoped they wouldn't be here long enough to need it. The sun was setting, but still casting plenty of light. The ocean was a slate stripe in the distance. Clouds gathered. A hint of the next storm, maybe.

She looked over the faces, made sure they were all here. Erik, as head of Semperfi, Bear sitting quietly at his feet. Anna, a couple of others from Semperfi. Tom wasn't here, which was just as well, Enid thought. The head of Pine Grove, the heads of the other households that had climbed up the hill.

All of Last House was here, just as she had asked. Mart, Telman, Neeve, Kellan. These latter folk stood apart, faces up but eyes downcast. Mart was in front of the group, protective. Enid wondered: Did he have any idea? Did he know what Neeve had done? She couldn't guess. But she liked to see the head of a house standing up for his people.

Enid studied the faces again. One was missing.

"Where's Juni?" she asked. "Jess, wasn't she with you?"

"I don't know. Guess it's been . . . an hour or so since I saw her? Since he"—he nodded at Teeg—"got back."

"I assumed she'd know she was needed, once Jess was here," Teeg said by way of explanation.

This was sloppy. Where had the woman gone off to? Enid was cranky at herself for not being well, for not paying enough attention.

"Can't we do this without her?" Teeg asked.

"No, we can't." Enid turned from the gathering, looking out, up and down the path. Maybe Juni was late, just catching up. Surely she wouldn't miss out on this kind of gossip.

Or maybe she would, if she knew what Enid was going to say.

"Why?" Teeg asked, then knew. "Oh. Wait. You're serious?" The realization settled in, and his expression turned stark. This might be his first case, but he knew the routine. "Really?"

"Really what?" Jess asked, full of anxiety.

"Has anyone seen her? Maybe on the road in or out of town, or heading up the river path? Anyone?" The tension in Enid's voice was plain, no doubt setting everyone on edge. Couldn't be helped. Time started ticking down in her mind. This was going to end badly, wasn't it?

Then Kellan pointed out to the shore. "There. Look."

Someone was walking far out on the marsh, toward the tide line, which was creeping in with the high tide, filling the flats with water. A line of footprints sunk in mud showed the route she'd taken, straight out.

"Where's she going?" Jess said wonderingly.

Away, away from everything. Enid let out a groan, "No, no . . . Teeg! Come on!" She ran. Probably shouldn't have; she was still woozy, but she did it anyway.

Juni didn't get to walk away from this.

Teeg followed her down the path, past the bridge, and out to the marsh. Enid was vaguely aware of Estuary folk following farther behind, as if they'd needed a moment to figure out what was happening. The dog was barking its head off.

The trek was hard. Even this late in the day, the sun beat down fiercely. The mud sucked at Enid's steps. But she kept on because she had no choice. Not if she wanted to see this through.

Juni kept walking, all the way to where waves battered, devouring mud, seaweed, trash. By the time Enid and Teeg reached her, Juni was knee-deep, waves lapping around her, soaking her trousers.

"Juni, get back here!" Enid commanded, as if her authority still held sway at the edge of the world.

The woman slogged on, pushing through water, incoming waves shoving her back. She swayed, about to fall over. Then she stopped, rooted, and let the water flow around her. Her arms hung at her sides, fingers trailing in the wet, her face tipped up to the sky.

The waves swept up and over Enid's boots. Still, Juni stayed planted.

Enid cursed and waded after her. Teeg followed only when she was already far out, as if he couldn't decide whether plunging into the ocean to pursue a murderer was part of the job.

The water was cold, smelling of brine and rot, and Enid was thoroughly sick of it all. Part of her wished Kellan hadn't seen Juni on the shoreline. That the woman had walked into the ocean and just kept going. She would have just vanished, and that was a mystery Enid might actually have walked away from.

But no. Enid chastised herself for being cruel. She was supposed to be better than that.

"Juni, come on, get out of there," Enid said.

"No. I don't have to go, I don't have to do what you say." Her voice was oddly calm.

Enid grabbed the woman's arm, hooked her own arm under Juni's shoulder in a bind, and hauled backward. Her own bruised shoulder twinged, and she winced. Teeg arrived and took up the other side; Enid didn't have to ask him to.

Juni screamed.

Screeched and thrashed, kicking water, soaking them all. If she used words, they were buried in the noise of outrage and sobbing. Grimly, Enid locked Juni in a hold and dragged. Between the two of them, they got her back to the sand, all of them thoroughly drenched. Enid thought they might need to use tranqs on Juni. But once out of the water, she stilled. Went limp in fact, a dead weight dropping to the ground. Finally exhausted, Enid couldn't keep hold of the woman and sank to the beach with her. Both of them sat there, wet sand plastered over them. Teeg, baffled, stood watch. Jess and Erik came running up. Bear trotted up as well, but skittered back from the water, wouldn't come any closer. The most sensible one of the bunch.

Juni was crying now, wasn't in any state to answer questions, but Enid had a lot of them. She stared out at the sea, catching her breath, putting her thoughts back in order.

Jess demanded, "What's this about? Why's she carrying on? What did you do to her?"

"I didn't do anything," Enid sighed. "It's all her."

"I don't understand," he said, lost.

"Juni of Bonavista," Enid said, all patience and sentiment gone. "Did you kill the outsider woman Ella?"

Slumped in the sand, face red and eyes swollen, she nodded and managed to croak out, "Yes."

Well, that was that. The party accompanying them had no response and just stared.

"Let's get her back home. I'll explain it all," Enid said. Still not able to rest. Wouldn't rest till she was back at Serenity with her family.

Nothing for it but to keep slogging.

JUNI WOULDN'T LOOK at anyone, not even Jess, no matter how much he hovered over her with hot drinks, dry towels, and deep concern. She wept, then finally quieted. She didn't seem to have any energy left for crying, for denials. She'd wrung herself out.

Enid didn't have a chance to change clothes, so her trousers, dried and crusted with brine and mud, chafed, making her feel even more hot and sticky. She imagined she stank as well. None of the households around here had a good shower. They mostly washed in the river. Didn't matter, since she didn't want to let the folk of Bonavista out of her sight, just in case they planned some great revolt. She had to stay right here until it was all finished.

Teeg leaned on his staff, standing watch. Seemed to be happy to have a solid, well-defined role to play. Not the floundering around and arguing they'd been doing for the past week. On the way back from the shore he'd kept looking at Enid, considering. Silently demanding she explain herself. She didn't, because she wanted to do it all only once. And then go home, at last.

The meeting, the great reveal Enid had planned, moved to the front steps of Bonavista. The observers hemmed Juni in, so maybe this arrangement was better. Let Juni feel trapped. This time when Enid surveyed the circle, taking count, everyone she needed was here.

Only thing left was to begin. Even though everyone already knew—the word had spread instantly.

Enid said, "I'm sure you've heard. But I want to lay it all out clear, so there's no question. Most of you know a body turned up here six days ago, washed down the river. Most of you had a chance to look at that young woman and the wound that killed her. Ella wasn't from here, but some of you knew her. The folk at Last House, yeah? Did some trading? Nothing wrong with that. It's allowed, as long as you have the extra without breaking your quotas. Salvage doesn't break quotas. And they do make very nice leather in the hills. I saw it.

"Should have been nothing wrong with it, but Ella was killed anyway, and I've been trying to figure out not just who did it, but why. But no one much likes to talk about so awful a thing. So here we are." Enid paced, looked at each of them. They were all uneasy. Waiting, wanting to be anywhere but here. Unhappy at what such a crime said about their community.

Enid approached the folk of Last House, and she stopped. Kellan cringed. Neeve touched his shoulder. She had on a neutral expression, but she must have known what Enid was about to say. What Enid had discovered, upriver. She'd been through an investigation before, when she cut out her implant.

Enid continued. "Ella and some of the others started trading with the settlement here. Maybe Ella liked it here. Maybe there was another reason, but she visited more and more. Neeve asked Ella to join Last House. Is that right?"

"We would have taken her in, if she wanted. I thought . . . I thought she wanted it." Neeve's voice was soft, but she always spoke softly. She revealed no emotion.

"Kellan, you didn't want Ella to join Last House."

"I didn't hurt her," he said sullenly.

Mart stepped in, put a steadying hand on the man's shoulder. "We know that, Kellan."

Enid nodded, gestured for Mart to move back. "I found the knife you were looking for. She left it back in the wild folks' camp before she came here. *Before* she was killed. It was another blade that killed her. And Kellan, you didn't want her here. Why?"

The question didn't seem to surprise him, or confuse him. He just hated it. He hunched over, hands pulled tight to his chest, and wouldn't look at anyone. Every time Enid and Teeg had questioned him, he hadn't wanted to talk. This time it didn't look like a conscious decision; the words were stopped up. He couldn't get them out.

Enid said, "Kellan, you're not in trouble, but I need your help. I'm trying to make things clear." Not for him, not for her—for everyone else. Everyone needed to hear this. "Please tell me. I think I already know."

"Because," Kellan said, and his mouth twisted up, his face wrenched in what might have been physical pain. "Because, because if she stayed here, folk would see what she was. They would *see*."

"See what?" Erik asked, baffled.

Enid held up a finger, a request for quiet, no more disruptions. No one spoke, but the question hung there. The question at the center of it all. "I know, Kellan. I know you were protecting Neeve. This whole time you were keeping her secret. I know. It's all right."

Neeve stepped beside Mart, displacing him, putting her hand where his had been on Kellan's shoulder while the man trembled with suppressed tears. Her expression remained cold.

Next, Enid turned to Juni of Bonavista. Took a breath, and asked the thing she wasn't sure of, that she needed most to know.

"And that's my last question. The one thing I haven't been able to figure out. Juni, how did you know that Ella was Neeve's daughter?"

There were gasps. Cries. Even more so than when Juni revealed herself as the murderer. Enid made note of the reactions, who was most shocked, and who wasn't shocked at all.

Juni—she wasn't surprised. She set her frown. Determined, unrepentant, she sat on the steps, her gaze blank, impassively bearing the scrutiny.

Mart stood open-mouthed. "What is this? What does that mean, what are you saying?" So, he hadn't known. All this time, only Kellan had known, and he'd kept the secret. She wondered how he'd found out. If he'd covered for Neeve back then, or if she'd confided in him—he was solitary, he wasn't likely to talk. A good person to tell secrets to. But she'd put him in a bind, if she'd told him and no one else.

"Juni, please answer." Enid spoke calmly, even gently. Nothing to get excited about, no reason to be angry. She was satisfied to see Teeg with his hand resting on the pouch of tranquilizers, just in case. Juni glanced over Enid's shoulder at him; maybe she was remembering this whole process from the last time.

She said, "I heard them. Kellan arguing with the girl, telling her to leave. Driving her off. I was down in the river channel; they'd not have seen me from up on the ridge. But I was there."

Enid remembered the spot upriver where the voices from Last House carried. Pure chance that she'd been there.

"You heard them argue. This would have been maybe ten days ago. Then what?"

"I climbed up to see. Wanted to see what she looked like. Kellan was gone by then, he drove her off. And she ran straight into me."

Enid could picture it: Juni would have followed that path along the water, the one that twisted around and climbed out of the channel when the river narrowed and met the forest. Ella likely would have been running for the trees there. They would have been surprised to see each other.

"She . . . she looked like Neeve when Neeve was young.

Not *just* like, but close enough." Juni chuckled. "Looked like both of us. Like my daughter would have. If I'd ever had a chance to have a girl." She sounded wistful, lost in the moment.

"And Ella might have thought she was looking at Neeve. Might have thought she knew you," Enid observed. The young woman would have been surprised if she didn't know Neeve had a twin sister. Might even have tried to talk to her, not understanding the danger. "You're pretty good with a machete, aren't you, Juni?" Enid said. Still calm, careful.

The air fell still, aching with the implication. No one breathed.

"I am," she whispered.

"You'd been cutting reeds, so you had it right there in your hand. You were angry because you realized what must have happened all those years ago, what Neeve must have gotten away with—"

"She spent all that time away . . ." Juni murmured.

"Yes."

"That girl. The moment I saw her, that young face, that long hair, just like Neeve's . . . She smiled at me like she knew me, and she was about to say something, and I couldn't . . . couldn't *stand* it. If she spoke, that would make her real. I didn't want her to be real. She should never have been born."

Worst of it was, she was right. Ella shouldn't have existed. But she did. "We're not dealing with should-haves, here," said Enid. "Ella was a living, breathing person. And you're a murderer."

Juni let out a forlorn, stifled sob. She knew very well what she was. "She didn't belong. Neeve should be punished, not me."

Out of the corner of her eye, Enid saw that Neeve was crying silently.

Enid had worried over this moment: When Neeve found

out what had happened to her daughter, heard the story herself, what would she do? Attack? Scream, start a fight, insist on blood? Enid was ready to step between them. Hoped Teeg was ready too, and wondered if maybe she should have warned him ahead of time after all.

But the woman simply stood, quietly mourning. Now Kellan had his arm around her. They comforted each other. Mart, though, had turned away. He'd had no idea, and now he had a problem to grapple with.

Enid had already decided: she wasn't going to lay judgment on Neeve for bearing a bannerless child. Whatever it was she'd gotten away with, or thought she'd gotten away with, was blown away like dust.

Besides, the looks the folk around Neeve were giving her now, the attitudes they'd throw at her for the rest of her life —well, that was likely punishment enough. Let the woman live with what she'd done.

Juni was another matter. There was a space around her. Even Jess had pulled away, probably unconsciously. This happened often with such cases, as if folk hoped to distance themselves from the crime, as if what Juni had become might be contagious.

There had to be consequences. Lots of investigators talked about making the guilty serve as examples, establishing deterrents. Determining which actions the community deemed out of bounds. Those were all useful conversations to have. But from some primal, gut emotion, Enid felt that people who'd committed such an act should have their life *changed* for it. They shouldn't get to go back, as if nothing had happened.

If any of her colleagues called this impulse revenge, Enid wouldn't argue.

The Coast Road communities didn't practice executions, though Enid had an urge to drop Juni in a very deep hole and walk away. Instead, she thought of the next worst thing.

"I'm going to send you away, Juni. I've got a place in mind, nothing at all like this. I'm pretty sure you won't like it. But that's the point, isn't it?"

"You . . . you can't. I won't go, I can't go into the wild, how will I live?"

"This isn't in the wild. Though Ella's folk seem to do perfectly well. No, you'll still be Coast Road. Just on the other end of it. And if you don't go, you doom your whole household to dissolution. You already know what that feels like."

She looked up at Enid in stark horror, eyes red, mouth open. "Jess?" she said, turning to look for him. But he'd walked away, was already on the other side of the house. She had no allies.

"You can't do this." Her voice was high, taut.

"I think I can."

The silence stretched on, and on. Neeve finally shifted. Stepped forward, toward Juni. Enid almost reached out, but the Last House woman stopped. Studied the murderer for a moment, then shook her head.

They were almost a mirror of each other. Neeve had always looked older, had lived a rougher life. But the last hour had aged Juni. They looked more alike than not. What did each of them see in that mirror, that none of the rest of them would ever know?

"I've always hated you," Neeve said to Juni. Then turned and walked away. The rest of her household followed her. The other heads of household left, to spread the story of what had happened.

Juni covered her face with her hands.

Erik was the last of the others to leave, and he sidled up to Enid, looking at his feet the whole time. "I'm sorry."

She tilted her head. "Why?"

He shrugged. "I brought this down on all of us. If I'd just let the house go, if I hadn't called an investigation—none of this would have happened."

"You'd have found Ella's body, called it just one of those things, and never thought about it again, is that it?"

He looked out at the shoreline, the lapping water, that convenient distraction. They never even would have asked the questions.

He asked, "Are we going to be okay? I mean, all of us along the marsh here. After all this. Are we ever going to be okay?"

"May take a little work. But most of you, yeah."

They'd need to look out for one another. But that was supposed to be the whole point, wasn't it? Looking out for one another. His nod was slow, hesitating. Like he wasn't convinced. Nice guy, but Enid was glad to see him go. She wanted to be alone. No—she wanted to be with her own people.

"One other thing, Erik—there's a young man from the camp upriver named Hawk. He's taken Ella's passing hard. He might come down here looking for some kind of revenge. Just . . . keep an eye out."

"So they really did care for her. Her people, I mean."

"Did you doubt it?"

He scuffed his feet and decided this was the moment to walk on.

Enid had to have one more conversation. Not for the case or the report, but for herself. She had to jog to catch up with the folk of Last House, already past the bridge.

"Neeve!" she called. At this, the men of the house closed ranks around the woman.

"Leave us alone, just leave us alone!" Kellan cried out, pressing hands to his skull and squeezing his eyes shut.

Frustrated and losing patience, Enid halted. She was being selfish. She should just leave them alone. But she needed to ask one last question. "I just need to speak with Neeve a moment. This isn't about the case; that's done. There's no more trouble. I spoke to the folk up in the hills about you, Neeve."

That sparked Neeve's interest. She lifted her head and put a hand on Mart's arm. "It's okay," she murmured.

Glaring, he obviously wasn't sure. But he stepped aside.

Enid guided Neeve away, off the path, walking through the scrub. "Walk with me, just a little ways." Enid figured taking Neeve away from her household, away from everyone, the woman would be more likely to talk.

Enid said, "I went to the camp up the hill. I talked to El Juez."

Neeve ducked her head to hide a smile. "He was just Rico back then. So he's in charge there now?"

"I suppose."

"Doesn't surprise me. He's easy to follow."

"You did. For a little while."

"Yeah."

"You wanted a child so badly, you cut out your implant. Then why did you leave her behind?"

Neeve wore a knitted shawl, same pattern as Ella's kerchief. Her hands picked at the stitches, stretching the yarn. Like she always needed something to do with her hands. "I wanted Rico to come here. We could say Ella was his, not mine. We could explain it all. We could have it all."

"Man like that was never going to come live here," Enid said. She'd known the man for just a couple of days and could tell that. "So why did you leave the baby behind?"

The smile vanished. Her voice broke. "Because if I brought her back, she'd be taken away. Someone like you would take her away."

"Then why didn't you stay there, with her?"

"Why are you asking? Ella's dead, it's all ruined, why do you care?"

"I'm trying to understand. It's part of why I do this job. I want to understand."

Neeve wiped her eyes, looked out at the sea. A few gulls dipped and turned. Their cries were high and rattling. "I never fit in there. I just didn't. I can't explain it, but if you were there you must have seen it. I kept . . . trying to change things. Make them better. Fix things. But they wouldn't change. I'd suggest a new way of cooking, or maybe try to plant some vegetables. Rico would just laugh. He loved Ella, he was a father to her. But I didn't fit in."

"And you fit in so well here."

"I know who I am here. I'm the woman who cut out her implant. And now I'm the woman who had a bannerless child."

It was a waste, Enid thought. A waste of a life. Two lives, counting Ella. It was all so . . . sad. She didn't think she understood it any better. But it was an answer.

"Thanks. That's it, I guess. You keep well." She turned to leave.

"You're not going to do anything to me? Exile me, disband the household—"

"Ban you from earning banners?" Enid said. "No. I'm not going to do anything you haven't already done to yourself. Good night, Neeve."

The folk of Last House stood on the path, watching Enid go. She glanced back once, then never again.

/////////////////////////////////////////////////////////////

DUSK HAD FALLEN. They couldn't set out for home until the morning. Enid wanted to scream, but there was nothing to be done. She was flat-out finished for today—only that afternoon she had collapsed on the marsh from heat exhaustion. She ought to be a little gentler with herself.

Least she and Teeg could have done was bring a car with them. But no, this was just supposed to be a simple case, no more than a day or two. But now they had to spend one more night in Bonavista's work house. They kept Juni with them, taking turns watching her. When it was Teeg's turn, Enid sought out Jess.

She had to resist the urge to apologize. "I'll have supplies sent to make up for what we used. I really wasn't expecting we'd be here this long."

He was putting on a brave face. But his smile wavered and his eyes were wet. "She did it to hurt Neeve, you know. Wasn't about the girl at all. I—I'm sure she didn't really mean to hurt anyone. Except Neeve, I guess."

Enid didn't know what to say. "Well. She's ended up hurting a lot of folk. Taking her away is the best punishment I can think of. No need to break up the whole house."

He nodded quickly, head bowed. Tom, their son, was nowhere to be found. He just hid, and that was all right.

They didn't get a nice cooked meal that night, and Enid wasn't going to ask for one. She spent the evening on the front steps of the work house, available if anyone wanted to talk. Visible, standing up for her judgment if anyone wanted to argue.

Nobody did.

After dark, bugs swarmed the porch light, and Enid hugged a sheet over her shoulders. The whole Estuary seemed asleep. But Enid wouldn't feel peace until she was far, far away. She kept double-checking shadows, sure Hawk was going to jump out of one, intent on revenge. She kept seeing movement in the edges of her vision; she felt unsettled.

Teeg came out after a while. Stood by the door, looking out in the same direction she did, expression locked in a frown.

"She's asleep, I think," he said finally. "Wore herself out."

Enid didn't have a lot of sympathy for the woman. Part of her still wondered if they shouldn't have let her keep walking out into the waves. Just let her disappear.

"The report on this one's going to be a trick," he said, the conversational tone forced. Trying to talk like nothing was wrong.

"I'll write it all up, you don't have to worry about it."

"But I'll have to sign off on it too—"

"You weren't even there." She hadn't meant to spit out the words so sharply.

He said, "I was wrong. That's what you want me to say, yeah?"

"I don't want you to say anything you don't want to. Doesn't much matter, does it?" She wanted a drink. A good cider from the orchards back home. Apples didn't grow in this region.

"You did it. You solved it. I knew you would, after the Pasadan case."

She was going to become the expert on murder, wasn't she? The specialist. The one committees called on when a body turned up. Be nice for them, having someone else to shove the problem onto.

"I never would have guessed it," Teeg said, shaking his head.

"Yeah. That's the problem, isn't it? We're not supposed to *guess.*"

"That's why you want to write the report. You're not going to have anything good to say about me."

She had planned on leaving him out of the report entirely, at least where finding Ella's murderer was concerned. That would speak for itself. "You care about the report that much?"

"Of course I care—"

"If you cared, you should have stayed to help." Except she couldn't imagine what he would have done at the camp, how he would have handled the gang that took her. Couldn't imagine him behaving in a way that would have encouraged El Juez to talk, to say the thing that parted the clouds and made the whole situation clear.

She couldn't imagine him helping, and that was a sad thought.

"Get some sleep, Teeg," she said. "I'll keep watch next."

"No. I'll watch. You need sleep more than I do."

Trouble was, she didn't think she'd be able to. Didn't make much sense to argue, though. They had a long walk ahead of them, come morning.

# Beginning

A light rain came through that night, and Semperfi's ruin crashed down in the middle of it. The screeching racket of it carried over the whole marshland. Enid bolted awake from her corner of the work house, blinking in darkness. In the opposite corner Juni was curled up, pressed to the wall, clutching a blanket to her chest.

"What was that?" the woman gasped.

Enid made a lopsided grin. "Doom," she murmured, and Juni's face fell.

Enid opened the door to go out; Teeg got up and followed her. The noise had stopped. The air was still again, but in the main house, lights were coming on, voices calling. Up the path to the hill, more house lights turned on.

"Stay here, " Enid ordered Juni, who cringed back against the wall. Then Enid grabbed a hand lantern from her pack and went out.

The crash drew people from up and down the road, so Enid and Teeg were part of a procession of folk with hand lanterns and questions. Their shapes and shadows moved ahead, beams of lanterns playing back and forth. Conversation was low and earnest.

They converged at Semperfi, at the pre-Fall house that had just collapsed into shredded timbers, scattered down the slope all the way to the river. Enid couldn't quite make out what happened, but if she had to guess, she'd say the muddy slope gave way, dropped the web of stilts, and the whole structure slumped downward. The floor tilted, the walls broke, and the roof fell. That was mostly what remained visible, the angle of that leather-wrapped, patched-up roof on a pile of splinters. As they'd all said, it was only a matter of time. A cloud of dust was still settling, carrying a stench of mold and old wood. There wouldn't be much to salvage here, but the wreck would keep Erik and the Semperfi folk busy for a time.

Enid felt weirdly glad that she got to see the end of the whole mess. "Well, that's that," she said.

Erik stood on the path, shining a light over it. With all of the handheld lights together, the ruin was pretty well illuminated. It would look entirely different in daylight, and probably sadder.

"Wait—what's that?" Enid focused her lantern on a spot near the top of the mudslide buried in torn roof timbers. A piece of fabric amid the broken wood, incongruously soft and delicate. She moved closer, to the edge of a collapsed wall, peering through the dark, sure her eyes were playing tricks. She couldn't be seeing what she thought she saw.

But she was. A rough-woven sleeve, an outflung hand at the end of it, pale against the soaked ruins. Enid knew exactly who it belonged to—the shadow she'd been watching for, over the past day.

Hawk had gone to ground in his usual hiding spot.

"Oh no," Teeg murmured behind her.

The hand wasn't moving. Nothing was moving. Since she couldn't assume the young man was dead, she blew out a breath and prepared to crawl along the broken pieces.

"Enid, wait—"

"I'll be careful," she answered. "Keep that light on him, will you?"

They all did, the whole gathering, and waited with such breathless silence, she could hear a faint rain pattering on the river at the base of the cliff.

Carefully, putting each foot down gently, holding on with both hands, and pausing to see if the structure was all going to slide out from under her, she crawled out to the body. Confirmed that yes, it was Hawk, with his floppy brown hair, though half of it was covered with blood now. She could see one of his arms, one of his legs, both twisted to awkward angles. But she guessed it was the blow to the head that had killed him. A piece of the roof might have come straight down on top of him. He likely had been asleep when it happened.

She held his wrist, waited for a pulse a lot longer than she really needed to, but she wanted to be sure. Wanted all the witnesses to be sure. In the rain, his skin was already cold. No life left in him at all.

With just as much care, she backed out of the ruin, testing each step, each broken board. When she reached solid ground again, she sat hard and caught her breath. She'd done a hell of a lot of work on this trip, she thought. More than earned her uniform. She really wanted that shower now.

"Enid?" Teeg put a hand on her shoulder, and she patted it reassuringly.

"I'm fine. Help me up." Grasping his hand, she got back to her feet. Regarded the gathering. Yet another time when all the Estuary's faces looked back at her, waiting for her judgment.

"Are you going to start another investigation?" Erik said, an edge to his voice.

Enid glared. "Why, you think you should be held liable for not knocking down this deathtrap earlier?"

The man stepped back, arm raised as if warding off a weapon. Enid—her voice, her presence—was sharp as a blade. The investigator shook her head. Exhaustion pressed her on all sides, and she couldn't afford to give in to it, not yet. Still so many miles to go.

"No, I won't start an investigation," Enid said, rubbing the mist of rain from her face. "This was an accident. A stupid, stupid accident."

"You want us to get the body out of there?" Teeg asked.

Enid shook her head. "Not till morning and full light. I don't want anyone else getting hurt."

With that, the gathering drifted off, knowing there was nothing more to be done just now. Anna touched Erik's shoulder and drew him back toward the main house. Their real house. Far from angry, the man seemed relaxed, the knots gone from his shoulders and neck.

Well, good for him.

Enid turned, was surprised to find Mart standing there, his lantern hanging at his side. Light pooled at his feet, but his face was in shadow. The rest of his household hadn't accompanied him; he stood alone, off the path. She stared stupidly at him for a minute, too tired to think.

"We'll do the pyre for him," he said softly.

She nodded. Her voice came out a whisper: "Good. Good."

Teeg had to lead her off, a tentative hand on her arm.

Returning to Bonavista's work house, Enid realized they'd left Juni unsupervised and half-expected that the woman might have fled. But no, they opened the door and she was still sitting in the corner, knees pulled to her chest and hugging a blanket. Maybe asleep, maybe not.

This gave Enid a little bit of hope for the long journey ahead, that at least Juni wasn't likely to run away and cause more trouble.

///////////////////////////////////////////////////////////

WHAT LITTLE SLEEP she got didn't seem to do Enid any good. Her body still felt drained, still moving only at half speed. She had to fight through a fog in her mind. She expected she wouldn't get a good night's sleep until she was back with Sam and knew how Olive and the baby were doing.

Some places still had working two-way radios, she'd heard. But Haven didn't have one, so even if she could find one this far out, she couldn't talk to home.

Enid and Teeg let Juni take a bag with her, whatever belongings she could carry. Wasn't much. A hairbrush, a change of clothes, a knitted scarf, a carved wooden mug, maybe something that Jess had made. She got a few minutes with her household to say goodbye, but only Jess and Tom came to see her off. Enid offered a quick word to the boy.

"I'm still putting in a good word for your work. This isn't on you," she assured him.

"Not that it'll do any good," he said, frowning.

Enid and Teeg stood apart to give the household privacy, but Enid did listen in. As part of the investigation, she assured herself.

"Did you really do it?" the boy asked, his voice tight and tearful. Juni didn't say anything. "But why? How could you?"

Unanswerable questions.

"I don't know," Juni said softly. Tom ran off, scrubbing his face, hiding his tears.

Jess looked back at Juni one more time. "I'll do what I need to, to keep the household together."

"Maybe you shouldn't. The place is cursed." Juni's mouth twisted as if full of a sour taste.

"I don't believe that. We'll keep our banners on the wall. It'll be enough."

The woman nodded, and they turned away from each other. Not even an embrace or a touch of hands.

They set off, Teeg and Enid taking up positions on either side of Juni, pressing her on. They had a long walk ahead of them.

"It's not fair," Juni muttered under her breath, only half an hour away from Bonavista. She repeated it like some kind of mantra. "It's not fair, it's not fair, it's not fair."

"You're right," Enid said curtly, cutting her off. "It isn't."

Juni didn't say another word.

///////////////////////////////////////////////////////////////

FINALLY, at the end of the day they arrived in Everlast, an actual town. It was like emerging from a shroud into sunlight.

Away from the coast, away from the wetlands—this place felt *stable*. No houses perched on stilts, no tumbling ruins, no waterlogged marshes constantly shifting.

But it wasn't the end of their trip. Teeg stayed with Juni while Enid checked in with the local committee for messages. Nothing personal had come from Haven, which she took as a good sign—that she wasn't too late. Even better, Everlast had a solar car on loan for committee business, and Enid laid claim to it.

Enid also asked that a medic go back to the Estuary as soon as possible, mainly to check on Kellan. The stress of the investigation had eaten at him, and Enid worried. Really, it might not hurt to get everyone looked over. A medic checked out her injury, admired the multicolored bruise covering her shoulder and upper arm. No, nothing was broken, but it would take weeks to heal. The medic handed her a salve and extracted a promise that she'd actually remember to use it.

After an hour's worth of work at Everlast, meeting with their committee and the medic, requesting that food be sent to Bonavista to replace what Enid and Teeg had eaten, and collecting all the other messages to be carried down the Coast Road, they set off. Juni remained sullen but cooperative. Teeg was thoughtful and quiet. Made Enid nervous.

Half a day of driving brought them to the Coast Road proper, then to Morada and the regional committee house. Two exhausted, grubby investigators driving up with a hunched, glaring woman between them attracted attention. When a pair of investigators based here walked up to meet them, Enid was relieved. She felt like she'd been carrying all this on her own.

Now, maybe, finally, Enid could be done with this.

"Wait here," she told Teeg and Juni, and went to meet her colleagues. One of them was Patel, Teeg's mentor. He'd have a particular interest, wouldn't he? With everything else, Enid hadn't had a chance to get her thoughts in order about Teeg.

"Enid," Patel said in greeting. Enid wasn't short, but Patel was half a head taller than her. An intimidating figure, with the uniform. He was intense, interested. "What happened? This was only supposed to take a couple of days. You've been gone a week."

She hesitated. "I don't know where to start."

"This was just a mediation, yeah?"

"It turned into a murder." She explained, trying to keep it simple, not sure she was making any sense. Most cases never lasted longer than a week or so. She'd been on this one too long.

"That's awful," said Denis, Patel's partner. A slim brown man with an eager gaze, scruffy chopped hair he must have cut himself.

"Yeah," Enid said with a sigh.

The closest thing the Coast Road ever got to a trial then ensued. In the pre-Fall world this would have been so much more formal, bound by rules and traditions and ceremony. The Coast Road didn't have much time, or call for anything like that. It was one of the things that encouraged towns to solve problems on their own. So solving them didn't become a production.

Murder was something that simply couldn't be solved, Enid was coming to believe. It could only be dealt with. The regional committee was there, along with the investigators who would take over the handling of the case, Patel and Denis. A handful of other investigators, some in uniform and some not. They'd already begged for copies of the report. One of them said, "I read your report on Pasadan from last year. You're becoming the expert on this." He smiled kindly enough, but the words sat like a rock in her gut.

Teeg still wasn't talking. He hung back from the others, arms crossed, answering questions in monosyllables.

The committee's meeting room had gotten chaotic, three committee members on one side of a long table, Juni sitting in a chair by herself, hugging her pack. An audience of investigators and assistants clustered in. Enid went over the details again and again, answered question after question. Teeg corroborated, answered some questions himself. Like what he'd been doing the three days Enid was gone in the wild. Asking the same questions of the same people, apparently. By then, they'd gotten used to not answering. So he decided Kellan was guilty and finished it himself.

Enid was still angry about that.

Ahn, the chair of the committee, peered through antique reading glasses and studied a set of notes Enid had copied from her book, right before the hearing.

"You went up to the hills, into the wild, to talk to witnesses?" The notes said so; the question was spoken in a tone of disbelief.

"I did."

"Was that necessary?"

Enid shrugged. "Wouldn't have been, if Kellan or Neeve had just told me the truth. But nobody talks, not about that sort of thing. I had to dig it up."

"Right. Well. You don't suggest that anything be done about Neeve's infraction?"

"I think everything's already been done that possibly can be. There's nothing left." Enid suspected word would get out: the bannerless child had been discovered. Twenty years later, maybe. But the pregnancy had been discovered, and such pregnancies always would be. A useful kind of tale, that.

"Right," the chair said. "About this next part—"

Juni burst in. "Can I appeal? Is there some kind of an appeal process? I want to tell my side of it." The whole trip here, Juni had likely been thinking of this, exactly what to say, exactly what her strategy should be. There was always a chance for appeal, wasn't there? She could request an investigation.

Ahn took off her glasses and stared at Juni. "You confess that you killed a young woman, direct and on purpose."

"Yes, but it wasn't like she was a real person."

Enid walked out of the room at that. She might have strangled Juni otherwise, and had her own murder investigation to face. The heat of her anger closed in on her like that moment on the marsh, right before she passed out, when her vision closed to nothing. She hardly noticed the silence, the wide-eyed expressions of a dozen faces watching her go. Teeg stood, but didn't try to stop her. She needed air, so she went to get it. Charged straight out and settled on the building's front steps and tried not to think about what was happening inside.

A long stretch after that, Patel came outside to sit with her. Enid had been watching traffic go back and forth. A crossroads passed through Morada, where the Sierra Road met the Coast Road. She'd seen horses, dogs, wagons, and even a couple of cars. All of it nice and normal. Soothing.

"Well, she's something," Patel said.

"I finally see why capital punishment was so attractive back in the day. It's not a deterrent, it's catharsis. I just . . . I'm angry."

"They're trying to decide where to send her. Whether she should be exiled out of the Coast Road entire."

Enid shook her head slowly. An indirect death was still death, and they were supposed to be better than that. "I think she should go to Desolata."

"Oh. I like that," Patel said.

"I put it in the report. Maybe I should tell them in person."

"I'll let them know, you don't have to worry about it. And how's our newly minted Teeg working out?"

"New as puppies," she said. "He left me, Patel. Let me walk into the hills alone. And I don't think he's sorry."

"Yeah."

"I miss Tomas," she said.

Patel persuaded her back inside to hear the verdict, and then went around the table for a whispered conference with the committee. They kept glancing at Juni, the perpetrator. Enid told herself she'd already left the case behind, that this didn't mean anything. But she ought to be here to see the end of it.

The chair announced, "It's been suggested we send you to Desolata when the next trading expedition heads out that way. You'll go along, and they'll leave you there."

Juni leaned forward. "Where's that?"

"It's the other end of the world."

"But why? Why are you doing this to me?"

Enid spat back, "Why did you kill Ella?"

Juni didn't have an answer.

"You can always leave, anytime you like," the committee chair said. "But nowhere else will take you."

///////////////////////////////////////////////////////////////

IT WAS OUT OF Enid's hands, then. The committee arranged the exile, asked Patel and Denis to take charge of Juni until the traders left for the long trip south. Juni would be cared for until then. Given a room and food. But nothing else. No one wanted even to talk to her. Enid decided she didn't need to see the woman again.

The whole process took long enough that she and Teeg spent the night at the town's way station, which had a hot shower. Enid would never get tired of hot showers. She tried not to take too long, not to drain the tank and leave nothing for the next person. But it was hard, and she still felt worn out and grubby when she finished. The clean clothes, though—those felt marvelous.

When she went out to the front porch to get some air, to watch stars come out, she met Teeg slouched on the steps, apparently with the same idea.

He held his brown investigator's tunic scrunched up in his lap.

Instead of his uniform, he wore a sleeveless linen undershirt. His arms were lean and strong, the brown skin shining with a glow of summer sweat. Elbows on knees, he stared out at the street, at the normalcy of it all. He didn't react to her approach. She was sure he'd seen her. Maybe he felt that nothing needed to be said.

"Hola," she said, when she got close enough that staying silent would be rude. "You okay?"

When he looked over, his lips were pursed, like he was working to keep his expression still. She didn't know what to say to draw him out. Finally, after too much silence, he reached out, handing her his tunic. "I've decided I can't do this."

She stared at the offering, leaving it hanging between them. "What do you mean?"

"I'm not meant to be an investigator. This proved it."

"One rough case and you're ready to give it all up? Is that it?"

When she refused to take the tunic from him, he let his arm drop, and his shoulders slumped. "I was wrong. I was wrong on everything. I don't want to do this."

She didn't know why she should feel panic at this declaration, why her immediate urge was to talk him out of it, explain to him all the ways he was wrong. Like she'd been telling him he was wrong all week. Maybe this time he wasn't wrong. But she didn't want him to quit, and she couldn't even say why.

"I think you're in a rush. You need to think this over. Talk to regional, talk to Patel."

"Already thought it over. Sorry, Enid. I know you're disappointed."

"I just want to understand." His handing over the tunic—

she felt like she'd failed. She was supposed to mentor him on his first case, yet here he was, ready to quit. She'd failed him.

His sigh was desolate. "I didn't follow you up the river because I thought you were wrong. I stayed behind because I was scared. And this job, this thing we do—you can't be scared and still do the work."

She couldn't argue with that.

"I hate that," he added. "That I didn't follow you. Thing is, even knowing how it all turned out—I still wouldn't."

He had the tunic wadded up like a rag, squeezing like he was angry at it. She wanted to take it, smooth it out, fold it neatly.

Neither of them had spoken aloud the obvious: that someone who didn't want to be an investigator absolutely shouldn't be one.

And Teeg didn't want it. He wasn't asking questions anymore.

"I'm not going to take that from you, Teeg," she stated. "Take it to the committee and talk it over with your folk. You're not thinking clear right now."

"I haven't stopped thinking about it since we left the Estuary. Done enough thinking about it." He bit the words off.

Enid didn't feel much like sitting and taking in the evening air anymore. She wanted to take a walk, even in the dark. She wanted to walk all the way back to Haven.

"Anyway, I wanted to thank you," he said.

"For what?"

"For making it all clear. What the job's really about."

"I'm not sure I know what it's about."

"The truth. Not justice, not the rules. Just truth, the very bottom of it."

That was a grand statement. She wasn't sure she agreed,

truth with a capital T. She smiled sadly. "Tomas always said it was about being kind. The only reason any of us is here is kindness."

"I'm not sure I know what that means."

"Yeah, I know. Neither do I. I'm leaving at dawn. I need to get home."

"I'm going to stick around here. Talk it over with folk, like you said."

"All right. Well. Come say hi, next time you come through Haven."

And Enid walked away.

///////////////////////////////////////////////////////////////

SIX MONTHS OR SO LATER, Patel found Enid in the clinic waiting room at Haven. Enid was balancing sixth-month-old baby Rose on her lap, distracting her before she got her first vaccinations. If the baby started happy, maybe this all wouldn't be too distressing. Olive refused to watch while the medics inflicted pain on their precious girl, so Enid did the deed. Someone had to.

Rose was beautiful. The most perfect baby ever. She had Olive's dark hair, already growing curls, and Berol's mischievous smile and bright brown eyes. Olive insisted the baby had Sam's good sense and Enid's bravery, but that was pure fancy. Already they could all see that Rose was who she was; she liked grabbing hair and beards and clinging to chairs. She babbled, but they could tell she listened close when anyone spoke.

"Who is this?" Patel asked, settling in the chair beside her.

"Patel, meet Rose. Rose, say hello to my friend Patel." Enid bounced Rose, held out her pudgy hand, smiled when Rose reached out her other hand herself, grabbing for Patel's fingers The investigator chuckled.

"I have a message for you, Enid, but maybe I should wait," Patel said, letting Rose grip his finger. People almost always reached for babies, Enid noticed. Even folk who didn't particularly get along with babies would hold a finger to them. The babies almost always reached back. The connection was primal.

"It's all right," she said. "It's obviously grim, might as well get it over with."

So he told her: after only a month at Desolata, Juni had walked into the desert and not returned. It happened sometimes, folk there said. Someone said they wanted to see how far they could walk. When really, they didn't want to come back at all. The woman had sentenced herself to execution.

Enid wasn't surprised, though maybe she'd hoped that Juni would find something useful to do with herself. Really, she wasn't sure Juni's story could have ended any other way. It was the woman's choice, she told herself. She could have lived. Just not the way she'd done before. And it was her choice to wreck that as well.

"Well. Thanks for letting me know," she said, and Patel nodded and left for the rest of his errands, giving Rose's little hand one last squeeze.

Rose was listening to it all. Not understanding, surely. She'd be all right, sheltered from the hardships of the world for as long as Enid and the rest of the family could manage it. But Rose lived with an investigator. Enid might not manage to shelter her for as long as she might wish. After Patel left, she kissed Rose's silky baby head, pressing her face there a long time to breathe in the scent of her, and Rose burbled happily.

SIX MONTHS BEFORE THAT, when she hadn't yet met Rose, Enid left Morada by car. Dropped off the car at Silt and continued on foot. This was the longest walk Enid had ever made in her time as investigator; the last ten miles back to Haven took forever. She kept speeding up, her feet shuffling to a jog without her realizing it, and she had to make herself go slow and steady, at a normal walking pace. She didn't want to collapse when she got home, or worse, before she got there. Might do that anyway. But if she did, the others would worry, and she wanted to avoid that.

There'd been no point in sending a message ahead, as she made various stops at towns and way stations. In fact, she was the one carrying messages. She would be delivering her own message, telling that she was on her way and hoping that everything was well.

That last day of travel, she wasn't going to beat sunset. Normally, dusk meant finding a way station, someplace to spend the night. But she was so close to Haven, she'd already passed Ant Farm and Potter, the outlying households that marked the edge of the region. Another hour and she'd be home. She wasn't going to stop now. This part of the world, the road was wide and well traveled. Plenty of electric lights glowed by the front doors of houses. One thing about walking in the dark: no one much was out and about, and the ones who were were clearly on their way to somewhere else. They saw Enid and waved; didn't try to stop and talk. She had no idea what she'd say if someone tried to stop her. How she was supposed to explain.

On the other hand, if she stopped to talk, someone might be able to tell her if the baby at Serenity had been born yet.

But no, she waved back and hurried on. Past the clinic, the original heart of the town. The pre-Fall cement building had been cared for and maintained and built onto, and wasn't sitting on a mud bank. No chance of it falling over.

Serenity was on the other side of town, down its own path. She reached the turn, came in view of Serenity's cottage, two stories, simple and neatly kept.

Home.

Somehow, now, at the end of the trip, Enid hesitated. Lights were on in the front room but not upstairs. This time of evening, everyone should be home. Everything looked normal. Nothing seemed out of place. Nothing told Enid what she might find inside. If her world had changed while she had gone.

She went to the door. Was about to touch the handle to open it when a sob rang out.

The sound of a baby crying.

Enid stopped, closed her eyes. Stood for a moment just listening.

All was well.

A noisy, demanding baby was a healthy one, and all was well. She was furious that she'd missed the arrival. Full of shame, regret at the broken promise, this empty hole in her gut that she'd missed a thing that might never happen again. But that all passed in a moment, in a flash, leaving behind joy.

She'd dreamed of this sound.

Carefully, she opened the door.